SOUTH BEACH

SOUTH BEACH

Aimee Friedman

SCHOLASTIC INC.

New York Toronto London Auckland Sydney
Mexico City New Delhi Hong Kong Buenos Aires

For my sister, Natalie — my favorite travel companion.

And with thanks to Craig Walker and Maria Barbo,
for their insight and encouragement.

No part of this publication may be reproduced, stored in a retrieval system, or transmitted in any form or by any means, electronic, mechanical, photocopying, recording, or otherwise, without written permission of the publisher. For information regarding permission, write to Scholastic Inc., Attention: Permissions Department, 557 Broadway, New York, NY 10012.

ISBN 0-439-70678-5

Copyright © 2005 by Aimee Friedman

All rights reserved. Published by Scholastic Inc.
SCHOLASTIC and associated logos are trademarks and/or registered trademarks of Scholastic Inc.

Book design by Steve Scott

12 11 10 9 8 7 6 5 4 3 2 1   5 6 7 8 9 10/0

Printed in the U.S.A.
First printing, March 2005

CHAPTER ONE
Spring Break

"Why is it snowing in *March?*"

Alexandria St. Laurent gave a deep sigh as she turned away from her window. It was a bleak, sleet-soaked Thursday afternoon, and she was in a pouty mood. She kicked off her fuzzy, camel-colored boots and collapsed on the bed beside her boyfriend, Tyler Davis. Tyler took a sip of his Heineken and lazily ran his fingers through Alexa's silky, white-blonde hair, which rippled out behind her on the velvet pillows.

"Alexa, this is New Jersey," he pointed out. "It's always cold in the spring."

"Don't remind me," Alexa moaned. She was sick to death of Oakridge, New Jersey, the quiet, leafy suburb where she'd lived most of her life. She was sick of her split-level house, her humdrum high school, and

1

most of all, the dreary weather. She craved sunshine and shimmer, tropical breezes and exotic intrigue. Alexa closed her eyes and stretched her arms high over her head so that her flat stomach peeked out from beneath her white cashmere V-neck. She was starting to drift into a pleasant daydream about lounging poolside in a yellow string bikini when Tyler spoke into her ear.

"Baby?" he asked hesitantly. "You don't really hate snow, do you? I mean, we're going skiing in two days, remember?"

Alexa opened her eyes and looked up into Tyler's earnest, handsome face. Right. Skiing. Back in January, they'd made plans to go to Aspen, Colorado, for their weeklong spring break. The idea had seemed so romantic to Alexa then — she and Tyler zooming down the ivory slopes every day, then fooling around in front of a roaring fire every night. Now, it just seemed silly. Who went someplace *wintry* for spring break?

Of course, back in January, she'd still been in love with Tyler.

Alexa watched as Tyler set his beer on the floor, then turned back to her, his lips curving up in a smile. "I can't wait," he said, leaning in and lightly kissing her neck. With one finger, he traced the thin gold chain around her throat. "It's gonna be so awesome."

Awesome. That was Tyler's favorite word. He used

it to describe everything from a good lacrosse game to a juicy hamburger to the way Alexa looked in her black Bebe halter dress. And every time Tyler said, "Awesome," Alexa felt like smacking him. But she always held back.

There really was nothing *wrong* with Tyler, Alexa mused as he stretched out beside her and began stroking her belly, his face buried in her neck. He was captain of the lacrosse team at Oakridge High, and had a body to go with that title — lean, toned, and broad-shouldered. With his wavy, dark-blond hair, sculpted jaw, and snub nose, it was no surprise he'd been asked to do a photo shoot for American Eagle — which he'd sweetly turned down because it conflicted with his history midterm. Everything about Tyler was sweet, from his toothy, aw-shucks smile to his impeccable manners. But that was also the problem, Alexa thought, as Tyler's lips slid down her neck to her collarbone. He was *too* sweet. Too perfect. Too predictable.

Now, for instance, as they lay entwined on her bed, she knew exactly how he was going to kiss her: tentatively, slowly, just this side of hesitant. As predicted, Tyler brushed his lips softly over hers, again and again, until Alexa finally took his face in her hands and pulled him in closer, deepening the kiss. He tasted of Heineken and cinnamon Altoids. Even though Tyler didn't really do it for her anymore, Alexa still let herself savor the delicious moment — the warmth of his breath against her skin, the feel of his body running the length of hers. She snaked her arms around him, pulling up his National Lacrosse Camp T-shirt. She slid her hands up and down his broad back. When she tried to tug the shirt off over his head, Tyler abruptly pulled back and sat up, his cheeks flushed.

"Alexa," he whispered, looking alarmed. "Isn't your dad downstairs?"

Alexa shrugged, rolling her eyes. Typical Tyler. He'd been just as stressed about pilfering the Heineken from the kitchen earlier, even though her dad had been safely sequestered in his sleek home office — and wouldn't have minded about the beer, anyway. Tyler simply didn't seem to get that Alexa's dad was possibly the chillest parent in the world.

Alexa was an only child, and her mom and dad were divorced. They'd split up when Alexa was seven, right after the family had moved from Paris to Oakridge for her father's architecture job. Alexa's dad was French, and his parenting style was totally laissez-faire: He basically let Alexa do her own thing, all the time. Alexa's mom was American, and she lived in New York City with her much younger boyfriend. She was a buyer for Henri Bendel on Fifth Avenue, and best showed her motherly affection by sending Alexa wrap dresses and slouchy boots on her birthday. Sometimes, Alexa craved a little more parental doting in her life. But other times — when there was a late-night party to go to, or a boy in her bedroom — she was grateful that her mother wasn't around, and that her father was so lax.

"My dad doesn't care what we do in here," Alexa said, reaching down to undo the top button of Tyler's baggy jeans. He was wearing his Tommy Hilfiger boxers, her favorite.

Tyler gently pushed her hand away, shaking his head. "It's just wrong," he said. "We can't have sex with your father in the house."

And it was at that very moment, as Tyler sat on her bed, his hair rumpled and his face bright red, that Alexa decided to dump him. Just end it, right then and there. Why should she waste any more energy secretly resenting him? Now was as good a time as any to make a clean break.

They'd been together since the beginning of their junior year, when Alexa had dared him to kiss her during the homecoming dance. At first, Alexa had found Tyler's naïveté and nice-boy vibe endearing. He'd been a virgin when they met — a status Alexa had happily relieved him of on New Year's Eve — and had never even flown in an airplane. Now, seven months later, she found those same qualities annoying. Alexa needed someone more interesting, more edgy, more . . . dangerous. Tyler was fun to cuddle with, but he didn't make her shiver with desire. She was ready to move on to new experiences and new adventures. And he was holding her back.

Her mind made up, Alexa inched away from Tyler and sat up against the pillows. She ran her pinkie over her bottom lip, fixing her smudged Bobbi Brown lip gloss. She felt a little nervous and fluttery, but once Alexa St. Laurent came to a decision, there was no reversing it.

"Listen," she began, looking directly at Tyler. He was sitting on the edge of the bed, facing her. "I've been thinking. . . ."

"What's up?" Tyler asked, reaching for his beer again.

"I was thinking we should . . ." Alexa paused for a moment, her heart pounding. "Take a break."

"Like . . . spring break?" Tyler grinned, tilting his head to one side.

Oh, God, Alexa thought. *He doesn't get it.*

"No," Alexa said. "A break from . . . this." She gestured to where they sat on her bed. "From us being together." Tyler was staring at her, seemingly dumbfounded, so she added, "As in, break up." It was a little harsh, but at least she was getting to the point, Alexa told herself.

Tyler's jaw dropped. "You mean . . . you don't want to date me?" he sputtered, his forehead creasing in confusion. Tyler wasn't exactly arrogant, but he knew he was Oakridge High's best catch.

At the sight of his baffled expression, Alexa felt a lump rise up in her throat. She didn't want to *hurt* Tyler. She really was doing this for his good as well as her own. Alexa bit her lower lip as she reached for Tyler's hand.

"I'm sorry," she whispered.

Tyler jerked his hand out of hers, and narrowed his eyes. He moved even farther away from her, so that he was almost off the bed. "There's someone else, isn't there?" he asked.

Tyler's reaction made sense, Alexa reflected. He couldn't have failed to notice the way guys gawked at her, whether in the Oakridge Galleria or in the halls of their school. And she knew for a fact that at least seven boys in the junior class — and two seniors — had crushes on her. Although Alexa soaked up the attention — and, sometimes, flirted back — she'd been perfectly faithful to Tyler. No, there wasn't someone else. Not yet, anyway.

"Of course not," Alexa said. "It's just that my feelings

have . . . changed." She swallowed hard, composing herself. "I did love you once, Tyler. But I feel like there's no spark between us anymore."

"But you tried to jump me, like, two seconds ago!" Tyler said, standing up and backing away from the bed. "I don't understand you, Alexa." He took a long drink of his Heineken, then set the bottle down on her desk.

"Maybe you never did," Alexa said softly. *That's why this is for the best,* she realized. Tyler Davis was simply not her destiny.

"But . . . but . . ." Tyler threw up his hands in frustration. "Why are you doing this *now?* What about our trip? What about Aspen? The plane tickets are booked, the ski lodge confirmed our reservation . . ."

Alexa twirled a strand of blonde hair around one finger. Breaking up with Tyler might have been painful, but the thought of not having to spend a snowbound week in Aspen was making her feel a whole lot better.

"We can cancel all that," she said. "I'll pay you back for my half."

"It's not about the money. . . ." Tyler shook his head, his light-brown eyes wide with disbelief.

"Or you could go with Jeff or Marc or someone," Alexa suggested. She did feel guilty that she was depriving Tyler of his first-ever chance to fly.

"My buddies already have their own plans, Alexa," Tyler said. He stared at her pink shag rug, defeated. "I can't believe you would do this to me right before spring break." He grabbed his North Face jacket off Alexa's desk chair and made his way toward the door, still shaking his head numbly. "I never even saw it coming. . . ."

Alexa sighed and eased off her bed. It wasn't the first time she'd broken a boy's heart, and they'd pretty much all reacted the same way. Alexa wasn't too big on warning signs.

She opened the door to her bedroom, and Tyler walked out into the hall. Before he could turn to go downstairs, she took his elbow and quickly kissed him on the cheek.

"Good luck, Tyler," she said. "You'll find the right girl. Someone who's a better match for you. I know you will." Tyler *would* be okay. Maybe she'd even done him a favor, in a way.

With that, Alexa closed the door on Tyler Davis and their seven-month-long relationship.

She leaned back against the door and surveyed her empty room. Alexa was a little shaky, but mostly she felt relieved. She'd done what she'd wanted. Tyler was gone, and it was time for a totally fresh start. In a matter of minutes, Alexa realized, she had completely turned her life around. And now that the difficult stuff

9

was out of the way, she had to admit it felt pretty damn . . . awesome.

Alexa walked over to the bulletin board above her desk, where she'd tacked up her favorite photographs. In the center was the black-and-white shot she'd taken of the Eiffel Tower on a rainy day. Alexa was born in Paris, and often visited the city to see her various cousins.

Alexa studied the other photos she'd snapped over the course of her many travels: a high-cheekboned couple at a sidewalk café in Rome, two men smoking cigars on the hood of a car in Cuba, a gaggle of school-children running down a bustling Tokyo street. Alexa's dad often went abroad for business or research, and Alexa liked to accompany him. If her father wasn't going anywhere during a school break, she vacationed with friends. Alexa adored traveling. She wanted to see the whole world before she was eighteen — and that was only a year away.

Alexa felt a pinprick of anticipation. Spring break would officially begin on Friday afternoon. Now that Tyler and Aspen were out of the picture, she was free to take off for the sun-drenched destination she'd been craving. It was too perfect. She knelt and rifled through her fringed hobo bag for her plush Poire phone pouch. Her best friends, Portia, Maeve, and Sabina, were flying to Cozumel tomorrow night, and Alexa knew they'd be thrilled that she could now join them. Alexa supposed that her friends *could* have fun on their own, but she was the true heartbeat of every party — the one who could transform an ordinary night into something unforgettable.

Sinking into her Pucci-patterned beanbag chair, Alexa flipped open her shiny silver Nokia and pressed "1" for Portia. Her friend answered on the third ring.

"'Sup, sexy?" Portia inquired.

Alexa could picture Portia so clearly — sprawled across her canopy bed in Juicy velour sweats, casually reaching for the remote to lower the volume on her Gwen Stefani CD. A heap of Miss Sixty jeans, patterned tights, and Lacoste polo shirts probably lay on the floor, waiting to be picked up by the housekeeper. Alexa had always thought of herself as fairly well off until she'd met Portia in ninth grade: Portia inhabited a whole other universe of wealthy.

"Get this," Alexa said, crossing her long legs. "I just broke up with Tyler. I'm single!" She giggled. Saying the words out loud to Portia made her moment with Tyler feel real — official. Only Portia knew how frustrated Alexa had been with Tyler these past couple of months.

"Wow," Portia said. "You did it. Congrats. Maybe now we can actually *see* you again."

Alexa fought down a sudden pang of guilt. True,

she hadn't been around that much this year — blowing off Maeve's Valentine's Day Jacuzzi party, ignoring Sabina's chirpy e-mails, skipping lunchtime manicures with Portia. Things always went that way whenever Alexa had a boyfriend: Her girlfriends' activities took a backseat to her romantic dramas. Alexa wondered, for a moment, if that made her a bad friend. After all, Maeve had a serious boyfriend, too, but she always made time for the girls. *Whatever,* Alexa thought, brushing the worry away. All the more reason for her friends to be psyched about her revised spring break plans.

"Exactly," Alexa replied brightly. "I canceled Aspen, so I am *all* about Cozumel, babe. What time do we leave tomorrow?" She could see it already — she and the girls crowding excitedly onto the airplane, beach towels and platform flip-flops tucked into their Vera Bradley quilted shoulder bags.

"Lex," Portia said gently. "I don't think there's any space left —"

"So I can fly out Saturday morning." Alexa shrugged. Leave it to cynical Portia to get hung up on some stupid obstacle. Alexa stood and headed for her desk, where she opened her PowerBook. "I'll look on Orbitz."

"I don't mean the flight," Portia clarified. "At the resort. When we made the reservations, they told us we were getting their last available room."

"So? Aren't there two queen beds?" Alexa asked

as her computer booted up. That was how her little foursome always arranged it when they traveled together — she and Portia in one bed, Sabina and Maeve in the other, everyone sniping about stolen covers and hogged pillows.

"Well," Portia said. There was a pause, and Alexa knew Portia was yanking on a chestnut curl of hair, her classic nervous gesture. Suddenly, Alexa felt kind of nervous, too. "Actually, our room is full," Portia went on. "We invited Delphine."

"*Delphine?*" Alexa repeated, gripping the phone tighter. Was Portia serious?

Delphine was the ringleader of what Alexa thought of as the second-tier crowd. They were the girls who wore last year's Uggs *this* winter, who still listened to Britney, and who hung around the fringes of Alexa's crew. As far as Alexa knew, Delphine would never have been beckoned to fill *her* place on a trip.

"Yeah," Portia said. "All her friends are going to Cancun —"

"*So* yesterday's spring break destination," Alexa filled in, rolling her eyes. She double-clicked on her Explorer icon, and it opened to the Orbitz site, her home page.

"Right. Delphine was not amused. She called me, basically begging to come with us instead." Alexa heard the click of a lighter, and Portia exhaling a long stream of smoke. "You had plans with Tyler, so . . ." She trailed off. "I'm sorry, Lex. I wish you could come. But it's just too late."

Alexa cupped her chin in her hand, staring blankly at the colorful Orbitz page. Portia did sound sincerely sorry. Still, Alexa couldn't help but wonder if this last-minute Delphine addition was also a dig at *her* — a form of revenge for how Alexa had behaved while she was with Tyler. Either way, the situation sucked. Alexa was *not* accustomed to being left behind.

She briefly considered asking Portia if there were other resorts with vacancies close by, or even if they could squeeze a cot into the room, but then she stopped herself. Alexa St. Laurent did not grovel. If her friends preferred to spend their break with some-one as dull as Delphine, that was fine by her. She simply had to make even better plans — on her own.

"Hope you'll still have fun without me," Alexa said, shrugging off her sinking spirits. "Listen, I need to run —"

"Wait, sweetie," Portia said. "I want to hear all the dirty details about Tyler."

"Another time," Alexa replied. "Ciao."

She shut her phone and flung it onto her desk. She was definitely pissed at Portia, but Alexa had more pressing matters on her mind right now.

On a mission, Alexa logged onto her IM account,

then scrolled down her buddy list, wondering who —
if anyone — hadn't yet made plans at this late date.
She knew Tabitha and Tracey had flown to London
last night, having secured special permission from
their teachers to bust out early. J.D. and Gavin were
friends of Tyler's — contacting them now would
be way weird. That left the second-tier crowd. And
how pathetic would *that* be? Alexa imagined asking
Delphine's cronies to include her in their Cancun
plans. *Not a chance,* she thought.

Numb, Alexa logged out of IM. The cold reality was
sinking in: She was going to be stranded in Oakridge
for a week, while her best friends and *Delphine* were
hooking up with hot college boys on the beach.

Alexa shook her head, banishing her self-pity. She
knew exactly what she needed right now: a hot, bubbly
bath and a glass of Merlot. Soaking in the tub always
cleared Alexa's head; if she relaxed and focused, she'd
come up with a fabulous alternate plan.

Slowly, Alexa took off her watch and her oversize
gold hoops, eager to slip out of her clothes and into
some scalding, foamy water. She unclasped her feather-
light gold chain, opened her desk drawer, and took
out her wooden jewelry box. She was about to drop
the necklace in when a piece of jewelry caught her
eye. A flash of hot pink amid all the glossy silver and
gold. Alexa smiled to herself. God. Her "Best Friends

Forever" bracelet. That tacky thing had been a gift from her old friend Holly Jacobson, back in the sixth grade. Alexa hadn't worn it in at least four years. She dug the bracelet out and slid it onto her slim wrist, studying the words on its side.

Best Friends Forever. That was how she and Holly would always sign their notes to each other. *That's what we were,* Alexa reflected. *Ages ago.*

When Alexa had arrived from Paris in the second grade, Holly had been the only kid in Oakridge Elementary who'd welcomed her warmly. Holly had offered Alexa a pumpkin brownie at lunchtime — Mrs. Jacobson always packed extra food — and their friendship was sealed. With her wide, sparkling gray-green eyes, sprinkling of freckles on her nose and cheeks, and straight, honey-brown hair, Holly was as innocent as she looked. Though timid and soft-spoken, Holly was also warm, genuine, and, once she opened up, a lot of fun.

Soon, Holly and Alexa were spending their weekends and afternoons together — making s'mores, painting each other's toenails, and trading secrets. In the fourth grade, on a pebbly path in the park, Holly patiently taught Alexa how to ride a bike. And, in the fifth grade, after Alexa had gone on a sort-of-date with David Metcalfe, she told Holly what it felt like to kiss a boy. At the time, Holly hadn't known anything about kissing. Now, as Alexa sat in her bedroom, she wondered if her old friend had *ever* been kissed.

Holly had always been a late bloomer, Alexa remembered as she spun the bracelet on her wrist. That was the main reason they'd grown apart. At the end of seventh grade, Alexa got her first real boyfriend, and suddenly, reading *Betty and Veronica* comics with Holly seemed kind of lame compared to French-kissing Eliot Johnson. By high school, Alexa had dumped Eliot, moved on to new conquests, and befriended Portia, while Holly started spending more time with her friends from the girls' track team. There had never been an official split — no screaming matches, no proclamations of a destroyed friendship. Their phone calls and e-mails simply got fewer and farther between, and soon Holly was just a face Alexa passed in the Oakridge High hallways.

Alexa thought back to the last time she'd seen Holly, at Monday's junior class assembly. Holly, wearing Puma racing pants, her hair in a ponytail, had shyly waved to Alexa from across the aisle and Alexa had nodded in return. It was weird how close the two of them had once been. Alexa remembered even going on a couple of weekend trips with Holly and her family in the summers — driving to a cabin the Jacobsons rented in upstate New York. Alexa and Holly would be squished in the backseat along with Holly's little brother, Josh, and her hyperactive puppy, Mia. Holly's parents would nag the kids about tightening their seat belts and the puppy would dig its claws into Alexa's knees. But she and Holly would laugh and gossip the whole ride away. They made good travel buddies.

Alexa sprung to her feet, flushed by a sudden inspiration. Travel buddies. Of course! Holly was the answer. She was far enough outside Alexa's social realm to be completely removed from the whole Delphine drama: *Holly* certainly wouldn't be smug about Alexa not having proper spring break plans. And if Portia, Maeve, or Sabina cocked an eyebrow at Alexa's traveling with Holly, Alexa could always write it off as a random flash of nostalgia.

Maybe it was the breakup with Tyler, or the sight of the bracelet on her wrist, but Alexa *was* feeling a little nostalgic. She remembered how affectionate Holly had always been, at least compared to cool-as-ice Portia. Alexa wondered what it would be like to take off on an impromptu trip with her old friend, for old times' sake. Impulsively, she grabbed the cell phone off her desk and scrolled down the names in her phone book. She was sure Holly was still in there, somewhere. Even though Alexa bought a new cell almost every year, she always transferred her old phone book over, not bothering to delete any names — except for ex-boyfriends, of course.

Alexa paused when she reached Holly's name. Holly might already have spring break plans . . . but most likely not. Alexa remembered how overprotective Holly's parents had been when it came to Holly doing anything even remotely adventurous. Chances were she was trapped in Oakridge, too. *Maybe we could help each other out,* Alexa thought. A small thrill shot through her. *Why* not *call?* she reasoned, clicking on Holly's name and pressing TALK. There was no harm in taking a chance.

CHAPTER TWO
Escape Plan

Holly Jacobson sprinted down the stairs two at a time and nearly collided with her twelve-year-old brother, Josh, who was deep into his Game Boy Advance.

"Hey, watch it, Nintendo-head," Holly teased, skirting around him.

Josh looked up from the game and stuck his tongue out at Holly. Then he pointed to the small square of shiny turquoise material that was tucked under her arm, and his green eyes widened.

"Is that a *bra?*" Josh asked, curiosity and disgust mingling in his voice.

Holly rolled her eyes. "No, you dweeb. It's a tankini." Could her brother get any grosser?

"Whatev," Josh replied, tromping up the stairs.

Growing up, Holly and Josh had been pretty tight — they could spend *hours* griping about how annoying their parents were — but ever since her brother hit puberty, Holly had felt totally distanced from him. Holly didn't have many good guy friends, and sometimes she worried that maybe she just didn't *get* boys. They all seemed to speak a different language from her. Which probably explained why her experience with boys was so utterly lacking.

Except for that one incredible summer, three years ago.

Holly headed down the hall into the kitchen. Her best friend, Meghan, sat at the table, munching on apple slices and idly flipping through her math textbook. Holly's open binder and textbook were on the table, as well; the two girls were *supposed* to be doing their precalculus assignment together that afternoon. But all they'd done so far, much to Holly's chagrin, was talk about Meghan's spring break plans.

"Here you go, Meggie," Holly said, tossing her friend the blue J.Crew two-piece. "It's all yours." She plunked down in the chair across from Meghan. "Well, for next week, anyway," she added with a grin, helping herself to an apple slice from the plate in the center of the table.

"Thanks for bringing this down," Meghan said,

holding up the tank and matching boy shorts. "It's so much more . . . *Cali* than my old black bathing suit." She shot a grateful smile at Holly. "You're the best."

Holly blew up her bangs. "It's not like *I'll* be needing any swimwear next week," she pointed out. She couldn't help the note of bitterness that had crept into her voice. She crunched hard into a shiny green crescent of apple.

On Saturday morning, Meghan, along with their other close friend, Jess, was leaving for Disneyland. Meghan and Jess had planned the trip back in February and assumed Holly would come, too. But when a hopeful Holly had broached the topic with her parents, they'd freaked at the mere suggestion. Three girls, traveling all the way to California? And spending a week alone, with no adults around? The idea!

So Holly wouldn't be joining them. Meghan and Jess had been upset, but not surprised. The same thing happened at the end of last summer, when Jess had invited the entire girls' track team to her beach house on the Jersey shore for a no-parents weekend. Holly had wound up stuck at home, helping her mom weed the garden while her friends went skinny-dipping and stayed up all night to watch the sunrise. Holly sighed at the memory. She was forever getting left behind.

Meghan frowned sympathetically, resting her elbows on her textbook and blinking her brown eyes at Holly. "Come on, H. Just ask them one more time. I bet they'd give in eventually, and you could still find last-minute tickets —"

Holly shook her head, her short ponytail snapping from side to side. "You know my parents never budge, Meggie."

It was true; Holly had long since learned to give up once her parents said no. But also, Holly realized with the slightest twinge of guilt, she wasn't sure if this *particular* trip was worth the fight. Holly fiddled with her chunky silver ring. She'd never admit it to Meghan or Jess, but going to Disneyland seemed sort of babyish to her. Disneyland was someplace you went with your parents when you were eight — not where you were supposed to go for junior year spring break. Holly would have loved to travel with her friends — and anyplace beat Oakridge — but did she want to incur the wrath of her mother just so she could go whirl around in a giant teacup?

Not really.

"It won't be the same without you," Meghan said. "You'd better call us every day."

"Believe me, I will," Holly groaned. "I'll need to vent to *someone* about Josh and the 'rents." Holly's mom was the assistant principal at Oakridge High, and her dad taught biology at the middle school, so they'd be on spring break, too. They always used their time off to catch up on errands around the house. And Josh would be busy prepping for his bar mitzvah next month. The whole Jacobson family, homebound together, for an endless week.

Holly glanced forlornly out the window at her slushy driveway. She wished she could be outside running, even in the snow. Her sneakers pounding the pavement, her breath coming in fast, smoky puffs. Holly loved the clarity and liberty running afforded her; she felt so free when she was in motion.

The sharp barks of her yellow Lab, Mia, punctured Holly's thoughts and she turned in her chair to see Mia bound into the kitchen. The dog had as much energy as her namesake, soccer star Mia Hamm — one of Holly's idols. Holly's mother was on Mia's trail. "She's giving me a migraine," Holly's mom said crisply as Mia dove under the table and nipped at Holly's feet. Holly bent and scratched Mia behind the ears.

"She probably wants to go out," Holly said. "Can I take her?" she added hopefully, eager for a chance to break out for a little while.

Holly's mom peered worriedly out the window at the gathering gloom. "Your father will take her. It's getting dark." Then she glanced at Meghan. "You should be heading home, Meghan. I'm sure your parents won't want you walking alone in the pitch-black. Or Mr. Jacobson and I can give you a ride —"

"Oh, that's okay, Mrs. Jacobson," Meghan said quickly, standing and pulling her fleece off the back of her chair. Holly watched thoughtfully as Meghan jammed her math books into her knapsack. Holly's friends always got flustered and über-polite around her mom — to them she was Mrs. Jacobson, big bad Assistant Principal. Both Holly's parents gave off that intense teacher vibe. Regardless of whether they were wearing pajamas or raking the leaves, they still behaved as if they were standing in front of a black-board, about to scold someone.

Meghan hugged Holly good-bye, thanked her again for the tankini, and dashed off. After Holly's mom returned to the den to watch the news, and Holly's dad shepherded Mia outside, Holly turned her attention to her math homework. But she couldn't concentrate. The house was warm and stuffy, and Holly peeled off her gray wool sweater, leaving only her ribbed Adidas tank over her flared cords. She undid her ponytail and ran her fingers through her straight, light-brown hair, which fell to just below her chin. Tossing down her pencil, Holly reached into her bookbag and pulled out her iPod. Holly was an eighties-music junkie; as she clicked over to the old Go-Gos song, "Vacation," she smiled wryly.

Vacation, all I ever wanted. Vacation, had to get away . . .

With the music blaring in her ears, Holly doodled a beach umbrella in the margin of her notebook, and then closed her eyes. She imagined herself someplace else — not Oakridge, not Disneyland. She was playing volleyball on a beach, the ocean breeze on her back, and her bare feet in the sand. . . .

There was a tap on her shoulder. Holly turned, and felt a knot of irritation rise up in her belly when she saw her mom standing there, holding Holly's red T-Mobile. *What now?* Holly wondered. Were they supposed to start dinner already? When Holly removed the tiny white earphones from her ears, she heard her phone ringing shrilly.

"You left it in the den," her mother said in an accusatory tone, handing Holly the cell.

As her mom walked out of the kitchen, Holly glanced down at the unknown number flashing on the screen. Bizarre. Usually, she only received calls from the people programmed into her cell. This number did seem vaguely familiar, but Holly couldn't place it. She bit her lip, a little nervous, then flipped open the phone.

"Hello?" she asked cautiously.

"Holly!" A girl's voice bubbled over the line, warm and fizzy. "It's me. Alexa!"

Holly's stomach tightened. Alexa St. Laurent? How random was *that*? She and Alexa hadn't spoken in years. Holly had deleted Alexa's number from her phone in the ninth grade, marking the final break from her former best friend.

"Holly? Are you there?" Alexa asked, after Holly had been silent for several long seconds.

Holly chewed on a thumbnail, now officially nervous. "Yeah. I'm here. Hi." What could she say? Why was Alexa even calling her?

"It's kind of weird to hear your voice." Alexa paused. "It's been forever, huh?"

"Tell me about it," Holly managed. Her tongue felt clumsy in her mouth. Was Alexa delusional or something? Did she think they were still friends?

"What have you been up to?" Alexa went on. "Still running track?"

"Yup." Holly thought about telling Alexa that she'd just been named co-captain, but she resisted. Would Alexa even care about something that didn't involve male models or designer labels?

"I always admired that about you," Alexa said. "I'm so lazy. Trying on Mavi jeans is my only form of aerobic workout."

Holly gave a hesitant chuckle. She was thrown by Alexa's sudden friendliness, but she also couldn't help feeling flattered by her words. Alexa had always been disarmingly charming.

"Well, you don't need to worry," Holly replied bashfully. "You're skinny, anyway."

Whenever Holly thought of Alexa, she first pictured the Alexa she'd known best — the short, slender, flaxen-haired girl in plaid skirts and knee socks, who spoke with a hint of a French accent and could make Holly burst into hysterical laughter just by crossing her enormous blue eyes. Then, Holly had to remind herself to replace the picture with the way Alexa looked now — tall and gorgeous, decked out in fur-trimmed tweed blazers and spike-heeled Jimmy Choos, striding through the Oakridge halls with her ever-present Starbucks latte and a boy at her side. Holly couldn't imagine the present-day Alexa ever crossing her eyes. Or trying to make Holly laugh at all.

"Thanks," Alexa said. "But lying around the house and stuffing my face with chips every day next week isn't going to help much."

Next week? Holly thought, confused. "Don't you have plans for spring break?" she blurted, regretting her words an instant later. Of course Alexa had plans for spring break. She was probably flying to Aruba or something. What a dumb thing to even ask.

"I did, but they fell through," Alexa replied with a sigh. "What about you?" she volleyed back casually.

"Um, not really," Holly said. A deep blush warmed her cheeks. Couldn't she have lied or something? Leave it to Alexa to make her feel like the biggest dork alive.

"I wasn't sure if you'd be busy or not," Alexa said. "But I had the craziest idea. . . ."

Wait a minute, Holly thought, suddenly wary. Where was Alexa steering their little chat?

"I was sitting in my room, thinking about how I used to go to the Catskills with you and your family. Those long car rides . . ." There was a note of wistfulness to Alexa's voice that Holly hardly recognized.

"I remember," Holly replied. She thought back to sharing a bunk bed with Alexa in the cabin upstate — trading ghost stories while the tree branches tapped against their window, frightening them in a delicious way. Back then, Alexa had practically been like Holly's sister. "That was a long time ago," Holly added quietly. She wasn't sure what purpose this trip down memory lane was serving.

"I know," Alexa said. "That's why I was wondering . . . wouldn't it be cool to go somewhere together this year? You and me. Like old times. But without

parents, of course. Just this total whirlwind getaway."
Alexa paused. "What do you think?"

Holly was speechless, but her mind was racing. *So
I'm your sloppy seconds,* she longed to retort. *Do I seem
like that much of a sucker?* Holly twisted the ring
around her middle finger, silently stewing. It was so
obvious. Alexa had called Holly, dripping kindness,
only because all her other plans hadn't worked out.
Did Alexa honestly think that after what had happened between them — and all their years of not
being friends — Holly was going to get all giddy at the
thought of their spending spring break together?
Holly took a deep breath, searching for a way to articulate her bubbling emotions. She'd never been very
good at confrontations.

"I — I don't think I'm up for that," Holly spoke at
last, her face burning. "I mean . . . we haven't talked in
so long. What made you even think to ask me?" God,
this was awkward.

Alexa sighed dramatically. "Oh, there was this boy
drama, and then all my stupid friends left me adrift,
and to be honest . . ." Alexa gave her small, tinkly
laugh. "I'm kind of sick of them, anyway. At this point
I would *completely* prefer to go away with you. If you'd
want to." Suddenly, Alexa sounded just the slightest
bit vulnerable, and Holly could feel herself starting to

soften. "Don't you remember how much fun we used to have?" Alexa went on. "Like the time we played Truth or Dare, and I dared you to crank-call my cousin Pierre in Paris and pretend to be me?" Alexa asked with another laugh.

Holly smiled, despite herself. "How could I forget?" she asked. "My parents saw the phone bill afterward and grounded me for a *month*." Holly remembered how she'd mimicked Alexa's voice into the phone, dropping in random French words that Alexa whispered to her, thoroughly fooling Pierre. Afterward, she and Alexa had fallen into a heap of laughter on Holly's bedroom floor. Alexa had often gotten Holly into scrapes that were wildly fun in the moment, but ultimately ended in some sort of parental disapproval.

"But it was worth it," Alexa mused aloud. "We had a good time."

"That we did," Holly had to admit. She'd always had trouble staying mad at Alexa — her boldness and energy could be irresistible. Holly glanced down at the beach umbrella she'd drawn in her notebook. She *had* been dreaming of an escape, hadn't she? But there was still the teensy problem of her parents. Maybe Alexa would at least have some ideas for how Holly could get away.

"So your parents probably haven't changed much, huh?" Alexa asked, as if she'd read Holly's mind. Her voice was full of understanding.

Holly bit her lip. Alexa knew about Holly's issues with her parents better than almost anyone, because she'd been there at the start. In the fourth grade, Holly's parents decided that Holly shouldn't go to sleepover parties. Alexa got to attend them all, and would always have some life-changing experience, like getting her ears pierced or seeing an R-rated movie. She'd fill Holly in on all the details the next day. It had been painful, but also sort of pleasant, to live life vicariously through Alexa.

"Yeah. Mom and Dad are pretty much the same," Holly replied with a sigh of resignation.

"So that's why you're home for the break?" Alexa pressed on gently.

"Basically," Holly confessed. "I can't even think of a place they'd let me go." She dropped her voice, glancing over her shoulder in case her mom walked in again.

"So let's brainstorm," Alexa suggested. "There's got to be somewhere!"

"The Galleria?" Holly asked with a snort.

"Stop it, Holly." Alexa laughed. "You can't spend spring break shopping in Oakridge like some old lady."

Old lady. Holly's heart leaped. How had it not occurred to her before? She'd totally forgotten about her grandmother, who lived near the ocean in Miami Beach. Holly's parents wouldn't hesitate to let her stay at Grandma Ida's over break. And Miami was gorgeous and sunny, and . . . Holly's pulse quickened as she remembered her last visit to Miami Beach, three years ago. It had been magical. That night on the beach, under the full moon . . .

Suddenly restless, Holly stood up. "There is one place," she said, as she began to pace the length of the kitchen. "My grandmother. She has an apartment in Florida. Josh and I visited her the summer I was thirteen." Alexa hadn't known about that trip, Holly realized, because by then, they'd stopped being friends.

"Your grandmother?" Alexa asked incredulously. Holly could practically read Alexa's thoughts: *That's the lamest plan in the history of spring break.*

"No, but listen," Holly went on, trying to maintain some dignity. "She's really cool. I mean, for a grandmother. And her neighborhood's nice. There are all these beaches, and you can take the bus down to South Beach. . . ." *What am I doing?* Holly asked herself. Was she trying to convince Alexa that they *should* go away together?

"South Beach?" Alexa cut in. Now, there was tremor of excitement in her voice. "South Beach is supposed to be this amazing up-and-coming spring break spot. And I think it got written up in *Elle* as one of the world's sexiest getaways!" Holly heard Alexa rustling about in her room, most likely going through her giant stack of fashion magazines.

"Here it is," Alexa said after a minute, then read aloud: "'South Beach, Florida. The land of rhythm, rumba, and rum margaritas!'"

"Does it really say that?" Holly asked, laughing.

"Let me finish," Alexa said. "'South Beach is a glamorous, glitzy town with an unmistakable Latin flavor. SoBe, as it's commonly called, overflows with sandy beaches for sun-worshiping, and spicy clubs for dancing the night away.'" Alexa giggled with delight. "And there's this photo of the ritzy Rose Bar, in the Delano hotel. Holly, it sounds perfect! Let's do it."

Holly was overwhelmed. South Beach did sound appealing . . . and very grown-up. Not Disneyland at all. Holly was still unsure about Alexa, but going to Florida with her would definitely be an improvement over staying home with her entire family.

At that instant, both Holly's parents entered the kitchen: Her dad walked through the back door with Mia, and her mom came in from the den and opened the refrigerator.

"Holly, would you start breading the chicken cutlets?" her mother asked, pulling out a carton of eggs as Mia barked loudly.

"Uh, hang on," Holly whispered to Alexa, flustered by all the commotion. She turned to her mom and said, "I'll be back in a second. I'm — I'm having an important conversation." Holding the phone to her ear, Holly hurried out of the kitchen and upstairs to her room. She was surprised by herself. When her mom asked her to get off the phone, she usually did it immediately.

In her bedroom, Holly shut and locked the door, then plopped down on her plaid bedspread. "Okay," she said to Alexa. "I'm back."

"Great," Alexa said. Holly could hear the clickety-clack of her fingers on a keyboard. "I'm on Orbitz right now. I can look up flights for Miami and —"

"Wait," Holly interrupted. This was moving way too fast for her. "I need to think about it a little. And ask my grandmother if we can stay with her. *And* ask my parents if I can even go." She dreaded the mere thought of that.

"Okay," Alexa said. "You think, and take care of all the yucky permission stuff. Meanwhile, I'm going to find us cheap flights. Call me back!" Then she clicked off.

Holly remembered her childhood nickname for

Alexa: "Little Miss Bossy." She wondered how that aspect of Alexa's personality might play out on their trip — if they did end up going.

Holly snapped her phone shut and stretched across her twin bed, hugging a stuffed panda to her chest. She looked at the framed photo that hung above the bed, of her, Meghan, and Jess. Sweaty and triumphant after a track meet, they stood with their arms around one another's shoulders. Holly's friends would probably freak if she told them she was going away with Alexa. They thought of Alexa and her impeccably dressed crowd as total snobs.

But now that the kernel of Miami Beach was in Holly's head, she could feel it expanding and growing, taking the shape of reality. She wanted to go, she realized. With or without Alexa. But, because Holly's parents didn't let her fly anywhere alone, Alexa's being there was a necessity.

If Holly was being completely honest with herself, her desire to go to Miami had something to do with a boy. The boy she'd met down there, three years ago. Holly felt a flush spreading up her neck into her face. She hadn't thought about Diego in a while. But talking about Florida had triggered all the old memories. They rushed back now, as vivid as ever.

Diego Felipe Mendieta. He'd been fourteen at the

time, but tall for his age. His skin was the color of cocoa butter, his eyes were black as olives, and his hair was dark and glossy. Whenever he smiled, the two deepest, most adorable dimples appeared in his cheeks. Diego lived in her grandmother's apartment building and he'd introduced himself in the lobby one day, which had absolutely floored Holly. Boys like Diego never talked to her. But the two of them had ended up spending the whole week together — surfing on Haulover Beach, bike-riding north to Sunny Isles, eating triple-scoop ice-cream cones on the boardwalk. Then, on Holly's last night, Diego had given Holly her first — and, so far, only — kiss.

Holly closed her eyes, summoning that one yummy memory. It had been around ten o'clock, a muggy, sticky Miami night. She and Diego had gotten choco-late chip ice-cream cones, and decided to bring them down to the beach. The full moon had cast its pale reflection on the surface of the ocean. Holly remem-bered the feel of the cold ice cream on her tongue and the foamy water on her bare toes. She and Diego had fallen silent, gazing up in wonder at the moon, and Holly had felt an odd shift between them — a kind of electric spark. She'd never felt that happen with a boy before. And she'd suddenly become aware of Diego's arm so close to hers. She'd resisted the urge to touch him — to rest her hand on the sleeve of his T-shirt — but then Diego had touched *her*. He leaned over, brought his fingers to her lips, and lightly wiped the corner of Holly's mouth.

"Ice cream," he explained with a half smile. Holly wanted to die of mortification, but before she could, Diego kissed her. Really kissed her. The fullness of his lips and the salty-sweet taste of his mouth, and his warm hand on her waist made Holly's knees wobble. She almost dropped her cone in the sand. Kissing was so much better than Holly had ever imagined — soft and warm and easy. She'd wanted the kiss to last forever, but Diego had gently ended it, smiled at Holly, and turned back to the ocean. Still, when they'd walked back to the building, their fingers had brushed together as if they were about to hold hands. And when they parted ways in the elevator, Diego had given her another kiss, this time on the cheek, and promised to stay in touch.

And they had, Holly remembered as she lay on her bed. They'd e-mailed and IMed for the rest of the summer and into the school year, trading reminisces about their week in Miami. Holly remembered how her heart would bang against her ribs whenever she saw his name pop up on her screen. But, as the year went on, their correspondence had petered out. After some time, Diego faded in Holly's mind, remaining a blissful, if distant, memory.

Holly opened her eyes and swung her legs off the bed. She looked at herself in the round mirror above her desk. Her green-gray eyes were very bright and her freckled cheeks dark pink. Holly *had* sometimes teased herself with the thought that she'd go back to Miami Beach one day and have a romantic reunion with Diego. But she'd gotten so busy with schoolwork and track, and sports camp in the summer, that there hadn't been another chance to visit Grandma Ida.

Until now.

Sure, things were weird with Alexa. The setup was far from ideal. But Holly knew she'd be insane to throw away this opportunity to reconnect with her old crush. Maybe it was fated that she see Diego again. There was a very good chance she'd run into him in Grandma Ida's building. Diego would be seventeen now, probably even hotter, and most likely an even better kisser. The answer was staring Holly right in the face. She grinned at her reflection. She was going to Miami.

"Holly Rebecca!" Her mother's voice thundered from the kitchen. "Are you still on the phone?"

"Are you upstairs?" her dad chimed in.

Holly took a deep breath. Right. She still had to

clear the hurdle of her parents. They'd probably be okay with the Grandma Ida plan, but the Alexa element was a wild card. Holly's mom had never been a fan of Alexa's; she had been ecstatic when the girls' friendship faded. Alexa was a good student at Oakridge High, and never got into any trouble, but, as assistant principal, Holly's mom had personally busted a few of Alexa's friends for smoking on school grounds. As far as Holly's mom was concerned, Alexa was still nothing but trouble. So Holly was somehow going to have to make her old friend seem otherwise.

Before Holly turned to go downstairs, she closed her eyes and rehearsed a brief speech in her mind: *Mom and Dad, I miss Grandma Ida so much! She must be lonely down in Florida. I thought, since I'll be on break next week, I could go see her. And I wouldn't be traveling alone. Alexa St. Laurent asked if she could come along, too. Just her, none of her friends. She's much more down-to-earth than she seems at school, and I think Grandma Ida would really like her. . . .*

Will that work? Holly wondered. Holly knew this sudden urge to see her grandmother might seem suspicious. But her parents would likely be so impressed with Holly showing, as her mother called it, "family commitment," that they wouldn't think twice.

Holly tightened her ponytail, straightened her shoulders, and strode out of the bedroom. She'd march into the kitchen, and sit her mom and dad down. She'd make this thing happen. She had to. Holly was fed up with watching her friends do exciting things while she sat at home, life passing her by. It was time to take her destiny into her own hands.

CHAPTER THREE
Like Paradise

"Welcome aboard American Airlines Flight 320, with nonstop service from Newark to Miami."

At the flight attendant's announcement, Holly fastened her seat belt and glanced at Alexa, who occupied the window seat next to her. It was Saturday morning, and the girls were on a plane bound for Florida. Holly couldn't believe this trip was happening. Everything had fallen into place so quickly, it still felt surreal.

Holly's parents had reacted exactly as she'd predicted — pleased about Grandma Ida, iffy about Alexa. But a phone call to Grandma Ida — who said she'd be delighted to host the girls — sealed the deal. In happy disbelief, Holly called Alexa (whose own dad, of course, had readily given his blessing) and they booked the tickets. There was no looking back.

Alexa plumped the airplane pillow behind her blonde head and gazed down at her shiny mauve nails. That morning, she'd made a last-minute run to Suzy's Salon for an emergency mani–pedi. One could *not* show up on the beach with pale, ungroomed winter feet. She'd invited Holly along, too, but — shocker — Holly had refused, claiming she didn't see the point. Alexa snuck a glance at Holly now, sizing up her outfit: pearl-gray zip-up hoodie, Gap jeans, Adidas sneakers. *Yawn,* Alexa thought. She hoped Holly wouldn't be too much of an embarrassment to her for the next seven days.

Alexa was wearing a fuzzy, champagne-colored cowl-neck, a corduroy miniskirt, and her chocolate brown, wedge-heeled Coach boots. It was one of her favorite winter outfits, but she was *so* ready to slip into something skimpier. She'd packed a pink halter bikini in her carry-on bag, so she would be able to change as soon as they got to Miami. Alexa imagined herself ambling along a boardwalk, clad only in her bikini, returning the smiles of passing boys. Of course, Holly was conveniently *not* in that picture.

"Flight attendants, please prepare for takeoff." The captain's voice came over the loudspeaker. Alexa felt Holly tense up beside her.

"Um, so this is it," Holly said, crossing her legs. She suddenly felt all-out nervous — about flying, as always, but mostly about Alexa. Sitting next to her felt familiar — as if they'd gone back in time — but also completely weird. They hadn't spoken more than a few words to each other since they'd met at the gate that morning: Holly's parents fussing over her while Alexa hid behind giant shades and sipped her latte. Their clumsy phone camaraderie from Thursday evening seemed to have evaporated. Now there was only stony silence.

What if we can't think of anything to talk about for the entire week? Holly agonized as the plane taxied down the runway. It was becoming glaringly obvious how little she and Alexa had in common — they barely knew each other now. And Holly kept thinking about what Meghan had said when Holly told her the news: "You know she's only going to want to do shallow things." Holly gulped, remembering how Alexa had invited her along for a manicure and pedicure that very morning. Meghan was right. This trip could be a disaster.

Alexa looked out the window, pretending not to hear Holly's stilted attempt at conversation. She was psyched to be getting away, but she was also wondering, for the umpteenth time, if taking this trip with Holly was a bad call.

"You're going with *her*? She'll be in bed by ten every night," Portia had warned Alexa on Friday morning.

Portia was right, Alexa thought. Holly had seemed *almost* cool on the phone on Thursday. But seeing her in the flesh reminded Alexa of how uptight her old friend could be. And the whole staying-with-Grandma plan *still* felt wrong. At least Alexa hadn't admitted that part of the scenario to Portia.

As the airplane gained momentum and began hurtling down the runway, Alexa felt a delicious tingle of anticipation and her anxieties melted away. This was the part she loved best about travel — the instant before takeoff. She settled back comfortably in her seat, feeling a renewed surge of hope about the trip. Then, she looked at Holly.

Holly was sitting ramrod straight, her fingers gripping the armrests. Her cheeks were drained of all color and her lips were white.

"Are you okay?" Alexa asked, leaning forward in concern.

"Yeah," Holly said. Then she shook her head. "No, I'm not. Oh, my God, imagine if we crash?" Holly had flown only a few times before — and had been scared out of her wits each time. And she didn't like the sensation of being trapped inside a small cabin for hours with not much room to move around.

The airplane lifted off the ground, its nose angled toward the sky. Holly reached over and clutched Alexa's arm, and Alexa tried as hard as she could not to laugh. Of course sheltered Holly would freak out on an airplane. It was kind of cute, if a little annoying. Alexa took Holly's hand and gave it a quick squeeze. "Relax," she said, hiding her smile. She hoped Holly wouldn't be scared of *everything*. Alexa didn't have much patience for fear.

The plane leveled off and Holly's crazy heartbeat slowed. She pulled her hand away from Alexa's, feeling like a baby, and stared down at her copy of *Teen People*, trying not to make eye contact.

"A drink would do you good," Alexa spoke, breaking the silence. She figured she'd at least *try* to make the plane ride fun. Alexa glanced around the cabin as the flight attendants began rolling their carts by. "It's too bad we can't order alcohol on board. I don't think my fake ID would go over well here, do you?"

"You have a fake ID?" Holly asked.

"It's a must," Alexa said, tossing back her long hair. "Don't tell me you . . . don't?"

"Um . . ." Holly said, just as a flight attendant stopped by her seat. Though she was relieved that she and Alexa were finally talking, this was one question Holly wanted to avoid. She hadn't ever thought of getting a fake ID, since she didn't drink.

Holly had gotten sort of drunk, once, off two beers at a party sophomore year. The slightly bitter flavor of the beer had been interesting, and the drinks had made

Holly's head whirl in an almost-pleasant way. But once had been enough.

Holly ordered an orange juice and Alexa got a Pellegrino. Alexa raised her cup and smiled. Maybe all Holly needed was some loosening up.

"A toast!" Alexa exclaimed. "To sunshine. And palm trees. And sexy boys!" She tapped her cup against Holly's. "God, I hope I'll have at least one good hookup," she said with a sigh.

"Wait . . ." Holly set down her drink on the folding tray. "Don't you have a boyfriend?" Whenever she'd seen Alexa in school that year, she'd been draped all over the studly lacrosse star, Tyler Davis.

"Past tense," Alexa said, her face lighting up. Though she'd had a few brief flashes of guilt, she hadn't given much thought to Tyler since Thursday. And he was behind her now — back on the ground. Far more intriguing boys awaited her in Miami. "Boyfriends are overrated, anyway," she added, sipping her drink.

"Are they?" Holly asked. She had no idea what it was like to have a boyfriend, but she guessed it must be pretty nice. To have someone you could kiss whenever you felt like it. Someone to go to the movies with on a Saturday night. Someone who'd drape his jacket over your bare shoulders if you got chilly.

Alexa nodded with conviction. "They're too . . .

intense. I think casual flings are the way to go." After her serious relationship with Tyler, she was more than ready for a few meaningless moments with boys she'd never see again.

"Oh," Holly said. She didn't have any experience with flings, either. Unless she counted Diego. At the thought of him, Holly's stomach gave a funny little jump. She eagerly peered out the window at the puffy white clouds. She might actually see Diego that very day. *And this time,* Holly thought, a little surprised by her own naughtiness, *maybe we'll do more than just kiss.*

A few hours later, the girls were in Miami, speeding toward Grandma Ida's in a cab. Holly's grandmother had offered to pick up the girls from the airport, but Holly had declined, thinking that might seem childish to Alexa. The cab was a mature — if pricey — alternative.

While Holly called her parents on her cell to assure them she'd landed safely, Alexa rolled down her window and drank in the passing scenery with glee. The avenue they were driving down was lined with tall palm trees. The buildings and Art Deco hotels were all pastel shades: pale peaches, light greens, sky-blues, and bright yellows. Bronzed boys in board shorts Rollerbladed by, and girls in bikinis flip-flopped lazily on their way to the beach. It was a perfect day for suntanning: The sky was a deep azure and the buttery sun felt warm as a caress. Alexa breathed in the salty tang of the ocean. She heard Holly shut her cell phone and roll down her own window.

"It's like paradise," Holly said, echoing Alexa's thoughts.

The one imperfection in this paradise, Alexa reflected, was that they weren't driving toward some luxury resort, but to Grandma Ida's. She didn't mention this to Holly, though. Holly would probably get all defensive, and Alexa felt there was enough tension between them already. She'd simply have to deal with the grandma sitch when they got there.

The cab pulled to a stop in front of a small, light-blue apartment house, and Alexa felt even more deflated. The place looked so ordinary. Her full lower lip plumped out prettily.

"Yes, this is it," Holly said, annoyed by Alexa's disappointed expression. Alexa had been the one to call *her*, asking to go on this trip. Now that they were in Miami, she was suddenly pulling a princess act?

They paid the driver and grabbed their bags — Alexa had packed twice as much as Holly. They straggled into the building's cool, airy lobby, and Holly felt a pang of anticipation mixed with anxiety. This was where she'd first met Diego that summer, right by the elevator. What if he walked through the lobby now? Holly glanced down, feeling plain in her jeans and hooded sweatshirt. When they made it to the elevator with no Diego in sight, she was relieved — but also disappointed.

They rode to the fourth floor in silence. Alexa gazed critically at a flyer in the elevator advertising a mambo class for seniors. What had she been thinking, letting Holly drag her here? Brooding, she followed Holly out of the elevator and down a corridor. Holly stopped in front of one of the gray doors and rang the bell.

The door flew open to reveal Ida Jacobson.

"Darlings!"

Petite and wiry, the very tanned, very wrinkled seventy-year-old had short, flaming red hair. She wore a leopard-print bathing suit, a purple sarong, and beaded floral slippers. Cat-eyed, white-framed sunglasses perched on top of her head, and blue dolphin earrings dangled from her ears. Alexa liked her immediately.

"Hi, Grandma," Holly said, stepping forward hesitantly.

"What beauties!" Ida flung her arms around Holly and Alexa at the same time. She smelled of Estée Lauder Pleasures and suntan oil.

She whirled on Holly, studying her intently. "Such a looker you are!" she exclaimed. "My Holly. Last time you were here, you were a little girl. You didn't have this"— she made an hourglass shape with her hands — "womanly figure!" Holly blushed to the roots of her hair. Ida patted her behind, apparently through with her, then turned to size up Alexa.

"And you're the infamous Alexa. Look at *you.*" Ida clucked her tongue appreciatively. "You must be beating the boys off with a stick!"

"Well," Alexa said, ducking her head and smiling. She didn't like to brag. . . .

"Come in, come in," Ida said, ushering them into the foyer. "Make yourselves at home."

Holly and Alexa stepped into the small, sunny apartment. Ida's living room was decorated in varying shades of purple. Magazines, books, and beach towels were strewn everywhere. A brightly plumed parakeet chirped shrilly from its cage in the corner. The air conditioner was going full blast. Holly looked around in wonder as she set her bags on the floor. At thirteen, the apartment had seemed fun to her, but now it was giving her a headache. She remembered that Josh had slept on the pullout couch in the living room, and she had gotten the spare bedroom down the hall. Holly figured she and Alexa would share that room now.

Alexa surveyed the decor, and her spirits lifted. Ida was a lot more interesting than she had anticipated. Staying here might be bearable after all. Besides, all she wanted to do now was change into her bikini, so she could head straight for the beach.

"What do you girls need?" Ida asked, hands planted firmly on her hips. "Something to drink, some cookies?"

"Is there someplace I can change?" Alexa asked, motioning to her numerous bags.

"Sure, the bathroom is right there, across from my bedroom." Ida pointed to a door off the living room just as the phone rang in the kitchen. Ida flew off, her sarong trailing behind her and picked up the phone. "Oh, hi, Miriam," Holly heard her say. "I'd love to chat, but I have guests. . . ." Holly tightened her ponytail nervously. Was it just her imagination, or did Grandma Ida sound a little put out by the fact that she and Alexa were here?

With a flourish, Alexa pulled her teensy metallic pink bikini and matching flip-flops out of her carry-on. Tucking them under her arm, she walked toward the bathroom. She didn't know why Holly wasn't also rushing to change; her outfit was *so* not Miami-appropriate. Alexa shut the bathroom door, turned on the light, yanked off her fuzzy sweater, and reached back to unhook her lacy bra. She was feeling sexier already.

In the living room, Holly sat gingerly on the sofa, twisting the silver ring on her finger. She wondered if Alexa planned to ditch her and go to the beach alone. After the awkward plane ride, it might be nice to get some space. Then, Holly glanced up and gave a start when she saw Grandma Ida's bedroom door open. An elderly man stepped out into the hall, and reached for the knob on the bathroom door. Had Alexa even locked it? Holly jumped up, ready to warn her, but she was too late. She heard Alexa emit an ear-piercing scream.

"Grandma Ida, there's a strange man in here!" Holly cried, pointing. The man apologized to Alexa, shut the door, and hurried into the living room, clearly embarrassed.

Ida came running in from the kitchen. "What's all this?" she exclaimed. Then, to Holly's surprise, she went up to the man and kissed him on the cheek. She turned to Holly, beaming.

"Holly, pancake, meet my special friend, Miles. Miles, this is my beautiful granddaughter, Holly. And I guess you've already met her friend, Alexa."

Miles was a handsome, seventy-ish, African-American man, with a close-cropped white beard and bright brown eyes. He wore a button-down Hawaiian shirt and Bermuda shorts. He tipped his baseball cap to Holly.

Holly stared back at him, wide-eyed. Grandma Ida had a *boyfriend*?

Ida's phone rang again, and Miles headed for it.

"That'll be Ruthie and Harry, wondering why we're late for canasta," Miles said to Ida over his shoulder. "And don't forget about bingo tonight, sweetie."

"Right," Ida said, looking frazzled. She turned to Holly. "So, bubeleh, can I get you some lemonade before Miles and I take off?"

"Uh . . . sure," Holly said, distracted. She was still trying to process someone calling her grandmother "sweetie." Holly's grandfather had died before she was born, so she'd always known Grandma Ida as single. Now, the fact that her grandmother apparently had better luck with guys than she did was making Holly feel just shy of pathetic.

Alexa emerged from the bathroom, still in her outfit from the plane, her lips set in a line. She wished she'd thought to lock the door. No way was she changing in that bathroom now — that old man barging in on her had totally killed her sexy vibe. Alexa walked over to Holly and Ida, and forced herself to smile as they explained to her that Miles wasn't a random stalker.

"That's good. Oh, Ida?" Alexa asked sweetly. "Where will Holly and I be sleeping? Can I change in there instead?"

Ida wrung her hands, her bracelets jangling. "Miles has sort of . . . spread out in the apartment," she explained. "A lot of his clothes and things are in the spare bedroom. Anyway, I thought you girls might be more comfortable sleeping right here on the pullout couch." She pointed to the sofa, then she bustled off to the kitchen again.

Alexa looked at Holly, horrified. Not only did they have to share a pullout, but they'd be stuck in the chaotic, crowded living room? Miles was hollering into the phone, and the parakeet was squawking. This would be a nightmare.

"I know," Holly muttered. She shrugged. "There's nothing I can do."

But maybe there's something I can do, Alexa thought. Ida came toward them carrying two glasses of lemonade, and Alexa studied Holly's grandmother carefully. It was obvious that Ida had a rocking social life, and didn't really need Holly and Alexa around. Alexa wondered if she could turn this situation to her advantage.

Ida handed the girls their lemonades, and motioned for them to sit on the sofa. She sat across from them in a lilac armchair.

Holly took a big gulp of lemonade. "This is . . . nice," she lied.

"Yes, thank you, Ida," Alexa gushed. "I hope we aren't imposing. Are you sure we're not in your way?"

"Not at all!" Ida said. "The more the merrier."

Miles hung up the phone and emerged from the kitchen. As he crossed the living room, he tripped over Alexa's open carry-on bag, but caught himself before he fell. Alexa and Holly gasped at the same time.

"Careful, honey!" Ida cried, leaping up.

"I'm okay," Miles said, looking humiliated again. Then he rushed out of the living room and back into Ida's bedroom.

Ida sat down and drew a deep breath, adjusting her sarong around her waist. "Well," she said, as if nothing had happened, "what kind of mischief are you girls cooking up for your stay in Miami?"

"Not much," Holly started to say — they had not, in fact, discussed any plans — but Alexa cut her off.

"We're going to be *so* busy," Alexa said, widening her pale blue eyes for dramatic effect. "We'll probably be in and out of the apartment a lot."

"Oh?" Ida tilted her head thoughtfully. "Well, that's fine. Miles and I aren't at home very much ourselves during the day."

Alexa nodded. "I meant at night. I love to stay out late dancing."

Uh-oh, Holly thought. She couldn't picture herself going out on the town with Alexa.

Ida twinkled merrily at Alexa. "You've come to the right place. Miami's full of discos. That scene's not *quite* for me anymore. But when I was your age . . ." Ida trailed off, looking misty-eyed. "I was quite the mover and shaker."

Alexa grinned. "Give me a crowded dance floor and a thumping rhythm and I'm in heaven," she said. It was true; she was in her element when dancing.

Ida held Alexa's gaze. "It's funny, dear. You remind me a bit of myself at your age."

Holly coughed, feeling a little jealous. Wasn't Grandma Ida supposed to say that sort of thing to her, not Alexa?

"But I hope we won't disturb you," Alexa was saying earnestly. "Like if we're coming in after midnight in our stilettos . . ." She leaned forward and stared at Ida, her expression concerned.

Holly shot Alexa a bewildered glance. She didn't even *own* stilettos.

"Me, I could sleep through a hurricane — and I have," Ida mused. "But Miles is a light sleeper. . . ." She tapped her finger to her upper lip, clearly considering Alexa's words.

"I'd hate for us to be a burden," Alexa added, laying it on thick.

A slow smile of understanding bloomed on Ida's face. "You two angels could never be a burden," she said. Then she paused. "Still, I want you to have the best possible time on your school break. And I am a little worried that we might get on each other's nerves — four people crammed in this little apartment . . ." She winked at Alexa.

Alexa latched on to this notion immediately. "Oh, I know! There's nothing like sharing a small space to make people *despise* each other." She winked back at Ida.

"We don't want that," Ida asserted, shaking her head.

Alexa held her breath, barely believing their luck. Ida totally *got* it. She didn't want the girls staying with her any more than they wanted to be there!

Holly glanced from her grandmother to Alexa, and felt a twinge of worry. Did Alexa want them to *leave* Grandma Ida's? That couldn't happen. Staying here was the most important part of their plan. Her parents wouldn't stand for anything else.

Alexa sighed. "Ida, we would love to stay with you, but maybe it would be best for everyone if we crashed somewhere else. At least for a little while?"

"We — we can't go somewhere else!" Holly jumped in, panicked.

Ida chuckled and leaned over to squeeze Holly's knee. "Listen, honey cake. If you and Alexa do decide to go someplace else, we'll still be able to see each other. You can still come over for dinner —" she gave Alexa a secret smile — "or cocktails! Any time you like."

"But Mom and Dad . . ." Holly trailed off in desperation.

"We don't have to tell your parents, do we?" Ida asked. "They can call you on your cell phone if they want to reach you. And if they ever call here, I'll just tell them you're at the beach!"

"You're a genius," Alexa declared, gazing at Ida with sincere admiration.

"And you're a girl after my own heart," Ida said, leaning over to pat Alexa's hand.

"Um, hold on," Holly said, interrupting their little love fest. "Where else could we even stay?"

"A luxury hotel in South Beach, silly!" Alexa said, springing up and walking over to her carry-on bag. She pulled out her new Time Out guide to Miami and started turning the pages. "There are tons of them. The Delano, the Shore Club, Mercury . . ." Alexa knew she belonged in a swanky place like that. She could see herself strolling into a dazzling hotel lobby, wearing her new strapless rose-colored dress.

"I can't afford to stay anywhere expensive," Holly protested. She'd brought along some of her baby-sitting money, but she wasn't expecting to spend most of it. She had assumed that food and board would be taken care of by her grandmother, but the game plan was rapidly changing.

"And a lot of those places might not have vacancies,

either," Holly added, seeing the sour look on Alexa's face. "Most schools have their spring break this week."

Alexa folded her arms across her chest and narrowed her eyes at Holly. "So what do *you* suggest we do?"

"I have an idea," Ida cut in. "I don't know if you girls will go for this, but . . ." She stood up, scurried over to a desk in the corner of the room, and returned with a thick leather address book. Holly looked on with trepidation as her grandmother flipped through it.

"Aha," Ida said, her finger resting on one page. "The Flamingo. My dear friends, Blanche and Seymour Gold, run this darling motel in South Beach, right on Ocean Drive. It's very affordable. Lots of young people stay there. And it's smack dab in the center of everything. What do you girls say?" She looked right at Alexa. "Should I give them a buzz and see if they have any free rooms?"

Alexa hesitated. The Flamingo? She couldn't remember reading about it in any of her fashion magazines or travel guides. But Ida was essentially handing them their getaway on a platter. Better to grab this chance while they could.

"The Flamingo it is!" Alexa said, flinging down her guide book and grinning at Holly. "Right, Holly?"

"I — I guess," Holly said. She couldn't believe

Alexa had basically convinced her grandmother to kick them out.

"Okay, darlings." Ida stood up. "Let me check in with Seymour. I think you girls will have much more fun staying there. But be sure to call me during the week if you need *anything* — a ride, or extra beach towels, or some advice from an old lady." She smiled mischievously. "And we can make a date for a girls' night out!" she added before heading into the kitchen.

Alexa clapped her hands together and started gathering up her bags, ready to go. She loved Ida, but she could love her even more from a distance.

Holly watched as Grandma Ida reached for the phone. Suddenly, a terrible thought struck her: If they left her grandmother's place now, she'd never get to see Diego.

There was still time to act. Maybe she could get Grandma Ida to check in with the Mendietas. If Diego was in this very building, why would Holly want to be anyplace else?

Casting all caution aside, Holly sprinted into the kitchen and took her grandmother's hand.

"Grandma Ida, can I ask you something?" she said breathlessly.

"Anything, muffin."

"Do you, um, ever speak to the Mendietas? You know, the Mendieta family on the third floor?" Holly willed herself not to blush and hoped her grandmother wouldn't guess at the truth behind her question.

"Oh, the Mendietas!" Grandma Ida said. "Such nice people. I remember, they had a girl and a boy. Very attractive family."

Holly nodded, every muscle in her body tensed as she waited for her grandmother's response.

"I do miss them," Grandma Ida went on.

"Why?" Holly asked, her voice tinged with worry. "Where did they go?"

"They moved down to South Beach, sugar." Ida winked at Holly. "A lot of people are heading there nowadays. It seems that's where all the action is."

Holly stared back at her grandmother as the words sunk in. So Diego was in the mythical South Beach — the very place she and Alexa were heading. It seemed this trip was moving in a direction Holly had never imagined. And she didn't know what to expect next.

CHAPTER FOUR
The Flamingo

Alexa fell in love with Ocean Drive at first sight. After Miles and Ida dropped them off, she and Holly paused on the corner in front of the Flamingo, taking everything in. There were funky hotels and hopping restaurants on one side and an endless stretch of beach on the other. People bustled past them, chattering in an array of languages. From a nearby restaurant came the jangly beat of a live merengue band. Shiny, candy-colored cars cruised down the streets, their tops rolled down to reveal svelte, tanned drivers. Alexa stared across the street at the shimmery blue Atlantic and shivered with anticipation.

"Don't you want to dive right in?" she murmured.

"First I want to drop off these bags," Holly said,

hoisting up her duffle. She still felt uneasy about this new turn of events. On the short ride over from Ida's, she'd called home again, to tell her mother they were settling in at Grandma's house. Her mom had bought every word. Little did she know Holly and Alexa were now walking under a hot-pink arch into the Flamingo, a dingy-looking, three-story motel that was nestled between two gigantic hotels on Ocean Drive. A passerby might never even notice it.

The motel's lobby floor was covered in bright yellow carpeting, and the retro, squiggle-shaped orange armchairs made Holly think of *The Jetsons*. The walls were painted with murals depicting flamingos on a beach.

Kind of kitschy cool, Alexa thought, raising an eyebrow. They headed for the front desk, where a rotund elderly man in a sun visor stood flipping through a guest book.

Suddenly, a shrieking girl streaked down the stairs and into the lobby, her curvy body wrapped in only a short beach towel. Hot on her heels came a buff, floppy-haired boy, adjusting a towel around his waist. They both dashed toward a back exit, and Holly heard the boy yell, "Last one in the shower buys the first round tonight!"

"There's a shower outside?" Holly asked Alexa, who grinned in return.

"Two, actually," the man behind the desk spoke. "Right by the pool. They're just for rinsing off, but the guests sometimes use them to wash up." He smiled at the girls. "You must be Alexa and Holly. I'm Seymour, Ida's friend. Welcome to the Flamingo."

After they'd checked in, Seymour showed the girls upstairs to their room — Number 7. It was tiny, with two narrow beds, a minuscule window, one dresser, and no bathroom. Even with the window closed, the sounds of Ocean Drive drifted into the room — Latin music, car engines, and flirty laughter. The floor had the same yellow carpeting as the lobby, and the bed-spreads were orange.

Okay, ew, Alexa thought, making her way across the room. What kind of hole had Ida sent them to? No wonder there were vacancies! When Alexa traveled, whether it was with her dad or with friends, she was used to staying in much more luxe accommodations. But as she peered out the window to the beach across the street, Alexa shrugged off her worries. So, the place was slightly declassé. She wasn't planning on spending a lot of time here, anyway.

"It's kind of gross, huh?" Holly asked guiltily.

"Who cares?" Alexa threw her massive suitcase onto the bed closest to the window — definitely the better-situated one. "We just need a place to rest our bodies after we're exhausted from too much partying!"

"Yeah," Holly said. Partying. "Like what kind of partying?" she asked tentatively as she placed her bags on the other bed. The two beds were practically crammed together, and there was hardly any space to navigate around them.

"Oh you *know,* Holly. Going to bars and stuff." Alexa rolled her eyes, unzipping one of her bags.

Holly watched with growing concern as Alexa began to unpack, removing heaps of clothing and tossing them onto the bed. The more clothes Alexa pulled out, the smaller the already-cramped room felt.

"Where are you going to put all that?" Holly asked.

"In the dresser," Alexa answered curtly, refolding a glittery black cardigan. She skirted around Holly and walked to the dresser across from Holly's bed. She began stuffing her things into the tight drawers.

Great. So where would Holly squeeze in her clothes? Holly remembered Alexa's words from earlier that afternoon: *There's nothing like sharing a small space to make people* despise *each other.* She and Alexa already seemed halfway there.

Their door was still open, and Holly heard laughter and strains of a John Mayer CD from the room across the hall. Then, a girl who looked to be about sixteen appeared in their doorway. She was Asian American and petite, with shoulder-length, shiny black hair and a wide smile. She wore a striped bikini and was barefoot.

"Hey," she said. "Anybody got a spare pair of flip-flops?" She motioned down the hall. "Eric from Number 2 puked all over mine on the way home from Ohio's last night so I had to get rid of them. Gross, right?"

"I do," Alexa said. She was kneeling at the dresser, surrounded by clothes and shoes. She held up a pair of red plastic flip-flops she'd gotten in New York City, then walked to the door and handed the flip-flops to the girl. "You can have these. I'm Alexa, by the way. And this is Holly."

"Daisy Moon," the girl said. "Did you guys just arrive? We got in last night from St. Louis. Spring break is going to *rock* this year!" She pumped her fist in the air, paused for a breath, then went on. "I'm across the hall in Number 6, with my friend Kaitlin."

On cue, a red-haired, chubby girl wearing shorts and a tight Señor Frogs T-shirt bounded over from across the hall.

"South Beach is the bomb!" Kaitlin exclaimed, after Daisy had done all the introductions. "We already checked out a bunch of places last night. Oh, and"— she lowered her voice —"speaking of 'check-ing out,' you girls need to meet the hotties in Number 5. I think they're down by the pool now."

"We're heading to the pool ourselves," Daisy said, stuffing her feet into Alexa's flip-flops. "Meet you out there in a few?"

Then they were off, their giggles echoing down the hallway. Alexa shut the door, and briefly met Holly's glance.

"They're . . . enthusiastic," Holly said. She got antsy around girls who acted so perky. But she was curious to see the pool and maybe get in some swimming. She opened her bag and pulled out her navy Speedo one-piece. After lending Meghan her tankini, the Speedo was the only item of swimwear she had.

Alexa didn't respond. She wriggled past Holly and back over to her bed, where she started changing into her pink bikini for the second time that day. Daisy and Kaitlin were a little "Rah-rah-sis-boom-bah" for her tastes, but they seemed like fun. More fun than Holly was being, in any case. And besides, she was intrigued by the hotties in Number 5.

The girls wordlessly changed into their swimwear, their backs to each other. Now that they were alone again, the tension between them was palpable. Alexa hurriedly tied the halter strings on her bikini, eager to get out of the room. She knotted her hair up in a bun and swung around to grab her Fresh Sunshield off the bed. Then she noticed Holly fiddling with her swimsuit straps as she frowned at herself in the mirror above the dresser. Alexa never would have guessed it, but Holly had a kick-ass body. It must have been all the running she did. She had shapely legs, a firm little butt, and perfectly proportioned boobs. Alexa, who was only an A cup, felt kind of envious; Holly managed to pull off being curvy and athletic at the same time.

"You should wear a bikini, Hol," Alexa observed. She was surprised at how smoothly the old grade-school nickname slipped off her tongue. Weird.

"I don't even own one," Holly said, turning away from her reflection. "I don't have the body for a bikini."

Alexa was about to disagree when there was a knock at the door.

"I'll get it," Holly said, heading for the door. *It's probably Daisy and Kaitlin with a cheer routine,* she thought.

She opened the door, and there stood two of the most delectable boys either she or Alexa had ever seen. And they looked exactly alike.

Both boys were on the short side, muscular and stocky, with curly dark hair and bright blue eyes. They wore swimming trunks — one had on a blue pair, the other had on white — and their smooth chests were nicely suntanned. Blue-trunks boy had obviously just gone for a swim; his wet shorts clung to his thighs, and he was toweling off his hair.

"You must be Alexa and Holly, our new neighbors," white-trunks boy said, flashing a grin that made the backs of Holly's knees tingle. "Daisy just told us about you. I'm Thomas Kalas and this is my brother, Aaron." He gestured to the wet boy, who gave Holly a quick, shy smile. "We thought we'd escort you girls down to the pool, if that's okay with you."

Twins! Alexa thought, sauntering over. Could life get any better? Both boys were equally smoking; Alexa didn't know which one to set her sights on first. She looked them up and down, and anticipation shimmied down her spine. She was going to kiss one of these boys tonight. She already knew it.

Holly, meanwhile, was feeling extremely self-conscious in her swimsuit. She crossed her arms over her chest, shifting her weight from one foot to the other. She wished she didn't find the twins both so cute. Aaron, in particular, was catching her eye — he seemed a little timid, and Holly was a sucker for quiet types.

"Come on, Holly," Alexa said, grabbing her sun-screen, shades, and towel. She followed the boys out into the hall. Holly scooped up her own pool gear and hurried after them, taking care to grab their only key from the dresser and lock the door.

The four of them headed downstairs and cut through the lobby to the back exit. As Thomas walked beside Alexa, his hand kept brushing against her thigh. *Accidentally on purpose*, Alexa thought delightedly. She noticed that Holly and Aaron had fallen into step behind them, and that Aaron was scoping Holly out. *Perfect*, Alexa thought. *One for each of us.* Still, there was a tiny part of her that wanted both brothers all to herself. She'd never hooked up with two boys at the same time, never mind twins. How much fun would that be?

The back exit led straight out to the pool area, which was fenced in, and faced the back end of Ocean Drive — hardly the glamorous view the motel's front entrance offered. The pool was a small square filled with murky-looking, greenish-blue water. Holly changed her mind about wanting to swim any laps. A boom box resting on a small round table blasted Dave Matthews. Kaitlin was sunning herself on a chair and sipping a Corona; there was a cooler packed full of them nearby. Daisy stood at the edge of the pool, playfully wrestling with a pale, brown-haired boy. The boy lifted Daisy in his arms and threw her in the water, yelling "Woo-hoo!" Daisy swam to the surface, splashing him, until he dove in after her.

"That's our buddy Jonathan. He's in our room, too," Thomas told Alexa and Holly, pointing to the brown-haired boy. "He's kinda hyper."

"I'd say so," Alexa said, watching as Jonathan dunked Daisy underwater. He was decent-looking, but too scrawny for her.

Holly stretched out on a beach chair next to Kaitlin, letting the sun wash over her. It was late afternoon by now, but still warm out. She tried not to think about how naked she was in front of all these boys. She wished she could look as carefree as Alexa seemed in her little bikini, chatting up a storm with Thomas.

Holly watched as Aaron dove headfirst into the pool, barely making a splash. He glided underwater for a minute, looking as graceful as an Olympic swimmer. Holly squeezed Neutrogena suntan lotion into her palm and slathered it all over her freckled legs. She was rubbing some into her arms when she noticed Aaron had swum up to the surface of the pool and was watching her. He slicked back his streaming dark hair and started floating on his back.

Blushing furiously, Holly slid her sunglasses on. There was no way this guy could be checking her out. He and his brother were probably both drooling over Alexa.

"Here," Alexa said, walking over and handing Holly

an ice-cold Corona. She sat down beside her. "Can you do my back?" Alexa asked, swiveling around so that her smooth shoulder blades were facing Holly.

Holly took a cautious sip of the Corona. It was cold and bubbly, tasting faintly of lime. She passed the bottle to Alexa and began massaging lotion into her back.

"I'm sorry, but that is so hot," Jonathan commented from the pool, squinting at Alexa and Holly. "Nothing like girls rubbing suntan lotion all over each other. Right, Aaron?"

"It depends," Aaron said. Then he glanced at Holly, turned red, and ducked back under the water. Holly's heart fluttered.

"Ugh, you are disgusting," Daisy said, slapping Jonathan's arm. "This isn't *Girls Gone Wild.*"

"Not yet," Jonathan smirked. "Who knows what tonight will bring?"

"You wish," Kaitlin said. "What are we doing tonight, anyway?"

Thomas strolled over and sat in the empty beach chair next to Alexa. "I thought we'd hit Lincoln Road first, maybe check out the scene there. Then come back and bar-hop on Ocean Drive. How's that sound?"

Alexa gave Thomas a slow smile. It sounded just right to her. Holly had finished her back, so Alexa lay down on her stomach, resting her chin on her arms.

"Great!" Daisy said, coming up out of the water and wringing out her black hair. "Kaitlin and I went to this rocking place on Ocean Drive last night. We can go back."

"We should start getting ready now, though," Kaitlin pointed out. "It's going to take a while waiting for turns in the shower."

"Are there only those two showers outside?" Holly asked, motioning over to the curtained booths at the far end of the pool area. The idea of showering outdoors seemed a little skeevy to her.

"And another inside," Thomas said. "There's only one bathroom per floor that all the guests have to share. Coed."

Terrific, Holly thought, taking the Corona from Alexa and swallowing down more than she had intended. *I'm going to have to share a bathroom with boys?*

Meanwhile, Alexa was thinking the exact same thing. Only she really thought it *was* terrific.

Once everyone went back inside, they worked out a schedule for the showers. Alexa ended up showering inside, while Holly and Kaitlin got the outdoor showers first. The boys and Daisy said they didn't mind waiting for the later shifts.

The temperature was starting to drop as Holly stepped into the shower booth. She wore her bathing suit and held a towel, shampoo, and soap. She glanced nervously at the empty pool as she drew the heavy plastic curtain across the rod. Trembling a little, she took off her Speedo and hung it over the rod along with her towel. It was weird to be completely naked outside, as night was falling. But she was a little buzzed from the Corona, so part of her was sort of enjoying the mild air on her bare skin. The sky overhead was turning fuchsia.

Holly switched on the water and closed her eyes as it rushed out of the shower head, beating a tattoo on her face and arms. Its coolness was refreshing. She stretched, raising her arms above her head as the water streamed down her body. She wished she'd had time to go for a run. Maybe tomorrow. She rubbed shampoo into her scalp and smoothed soap all over her body, feeling clean and energized after her long, crazy day. Holly let a giggle escape her lips. Just this morning she'd been in New Jersey, listening to her parents nag her, and now here she was, taking a shower outside. Who would have guessed it?

Holly rinsed herself and reluctantly shut off the water. She wanted to linger longer, but she knew other people were waiting. She was reaching for her towel when the curtain suddenly slid open from the outside. Aaron stood there, his mouth open, a towel slung around his hips.

Holly gasped, frozen. She was totally nude, sopping wet, and had absolutely nowhere to hide. She watched in shock as Aaron's eyes swept over her body, and she thought she saw the corner of his mouth curl up in a smile. But it was so quick, she was sure she'd imagined it. Then, she sprang into action and grabbed her towel, wrapping it around herself as fast as she could. Her swimsuit fell onto the shower tiles. She bent down and snatched it up, along with the soap and shampoo.

"Oh, man, I'm so sorry," Aaron said, covering his eyes. "I honestly had no idea someone was in here. Kaitlin told me the outside shower was free."

Holly was shaking uncontrollably. A random boy had seen her *naked*. It had to be the single most embarrassing moment of her entire sixteen years.

"She — she must have meant *her* shower," Holly stammered. She felt goose bumps rising up on her arms. "I have to go," she said, pushing past Aaron and running like mad back toward the motel.

"What's the matter with *you*?" Alexa asked as Holly burst into the room, her teeth chattering and her eyes enormous. Alexa had long since finished her shower and was standing in front of the mirror, wearing a delicately beaded baby-blue camisole from Arden B. over a ruffly white miniskirt and high-heeled metallic silver mules. She held a Nars eyebrow pencil in one hand, in mid-makeup procedure.

"Aaron just saw me naked!" Holly exclaimed. She hadn't planned on telling Alexa, but it was impossible to keep the humiliation to herself.

Alexa threw her head back and laughed. "You're so lucky!" she said. "Now he's going to want you even more."

"He doesn't want me," Holly mumbled. What was Alexa talking about? She stepped around Alexa to get to the bed, and her half-unpacked bags. Then she noticed the window shade was up and the window was wide open. Holly could hear horns honking and a group of guys drunkenly singing a Black Eyed Peas song down on Ocean Drive.

"Oh, my God, Alexa, close the window," Holly gasped, wrapping her towel around herself even tighter. "What if someone sees us changing?" She'd had enough exposure for one night.

"Would you chill?" Alexa said. "I like seeing the beach when it's dark." But she climbed over her bed and did as Holly had asked, rolling her eyes all the while.

Holly turned her attention to her bags. She was so eager to get into some clothes — any clothes — that she pulled out whatever she could find: red capri pants and a white sleeveless T-shirt. She dressed quickly and was jamming her feet into black slides when she heard Alexa clear her throat. She was standing by the dresser, looking Holly up and down.

"Uh-uh," Alexa said. "You are *not* wearing that on our first night out in SoBe."

"Why not?" Holly asked, feeling defensive. Her outfit might not be as slinky as Alexa's, but it wasn't hideous or anything. Couldn't Alexa just lay off?

Alexa tossed her mascara tube down with a clatter, then walked over to Holly's bed. She started sorting through Holly's clothes, shaking her head in exasperation. She refused to be seen with someone who couldn't dress well. Finally, Alexa plucked out a strappy black tank top and held it up. "This isn't bad," she said.

Holly took the top from Alexa. Jess had convinced her to buy it on sale from Urban Outfitters last year, but Holly didn't wear it very often because it was more low-cut than most of her tops.

"Put that on with the capris," Alexa ordered. "I'll get you some accessories."

"Look, Alexa," Holly began, trying to stand her ground. Just because Alexa used to boss her around when they were little didn't mean the same rules had to apply now. "I think my outfit's fine." Though, even as she spoke, she was thinking that the black top *would* look pretty nice with the red pants.

Alexa didn't respond. She was back at the dresser, where she started looking through an array of earrings, bracelets, rings, and belts. She selected a pair of dangly silver earrings and a sparkly belt.

"Holly," Alexa said as she walked over, slipped the earrings into Holly's ears, and looped the belt around her waist. "You need to trust me on this. You want some boy attention tonight, don't you?" She looked at Holly's amended outfit approvingly. "When you change your top, I'll do your makeup," she added, heading back to the dresser.

Holly was preparing to protest when suddenly a crazy notion struck her. Diego lived in South Beach now. What if she ran into him in a bar? She'd want to look her best. So Holly took off her T-shirt, slipped on the black tank, and joined Alexa at the mirror. She had to admit that the outfit she had on now was definitely more going-out appropriate. And the long silver earrings looked dramatic with her short hair. Holly let Alexa line her eyes with black pencil and swipe some gloss on her lips. The makeup felt thick and unfamiliar on Holly's face.

"See?" Alexa said. "Much improved." Done with Holly, she applied Trish McEvoy gloss to her own lips, sprayed herself with True Star, then stepped back and smiled at her reflection, satisfied. Her skin was glowing from the shower and her still-damp, wavy flaxen hair tumbled over her shoulders. She was primed for a night out in the country's most sizzling party town.

"You girls all set?" Kaitlin called from outside their door. "The boys are almost ready, so we're heading off soon."

"Wait for us!" Alexa called, slipping on her dangly sapphire earrings.

Holly hurriedly brushed her hair, put on her silver ring, scooped up her tiny black bag, and headed for the door. Alexa picked up her silver clutch and followed Holly into the hall, locking the door behind them. Kaitlin, Daisy, and the boys slowly congregated, teasing and laughing. Holly made a point of not looking at Aaron as the raucous group of seven made their way downstairs and into the lobby.

"Let's get this party started!" Jonathan called as they left the Flamingo.

Alexa, who was walking ahead of everyone else, stopped to soak up South Beach at night. Darkness had fallen, and Ocean Drive was neon-spangled and fiery with color. Every bar and restaurant was brightly lit, with people pouring in and out in big groups. The cars driving by blared hip-hop, and the streets were throbbing with beautiful, scantily clad people. The very air felt seductive, alive, magical. *So* this *is South Beach*, Alexa thought. It was just as she'd imagined it. She held her breath, anticipating the delicious night ahead. All she had to do was dive in.

CHAPTER FIVE
The Truth About Body Shots

"Check her out — think those are real?" Jonathan asked, pointing to a woman who had emerged from an elegant, Art Deco–style hotel. The group from the Flamingo was heading up Collins Avenue toward Lincoln Road. Alexa and Daisy were in the lead with the boys, and Kaitlin and Holly were trailing behind.

Holly turned to look. The woman was petite and deeply tanned, with long, frosty blonde hair. She was walking next to a suave older gentleman, and she wore a gold sequined sundress that hugged her curves and barely covered her enormous breasts. Holly tried not to stare. She'd never seen anyone like that back in Oakridge.

"If they look that good, who cares?" Thomas laughed.

"Whatever," Alexa said, flashing Thomas a flirty grin. "Nothing's better than the real thing."

Alexa couldn't help it; South Beach's sensual vibe was making her feel reckless. She, too, glanced back at the woman in gold. The woman's older boyfriend was now guiding her into a white stretch limo, which promptly slid off into the glittery night. Alexa wondered what sort of exciting places the woman and her sugar daddy were heading toward. For a second, she imagined herself in the backseat of a limo, sipping Cristal and being fed black caviar by some rich and famous guy — though preferably one who was under forty.

"You're right about that," Aaron said, nodding in agreement with Alexa as the group crossed Collins over to Washington Avenue.

Holly unintentionally locked eyes with Aaron, and her cheeks reddened. It was hard not to think about the fact that he had recently seen *her* non-enhanced boobs. As they walked up Washington Avenue toward Española Way, Holly willed herself to relax. She was not going to have any fun tonight if she kept obsessing over the shower incident. All around her, gorgeous guys and girls were working it, strutting along in their most sultry outfits and heading toward various glam locales. Holly had never experienced this sensation before: Every person in the vicinity was going out to have a good time. There were definitely no home-bodies in South Beach. It was exhilarating — and a little intimidating.

By the time they reached Lincoln Road, an out-door pedestrian mall full of trendy shops and cafés, Holly felt a little calmer. The group nabbed a big out-door table at a restaurant on a bustling corner. They ordered a pitcher of sangria and a bunch of appetizers to share, then settled back to watch the parade of people.

Alexa spotted musicians strumming their guitars in the street, mimes performing, and lots of wide-eyed wandering tourists. Alexa decided to come back here and take photographs of all the fascinating passersby. When she saw several more flashy couples — usually a stunning, voluptuous younger woman and a well-dressed older man — she smiled to herself.

"What's up with all the sugar daddies?" Alexa asked the group at large. She reached over and grabbed a mini-slice of pizza from all the food in the center of the table. She and Holly hadn't had time for lunch that day, and Alexa was ravenous. She noticed that Holly, though, was only picking at her food and hadn't poured herself any sangria.

"I think it's a South Beach thing," Kaitlin said. "There's a lot of bling here."

"Last year we went to Daytona Beach for spring

break and it wasn't like that at all," Daisy said, nibbling on a chicken wing. "But, oh, my God, Daytona is amazing! Remember when those guys did body shots off us, Kait?"

"Duh. Of course I remember. That was the best night of my life!" Kaitlin exclaimed, tossing back her red curls.

Everyone at the table laughed, and Jonathan whistled loudly. Only Holly was silent.

Kaitlin noticed Holly sitting quietly and leaned across the table, grinning.

"Holly!" she said. "What's up? Haven't you ever done a body shot?"

"Well . . ." Holly hedged. Done them? She'd never even *heard* of them before. She felt a dead-giveaway blush creeping into her cheeks.

"Oh, my God, do you even know what they *are*?" Daisy squealed. The rest of the group broke up laughing again. Except for Alexa, who was watching Holly carefully.

"Wow, welcome to reality!" Jonathan called to Holly from down the table. "What planet have you been living on?"

"Hey, shut up, bro," Aaron said, jabbing his shoulder.

"Yeah, shut up everyone," Alexa said imperiously. She leaned forward and squeezed Holly's elbow. It was embarrassing how innocent Holly could be, but

Alexa suddenly felt protective of her old friend. Holly pulled her elbow away, regarding Alexa suspiciously.

"There are lots of ways to do a body shot," Alexa explained. "But *I* have a preferred method." She grinned. "You know when you do a tequila shot — with the salt and the lime?" Holly didn't know, but she nodded, anyway.

"Okay. So the guy puts some salt on your belly or your leg," Alexa went on, caressing her own leg to demonstrate. "Then he pours a shot of tequila on your stomach. He licks off the salt, and does the shot off you. If you want, you can hold the wedge of lime in your mouth for him to take out with *his* mouth when he's done. It's very sexy!" Alexa giggled, thinking back to her first body-shot experience, when she was in Turks and Caicos with Portia two summers ago. Sure, it had felt a little trashy, but it was definitely memorable.

"I'll drink to that," Thomas said, reaching for the sangria pitcher. He'd already had three glasses.

Holly nodded again. Body shots sounded disgusting to her, but she didn't say that. She was sure everyone already thought she was a total prude.

"You have a lot to learn," Daisy said, patting Holly's shoulder. "But that's okay. We're gonna have fun teaching you."

Once again, Holly wondered if it was her imagination, but she thought she saw Aaron smiling.

After dinner, the Flamingo group tried to get into Rumi, a swank-looking club off Lincoln Road, but the bouncer standing in front of the velvet rope chuckled and told them, "Go back to high school." Alexa was miffed, since she was sure she looked better than the twenty-something models who were lined up outside, chain-smoking.

"Asshole," Kaitlin muttered, striding back toward Washington Avenue. "Come on, you guys. Let's go to Ohio's."

Ohio's was a lively bar on Ocean Drive, right near the Flamingo. There was a line outside, too, but the crowd here was definitely more casual: boys in cargo shorts and white hats; sunburned girls in halter dresses. The bouncer was a tall, dark-skinned guy who wore a newsboy cap over his long dreadlocks. And he seemed more laid-back than the Vin Diesel wannabe at Rumi, Alexa observed as she and the others got in line.

Alexa and Thomas were in front, with Kaitlin, Daisy, Jonathan, and Aaron right behind them. Alexa craned her neck, looking for Holly, and felt relieved when she saw her standing by Jonathan. Alexa could just picture Holly getting lost and wandering the streets alone all night. The line surged forward. Alexa stepped up to the bouncer, gave him her most dazzling smile, and flashed her fake ID. She'd gotten it two years ago in New York City, and, according to the birth date, she was twenty-three. She knew she could pull off that age, especially in her flouncy skirt and heels.

The bouncer smiled back at her, obviously charmed. He barely glanced at the ID, and waved her in. As Alexa sauntered through the door, she saw throngs of rowdy kids grouped around the long, curved bar. Most everyone seemed to be her age, or maybe in college. Straight ahead, the room opened up to a good-sized dance floor. The DJ was spinning Pitbull — the perfect music to welcome her to Miami, Alexa realized with a grin. People were dancing in big groups, and couples were grinding. *Spring break has officially begun*, Alexa thought, and headed straight for the bar.

Meanwhile, outside, Aaron, Kaitlin, Daisy, Jonathan, and Thomas were flashing their own fake IDs at the bouncer. Holly watched them troop into the bar. She'd purposely stood at the back of the line to avoid being near Aaron. As she stepped forward, there were serious butterflies in her stomach. It hadn't occurred to her until now that the bouncer might not let her in. She remembered her conversation with Alexa on the plane. *Why didn't I ever get a fake ID?* Holly berated herself. Of course, she never anticipated ending up in a situation quite like this one.

Her palms clammy, Holly reached into her purse and pulled out her New Jersey driver's permit. She glanced down at it, then quickly stuffed it back in her bag. The bouncer would never let her in if he saw she was sixteen.

"Um, hi," she said. She hadn't noticed from the back of the line how tall the bouncer was. "I feel really stupid, but I forgot my ID in my motel room. . . ."

"Sorry, miss," the bouncer interrupted. "No ID, no entrance."

Holly was seized by panic. She couldn't be left outside the bar like a loser. "But — but I swear I'm twenty-one! And all my friends just went in and . . ." What was she going to do? Did the rest of the group even realize she was stuck out here?

"Rules are rules, miss," the bouncer said, shaking his head. "I can't let you in. Now, please step aside."

A sharp elbow in Holly's side sent her stumbling out of line. She whirled around and saw a long-faced girl with her hair in pigtails saunter by, shove her ID in the bouncer's face, and amble into Ohio's, shooting a snide look back at Holly. There were titters from other people on line, who had clearly witnessed Holly's exchange with the bouncer.

Near tears, Holly walked to the corner, away from the laughter. Suddenly, a boozy-looking boy with curly orange hair, wearing a backward Red Sox cap, came over to her.

"Hey, you," he said, slinging an arm around Holly. "What's wrong? Why didn't the bouncer let you in?"

"Leave . . . me . . . alone," Holly said through gritted teeth, trying to get his arm off her. She was shaking a little. This creep was the last thing she needed right now.

"Yeah, baby," Red Sox boy went on, as if she hadn't said anything. "I can make your night a whole lot better."

Boy attention. Holly *had* wanted boy attention, but not this kind. She shoved him away as forcefully as she could. Fortunately, he was so drunk he stumbled off the curb and wobbled away, but not before yelling, "Good luck scoring tonight!" back at her.

Hot tears pricked at Holly's eyes. She turned to face the beach across the street, telling herself not to cry. God, she missed her friends. She'd give anything for Meghan or Jess to be here. *They* wouldn't have even wanted to go to a place like Ohio's. They'd decide to go back to the motel room, where they'd stay up late eating junk food and talking.

But I can't go back to the Flamingo, Holly thought

miserably. *Alexa has the only key to our room.* The full reality of the situation hit her, and she almost started crying all over again. *I'm stranded in South Beach.*

"Can I get you another drink?"

A short, muscular boy with a blond buzz cut, wearing a white polo shirt, leered at Alexa. She'd been hanging out at the bar, sipping a dirty martini, when he'd loped over to her. Thomas, Aaron, and the others stood nearby, fighting for a bartender's attention.

Buzz-cut boy practically screamed "Delta Gamma Phi," Alexa thought as she sized him up, but he wasn't terrible. And she could get a free drink out of him. What was so bad about that? The sangria at dinner, combined with the martini she had now, made her feel warm and open to anything.

"Sure," Alexa said, taking another sip of her drink. "How about a Cuba Libre?"

"What's that?" the frat boy asked.

Alexa resisted the urge to roll her eyes. "It's a rum drink," she said.

"Rock on," the boy said, reaching for his wallet. "I'm Colby." Then he leaned in and kissed her quickly on the lips. "And you're beautiful," he breathed.

Hmm, Alexa thought. Colby was so not her type, but it looked like the night was getting interesting.

As Colby tried to flag down one of the bartenders, Alexa turned around to see Thomas and the others making their way toward her.

"This place rules," Thomas commented.

"We told you guys!" Kaitlin said, grinning at Alexa. "Are you having fun yet?"

Wait, Alexa thought, as she studied the crew around her. *Thomas, Aaron, Kaitlin, Daisy, Jonathan . . .*

"Where's Holly?" Alexa asked.

The other kids looked at one another, shrugging.

"She was with us outside." Daisy pointed to the door. Then her eyes grew wide. "Oh, no, do you think she couldn't get in?"

Why would Holly not get in? Alexa wondered. *She looks good — I made sure of that.* But then she flashed back to their conversation on the airplane that morning. Holly must *not* have had a fake ID, Alexa realized. She'd probably tried to get in without showing any ID — or worse, by showing her real one. Alexa pictured Holly, scared and alone outside the bar. She had to rescue her.

"I'll be right back," Alexa said, finishing her drink. She waved to Colby, but his back was to her, so she dashed off. Whatever. Either she'd meet up with him when she got back, or she'd find another frat boy. They were a dime a dozen in here.

Alexa elbowed her way outside. The cool, salty air

felt soothing against her sweaty skin. There were even more people gathered outside the bar now, but Alexa saw Holly right away. She was standing on the corner, looking dangerously close to tears.

"Holly!" Alexa cried, hurrying over. "I'm sorry we went in without you!" Impulsively, she flung her arms around her old friend.

Holly took a big step back, not ready to be hugging Alexa anytime soon. What was up with Alexa acting like they were pals, especially after she'd abandoned her outside? As far as Holly was concerned, this night was over.

"Can you give me the key?" Holly asked, her lips quivering. "I'm going back to the motel."

"Are you nuts?" Alexa said. "It's our first night of spring break! You can't go to bed early."

"Well, I can't go in *there*," Holly said, pointing to the bouncer. Her voice broke. "I don't have a fake ID, Alexa! I told him I left my ID in the motel, but he wouldn't let me —"

"I figured," Alexa said. She piled her hair on top of her head and took a deep breath. This called for some serious measures. There was no way she could let Holly mope back to the Flamingo wrapped in self-pity. *If I'm going to have the night of my life*, Alexa thought, *Holly should at the very least be able to witness it.* She let her hair fall gently back to her shoulders.

"Come with me," Alexa said, grabbing Holly's wrist and steering her toward the entrance of Ohio's. Holly followed grudgingly, and waited in line again until they made it back to the bouncer.

"Hi there," Alexa said, lowering her lashes. "Remember me?"

"Could never forget you." The bouncer grinned.

Alexa fingered the spaghetti straps of her beaded cami. "Listen, my best friend here"— she linked her arm through Holly's —"left her ID back at the motel! Don't you feel sad for her? And I can't have a good time unless my best friend is with me. . . ."

Holly wanted to laugh at the irony of the best friend reference, but she knew she should keep a straight face.

The bouncer didn't budge. "I can't let someone in without an ID, honey."

"Forget it," Holly said, trying to extract her arm, but Alexa wouldn't let her go.

"I love your accent," Alexa told the bouncer. "Where are you from?"

"Haiti, originally," the bouncer replied.

Why is she asking him that? Holly wondered, still trying to remove herself from Alexa's grip.

"So you must speak French, then!" Alexa said. When the bouncer nodded, Alexa immediately launched into fluent, beautiful French.

"*S'il vous plaît, monsieur. J'ai besoin de mon amie! Je vous promets qu'elle ne boirera rien.*" As she spoke, she batted her lashes. French was her first language, and she spoke it even better when she was a little tipsy.

"What did you just say?" Holly hissed. She took Italian in school, so she hadn't understood a word.

The bouncer's face broke into a huge smile. "*D'accord,*" he replied, stepping aside to let them in. "Go in, *chérie.* Both of you. But keep to that promise," he warned Holly.

"What promise?" Holly asked Alexa once they were safely inside.

"I told him you wouldn't drink!" Alexa laughed. "But he'll never know. Come on. Your first one's on me!"

After Alexa had treated Holly to a Cuba Libre — and downed her own, which Colby had waiting for her — they all hit the dance floor. The crew from the Flamingo formed a big circle, and Colby joined some of his buddies, but hovered near Alexa. The dance floor was packed with wriggling, sweaty bodies. Alexa closed her eyes, threw her arms up, and began to rotate her hips, letting the hip-hop beat course through her. As she twirled around, her skirt flared up naughtily. She felt good and drunk now, which loosened her limbs and made her moves even more fluid. Practically every boy on the dance floor was watching her, which she could sense even with her eyes closed.

Holly was so grateful to be inside Ohio's that she cast aside her usual inhibitions and started shaking her shoulders and wiggling her behind. Kaitlin and Daisy shook it next to her, and Jonathan swayed, clearly lacking any rhythm. The twins danced side by side, dipping and curving their arms, raver-style. Holly grinned. She'd never gone out dancing before, but here she was, at a real club, and sort of enjoying herself. It didn't hurt that she'd drunk half of that Cuba Libre — she hadn't wanted any of it at first, but the sweet liquid had slid down her throat too smoothly to resist.

The DJ switched to Outkast and the crowd cheered. Holly turned to look at the rest of the dance floor, and suddenly felt a pair of hands on her hips. She gasped and whirled around, only to find herself pressed up against Aaron's chest. He kept his hands tight on her hips and began moving in time with her. It was obvious Holly didn't know what to do with her arms so Aaron took them and draped them around his neck, then pulled her in closer. Their faces were only inches apart. She could feel his breath on her ear.

What is going on? Holly thought frantically. Did Aaron like her? He was probably just drunk. But did he want to kiss her? Did *she* want to kiss him? Holly imagined his mouth on hers, and her heartbeat sped up. It would probably feel nice. But then she thought back to her first kiss. That had been such a wonderful, dreamlike moment. Holly didn't want her second-ever kiss to be in a skanky club, with some boy she barely knew. Especially not if Diego was in this same city. She'd much rather save up her kisses for *him.* Holly started to back away, shaking her head.

"What's the matter?" Aaron whispered, stroking her bare arms. Suddenly, he didn't seem so shy.

It was too much. Holly loosened his hold on her arms, mumbled, "Sorry," and walked backward, letting the crowd swallow her. Her face burning, she pushed past the hordes of dancers and went back to the bar. Now, she was regretting that Cuba Libre. She asked the bartender for a glass of water and gulped it down while watching the dance floor. Maybe the bouncer had been right in the first place. She didn't belong in here. She should go back to Grandma Ida, and play canasta with her and Miles in peace.

Holly's eyes fell on Alexa. She was sandwiched between Thomas and Aaron, dancing sexily. Holly felt a pang of jealousy. Naturally, Alexa was making sure that all the boys flocked to *her.* Suddenly, Holly was feeling strangely possessive of Aaron. She set down her water and considered going back to the dance floor, but there were so many people crowded around that she couldn't move. So Holly stayed where she was, and kept watching.

Out on the dance floor, Alexa was eating up the twins' attention. Thomas was facing her, their foreheads touching as he moved his hips against hers, and Aaron held her waist from behind, dancing just as close. She dipped her head all the way back, her hair spilling everywhere, and smiled up at Aaron. When he leaned toward her, his lips parted, she straightened up again. It was Thomas she really had her eye on.

Aaron drifted into the crowd and started dancing with another girl, so Thomas and Alexa wrapped their arms around each other. Alexa shivered at his nearness. She could smell the alcohol on his breath. He lifted her chin and lowered his lips to hers. She responded to his kiss, fiercely. Soon, they gave up dancing and stood pressed together, kissing. Alexa smoothed her hands up and down his chest. Thomas ran *his* hands along her waist and cupped her behind. Alexa was thrilled. Tyler and his hesitant kisses were out of her life. She'd moved onto bigger and better things.

"Get a room, you two!" Jonathan called, dancing over to them with Daisy.

Thomas and Alexa pulled apart. Alexa licked her lips and stared at Thomas, wanting more. Thomas looked flustered. His sweaty shirt was sticking to his chest and his eyes were glazed over.

Alexa stood on her tiptoes and nibbled Thomas's ear. "Why are you stopping?" she whispered.

"I need to take a break," Thomas said. "I think I drank too much."

"Are you going to be sick?" Alexa asked, stepping away from him and cringing.

Thomas shook his head, but he lurched away from her unevenly. "I'm just going to the bathroom. I'll be back." He squeezed her arm. "Wait for me."

The too-drunk thing was a bit of a turnoff, Alexa thought, but who cared? It wasn't like she was sober herself. She started dancing again, alone. Oh God, she *was* drunk. Her head was suddenly spinning so badly she felt like the room was tilting. But it was fine. She knew what she was doing. Kind of.

Then she felt a guy's arms go around her, and a pair of lips against her throat.

"That was quick," she said, turning and expecting to see Thomas. But instead there was Colby, along with three other drunken frat-boy types. One of them was eyeing Kaitlin and the other two were gawking at Alexa.

"We've been watching you dance all night," one of Colby's friends slurred to Alexa. "Is that guy your boyfriend?"

"No!" Alexa said as emphatically as she could, considering her own speech was a little on the slurred side. "I do NOT have a boyfriend."

"Good," Colby said. He came up to her and planted a long, wet, sloppy kiss on her lips. Alexa drew back, caught off guard.

"Could you not shove your tongue down my throat?" she asked, but Colby didn't hear her. Or maybe she hadn't even spoken. Her head was spinning even more now. She glanced to her left and saw Kaitlin was making out with one of Colby's friends. Beside them, Jonathan and Daisy were going at it, looking like they needed to get a room themselves. *Everyone's hooking up,* Alexa thought. Suddenly, she felt tired. She wondered where Holly was, and if she still wanted to go back to the motel.

"Hey, come with us," Colby said, taking her hand and leading her to a table near the bar.

"Okay," Alexa said, trying to perk up. This was *fun.* This was what she wanted to be doing. Why did she feel so turned off by the whole scene?

"Do you know what body shots are?" Colby yelled above the din. He took her by the waist, lifted her, and set her down on the table.

Alexa nodded, thinking back to what they'd talked about at dinner. Colby eased her back so that she was half-lying on the table, and Alexa rolled up her cami, exposing her midriff. She noticed that Colby and his friends were now all holding shot glasses full of tequila.

"Can I do some off your stomach?" Colby asked. "I'm just gonna get some salt and limes from the bar."

Alexa paused for a moment, considering. It would be kind of funny to have Colby licking salt off her belly. But then she looked across the room and saw Holly, standing by the bar. For a second, she and Alexa made eye contact, and then Holly looked away again. Alexa felt a flash of sobriety. Was Holly *judging* her? For an instant, Alexa saw herself through Holly's eyes: trashed and half-clothed and lying on a table in front of three horny boys.

"Get away from me, you gross-out morons," Alexa managed to say, standing up and pushing Colby aside. She flung her hair back, readjusted her top, and made her way toward the bar.

At the bar, Holly gazed sadly into her glass of water. Alexa was out there having a blast — hooking up with boys, dancing, being wild — while she was stuck in a corner, playing the wallflower role to the hilt. Holly wished some of Alexa's sparkle and spontaneity might rub off on her. She just felt so bland.

"Hey," Alexa said, appearing beside her. She looked a little woozy, Holly noticed.

Alexa reached for her clutch, which she'd stashed in the corner. "Do you want to head out?" she asked Holly.

"Aren't you having fun?" Holly asked, gesturing to the dance floor.

"Of course," Alexa lied. "But you need to end the night when it's at its peak. Stay out any later and you're, like, desperate."

"I guess," Holly said, her eyes scanning the dance floor for Aaron. He was nowhere to be seen. She shrugged, and slid her bag onto her arm. "Okay. Let's go."

They left Ohio's, waved to the bouncer, and walked slowly back to the Flamingo. This time, Holly noticed that the silence between them didn't feel uncomfortable. They were just being quiet, letting the ocean breeze wash over them. The loud music from different clubs blurred together as they passed. It felt good to be getting away from that blur, for now. Holly looked at Alexa. Her eyes were half-closed, and her hair was tousled.

"I can't believe you made out with all those boys," Holly said to Alexa quietly. She felt dumb bringing it up, but her curiosity was nibbling away at her.

"Only two," Alexa sighed. She'd done better. Once, on a good night in Cannes, she'd kissed five.

Two more than me, Holly thought. Maybe she should have let Aaron kiss her. But, no. Her first instinct had been right. It was Diego's kisses she wanted to savor. If only she knew for sure that she'd be seeing him before she went home.

"But it felt . . . not as good as I'd thought it would," Alexa added, startled by her own honesty. "I mean, at first it was great. But then, I don't know. I wish I hadn't been so drunk." She wasn't sure why she was saying these things to Holly. They were things she wouldn't admit even to Portia. What was *with* her tonight?

It was Ohio's, Alexa told herself as they walked into the Flamingo. The place was off. Not her. Tomorrow night, they'd go someplace much more glamorous and classy. Then, she'd be back to her old self.

After all, she couldn't leave South Beach without breaking her Cannes record.

CHAPTER SIX
Looking for a Boy

"How hung over do I look?" Alexa asked Holly the next morning. They were on the beach, sprawled out on towels while the ocean lapped at their toes. It was another blindingly gorgeous day.

"Not bad," Holly said, taking off her sunglasses to get a better look at Alexa. "Maybe a little tired." Alexa was wearing a canary-yellow string bikini. Her hair was swept up in a bun, and with her oversize shades on, she looked like a mysterious old-time movie star.

"Well if I'd gotten more *sleep* . . ." Alexa said in an accusatory tone. She shot Holly an evil glare, then tilted her face back up toward the lemony sun.

Much earlier that morning, Holly's miniature travel alarm had gone off, startling both her and Alexa awake. When she was going to bed at two A.M., Holly had ambitiously set the alarm for seven thirty, thinking she'd go for an early run on the promenade along the beach. Of course, she hadn't counted on feeling like utter crap when the alarm went off. Alexa, pissed, had thrown her lone pillow at Holly's bed, and was unable to drift off again. Holly turned off her alarm and fell into a restless sleep, deciding she'd go for a run some other day. Now, four hours later, both girls were groggy and grouchy — and Holly was feeling guilty about her laziness.

"Sorry," Holly said defensively as she readjusted the straps on her Speedo. "I'm just trying to keep healthy and active." Ever since Alexa had rescued her outside Ohio's last night, Holly had been feeling a bit warmer toward her old friend. But now, her irritation had returned.

Oh, please, Alexa thought, reaching for the large iced cappuccino she'd stuck in the sand beside her. Being healthy was so not the point of spring break. Leave it to holier-than-thou Holly to try to stick to her exercise regimen, even after a night of drunken debauchery. Alexa took a long sip from the straw. It was her third coffee of the morning, but it wasn't helping. Her head still throbbed and she felt fuzzy, as if she were experiencing the world through a layer of cotton.

"I need a little hair of the dog," Alexa mused aloud.

"Hmm?" Holly asked, distracted. She'd seen an olive-skinned boy coming out of the water, and thought, for a moment, that he was Diego.

"Another drink," Alexa explained patiently. "Like a mimosa or something."

"Oh." Holly squinted at the boy, confirming it wasn't Diego. He walked past Holly's towel to his waiting girlfriend, who said something to him in Spanish as he approached. Holly glanced around the beach. It was still relatively early, but the stretch of creamy white sand was dotted with serious sunbathers — all toned and bronzed. Holly felt very pale and freckly amid all the golden brown bodies.

"Plus, I have to pee," Alexa complained. "Stupid coffee." She stood up and flung her empty container into the nearest trash bin.

"Do you want to go back to the Flamingo?" Holly asked. They'd walked to a beach that was several blocks north of the motel, not wanting to see any of the kids from the night before.

Alexa couldn't bear the thought of facing Thomas. She shook her head, remembering how drunk and red-faced he'd looked in the bar. "I need a break," she groaned.

"Maybe we can go to one of those places back there," Holly said, rolling over and pointing to the grand hotels along the boardwalk. "They'd probably let us use their bathroom, right?"

Ooh, Alexa thought, intrigued. She'd been dying for a chance to get into one of those fabulous retro-glam hotels, especially after enduring almost a full day at the Flamingo. Brushing her teeth in the teensy hall-way bathroom that morning had been anything but fabulous.

They put on their flip-flops, stuffed their towels into their beach totes, and trekked over to the board-walk. Alexa spotted a sign for a hotel called the Oceania and pointed it out to Holly. Behind the sign lay a winding path that led off the boardwalk. Alexa and Holly exchanged a quick glance, then, in silent agreement, stepped off the boardwalk and onto the path to the hotel.

The path led to an elaborate, palm tree–bedecked fence. The fence door opened easily from the outside, so Alexa and Holly simply slipped in, and found them-selves inside a jaw-dropping pool area. In the center was an L-shaped, bright blue pool with painted tiles on the bottom. Alexa remembered the mildly gross pool at the Flamingo and wanted to die. Here, reed-thin women in gold lamé bikinis floated in the glimmering water on inflatable rafts, sipping fruity cocktails and dozing. Around the pool were an array of hammocks and cushioned lounge chairs where other lucky, pampered guests munched on hors d'oeuvres brought to them by uniformed waiters. The whole area was surrounded by giant palm trees and exotic plants, which gave the place a tropical, rain-forest feel.

Alexa and Holly exchanged another glance, and this time they were both grinning. Alexa had arrived at her South Beach fantasy. *This* was where she should have been staying. And, by the looks of it, Holly was just as enchanted by the scene before them.

"Forget the beach," Alexa whispered excitedly. "Let's hang out here!" She wanted to dip her toes in the cool, chlorinated water, and have one of the wait-ers bring her frozen grapes on a platter. Her hangover seemed to have magically disappeared. *All I needed was a little luxury,* Alexa thought.

"We can't use the pool!" Holly protested. She glanced over her shoulder, paranoid, as a waiter saun-tered past bearing a tray with hummus and pita wedges. "We're not guests here, Alexa. Besides, I thought you just had to go to the bathroom."

"The trick is to act as if you belong," Alexa replied, pushing her shades on top of her head and striking a supermodel pose. She took Holly's hand and led her past the pool. "They don't know we're not staying here. Come on, let's go inside and find the little girls' room, and then we'll come back."

The hotel itself lay straight ahead — a multistory pink-and-white confection. The rooms all opened up onto delicately latticed terraces that overlooked the pool. As Alexa and Holly neared the hotel, Alexa imagined what those rooms must look like inside: spacious and light-filled, with crisp, king-size beds, plush sofas, plasma TVs . . . *Next time,* Alexa told herself. *Next time I'm in South Beach, this is where I'll stay.*

But, for now, sneaking in would do just fine.

They walked up a short flight of stone steps and were about to open the hotel's double doors when a dark-haired skinny boy in swim trunks burst out of the hotel, his shoulder knocking against Holly's. Holly's stomach tightened and she stopped in her tracks, glancing sideways at him.

"Diego?" she whispered, hardly able to believe it. Would she really find him so easily?

The boy stopped and brushed his straight hair off his forehead. Holly saw he had narrow green eyes and his nose was larger than Diego's. But she could've sworn . . .

"Sorry," the boy said, shaking his head. "Rodrigo." Then he ambled toward the pool, shooting a confused glance back at the girls.

Alexa took Holly's arm and dragged her into the hotel. "Who's Diego?" Alexa asked. "Could you not humiliate us like that?"

"No one," Holly sighed as they entered the air-conditioned, carpeted lobby. She felt like a humongous fool. Why would Diego be here, in a hotel? He *lived* in South Beach! *I'm an idiot,* Holly thought.

Numbly, she followed Alexa through the lobby, past a tinkling fountain and gilt-framed paintings of seascapes. *Why am I obsessing so much?* Holly obsessed. *I'm thinking every boy I see is Diego.* She waited while Alexa politely asked the concierge where the rest-rooms were. Then, as they left the concierge's desk, Holly noticed a phone booth nearby. On a shelf beneath the phone sat a thick white-pages directory. *That's it,* Holly thought, suddenly relieved. She'd look up Diego in the phone book. That was the mature, logical thing to do — much more practical than hoping she'd bump into him at random.

But I'll do it later, Holly thought as they walked into the restroom. *Not with Alexa around.* Before leaving Oakridge, Holly had briefly mentioned to Meghan and Jess that she hoped to reconnect with her First Kiss boy on this trip. They'd thought it was a romantic mission. But Alexa would probably tease Holly merci-lessly for harboring a crush on a guy she hadn't seen in three years. *Maybe it* is *borderline pathetic to look for him,* Holly reflected. *But I won't forgive myself if I don't try.*

The ladies' room was just as deluxe as the rest of the hotel, complete with gleaming chrome surfaces, sinks in the shape of swans, a fully stocked table of grooming products, and an attendant handing out towels and mints. After Holly and Alexa were finished (and Alexa had tipped the attendant), they strolled back into the lobby.

"Pool time!" Alexa said gleefully. She'd reapplied her lip gloss and dabbed powder under her eyes and was now feeling much more up to snuff.

"Uh . . . give me a minute?" Holly said, tugging on her tote. "I need to call my parents."

In truth, Holly did need to call home — her dad had already left her two messages that morning — but she wanted to do a little Diego detective work first. And she was sure that the mere mention of parents would get Alexa out of her hair, for the time being.

"Oh, totally stay here. You do not want to make that phone call outside," Alexa said. "If someone overheard you saying 'Hi, Mommy, how's New Jersey?' that would give us away instantly."

"I don't call my mom *Mommy*," Holly muttered. Could Alexa be any more condescending? And just when Holly was starting to almost tolerate her.

"Right. I'll go outside to snag us a prime spot," Alexa said, walking toward the double doors. She waggled her fingers back at Holly. "If you come out and find me kissing a boy in the pool, don't bother me!" she added, then flounced off.

Perfect, Holly thought. She glanced around furtively as she made her way back to the phone booth. There were guests strolling in and out of the lobby, and waiting to speak to the concierge. Holly tried to act natural as she slipped inside the booth and reached for the white pages. What was it Alexa had said? *Act as if you belong.*

Holly opened the directory and turned to the "M" section. She tried to tune out the loud, obnoxious woman at the concierge desk. Wearing a silken head wrap and a flashy diamond choker, the woman was berating the poor concierge about delivering her package to the wrong room. "Don't you know who I am?" she shrilled.

Who cares? Holly fumed silently, struggling to focus on the task at hand. She scanned the page in front of her. Unfortunately, there were several Mendietas in South Beach. Ana Mendieta, Carlos Mendieta, Juan Mendieta . . . no Diego. But if he were living with his parents, Holly realized, he wouldn't be listed under his own name. Holly tried to remember the name of Diego's father or mother, but came up blank. For some reason she could only think of her own parents' names, Lynn and Stanley. At the thought of her parents, Holly felt newly determined. She certainly wasn't going to be hooking up back in Oakridge. She'd better act now, while she had some modicum of freedom.

Holly pulled her cell phone out of her tote and started punching in the number of Ana Mendieta. She'd just go down the list and call everyone, asking to speak to Diego. Holly's heart was in her throat as she pressed the last digit. *Am I being brave or crazy?* she wondered. But it didn't matter either way. In a few seconds, she might be hearing Diego's smooth, mellow voice. Her spring break romance was just a phone call away.

Out at the pool, Alexa casually set her straw tote on one of the lounge chairs and patted her thick blonde bun to make sure it was still in place. She removed her sunglasses, slid off her flip-flops, and strode toward the pool, wiggling her hips as she walked. Out of the corner of her eye, she saw boys watching her with interest, and she felt her spirits lift. She was sure she didn't look tired anymore.

Alexa glided down the tiled steps into the water, which was just the right temperature: cold enough to wake up her skin, but warm enough to feel relaxing. She submerged herself completely, sinking into the water's cool embrace. Then she drifted back up, happily drenched, and swam a few paces into the deep end. Alexa, unlike Holly, was not a great swimmer, but she adored pools — the gentle caress of the water, the other half-naked bodies so nearby. An empty inflatable lounge floated toward her, practically begging her to climb on. How could she resist? Alexa put her hands on the float and hoisted herself out of the water. She slid onto the lounge slowly and, she hoped, seductively.

She'd just gotten settled when a mustachioed waiter near the pool's edge caught her eye and smiled.

"Can I get you anything, miss?" he asked, nodding toward the pad and pen in his hand.

It's working! Alexa thought. Nobody doubted that she belonged here. This really had been a brilliant plan.

"I'd love a Bellini," Alexa replied without missing a beat. She'd never had that drink before, but had always liked the sound of it: white peach nectar with sparkling white wine.

"Anything else?" the waiter asked, scribbling down her order. "Black olive tapenade on toast points? Hummus dip with whole-wheat pita? Blue corn chips with homemade guacamole?"

I should probably get some food in my stomach, Alexa mused. *To help my hangover and all.*

"I'll have the tapenade," she said, trailing her foot through the water.

"Very good." The waiter walked away, and returned shortly with her Bellini and a miniature platter of toast points with black olive spread.

Alexa nibbled on a few toast points, then left the platter by the side of the pool as she drifted away on her float. She wondered, fleetingly, how she was going to pay for the food and drink once the waiter returned with the bill. She was sure that most guests at the pool simply charged the food to their rooms. Using her credit card would be way suspicious, and she didn't have any cash on her — she'd spent it all on coffee that morning, and needed to hit an ATM. Alexa shrugged, and her concerns flitted away. She'd come up with something. She always did. She lifted the champagne glass and took a long sip, savoring the chilled, peachy flavor and the undercurrent of white wine. Just what the doctor ordered.

"Good choice." The man floating on an inflatable lounge beside her spoke up. "Bellinis are my favorite daytime drink."

Alexa cocked an eyebrow as she turned to look at her neighbor. Was he hitting on her? He looked to be in his twenties, and was definitely hot, in a Ken-doll way: blond hair, blue eyes, sparkly white teeth. His swim trunks, she noted with approval, were Calvin Klein. Alexa gave him her most radiant smile. *Here* was a classy guy. She wanted to cringe at the memory of last night's frat boys.

"It's yummy," she replied, delicately licking her bottom lip and lowering her lashes.

Ken-doll smiled. "So are you enjoying Miami? I come here at least once a year. It's a great city."

"Sort of," Alexa said with a roll of her eyes. "My friend and I went to this trashy place last night and I'm just so *over* that beer-guzzling scene." She gave him a long, meaningful look that said *you and I are different.*

Ken-doll nodded sympathetically. "There's a lot of that here," he said. "But there are also some fantastic night spots." His face lit up. "I don't know what you were planning for tonight, but I'm going to a Cuban place in Little Havana called Esta Noche. It's a restaurant, but at eleven the bottom level turns into a very sophisticated dance club."

Alexa's heart raced as she took a gulp of her Bellini. He was asking her out for *tonight*? This had to set a record for world's fastest pick-up, and he was totally smooth about it. This was exactly the kind of guy she'd been looking for!

"That sounds incredible," Alexa said softly. She

remembered reading about Esta Noche in her guide-book — it was supposedly Little Havana's best new spot for Latin dancing. Alexa had been to the real Havana once — a couple years ago, with her dad, when he'd gone for architectural research. Their trip had been one of Alexa's most fascinating journeys yet, and had piqued her interest in Cuban culture. She imagined herself and Ken-doll, in a dark, chic club, salsa dancing.

"You should join us," Ken-doll said, waving toward someone poolside. "Luis and I will be getting there around ten."

Luis? Alexa thought, following Ken-doll's gaze to an extremely handsome, brown-skinned man who was toweling himself off near the pool. The man lifted his hand and smiled at Ken-doll.

"Careful, honey," Luis called over. "You look like you're getting a little pink."

"Am I?" Ken-doll asked in response, looking down at his fair chest.

Oh no, Alexa thought, comprehension dawning. Ken-doll wasn't hitting on her at all. He was gay. And, obviously, had a very hot boyfriend.

Alexa's face flamed. He'd just been making friendly conversation, and she'd practically thrown herself at him! How out of it could she be? Was she turning into Holly? *Or maybe,* a nagging voice sounded in her head, *you're so self-centered that you always assume every guy is into you.*

Just then, she saw Holly approach the pool, looking as wan and depressed as Alexa herself was feeling.

Holly padded over to where Alexa floated, and kneeled by the edge of the pool. She had called all the Mendietas in the phone book and gotten a bunch of busy signals, a few answering machines, someone who couldn't speak any English, and a grouchy man who said he knew no Diegos. Worse still, she had then called her parents, who kept asking specific questions about Grandma Ida. And *then* she'd had to call Grandma Ida, to make sure all their stories were straight. Holly felt depressed and drained. She noticed Alexa looked kind of limp, too.

"What's wrong?" Holly and Alexa asked each other at the same time. They smiled.

"You go first," Holly said.

"Well . . ." Alexa hedged. Ken-doll was still floating nearby. She couldn't exactly explain the whole humiliating incident to Holly now.

"Hi there," Ken-doll said to Holly with a little wave. Then he looked at Alexa. "Is this the friend who suffered through the trashy place with you?"

"Yup," Alexa replied, careful not to make eye contact.

"Well, you girls should most definitely investigate Little Havana tonight," he said. He paddled the water with his hand and his float drifted off in the direction of Luis. "Nice chatting with you," Ken-doll called to Alexa.

"Nice chatting," Alexa repeated dazedly.

"Little Havana?" Holly asked Alexa. Her eyes lit up at the mention of the Cuban neighborhood. She kicked off her flip-flops and swung her legs over the pool's edge, dangling her feet in the water. "What's there?"

"This dance club called Esta Noche," Alexa replied, sipping her Bellini.

Holly let out a big breath, newly hopeful. Diego was Cuban American, and she had a vague memory of him offering to teach her Latin dancing. Of course, at thirteen, she'd been too timid, and had declined. But now, Holly was feeling bolder. Was there a chance that Diego might be at Esta Noche tonight? After her unsuccessful sleuthing, she was willing to try another tack.

"We should go!" Holly exclaimed. "Little Havana's kind of far. I mean, we can take a cab, but that might be expensive. Maybe Grandma Ida would let us borrow her car or something. . . ." She was babbling, she realized, but this new opportunity seemed very promising.

Alexa observed Holly's glowing face. She didn't get it. Why was Holly getting so bubbly about Little Havana? She'd looked suicidal two seconds before.

"Would Ida really let us use her car?" Alexa asked. A set of wheels would certainly afford them a new kind of freedom. Alexa had just gotten her driver's license, and thought of her yellow VW Bug back home with a pang of longing.

"Definitely," Holly replied. "She said we should call her if we needed anything, right?"

"True," Alexa said, warming to the idea. "I've been Latin dancing a couple times before and it's a lot of fun."

"And we already know someone who'll be at the club!" Holly enthused. "That guy you were just talking to. He seemed nice." She smiled at Alexa and dropped her voice. "Too bad he's not into girls, right?"

"Wait, you *knew?*" Alexa asked, almost falling off her floating lounge.

Holly shrugged. "It was pretty obvious." She gave Alexa a look that clearly meant *I'm not as dense as you think.* Then she pointed to the Bellini in Alexa's hand.

"Did you order that here?" Holly asked.

"Uh, yeah," Alexa said. "And that." She gestured to the platter of toast points next to Holly. She didn't mention the tricky issue of payment.

"I'm kind of hungry," Holly said, looking around for a waiter. She needed sustenance after her phone ordeals.

"Holly?" Alexa began apprehensively, but then the

same mustachioed waiter who'd served Alexa appeared at Holly's side, pen and pad at the ready.

"Do you have a burger or something?" Holly asked, shielding her eyes from the sun as she looked up at the waiter. She just wanted ordinary food — nothing fancy.

The waiter blinked in shock, as if Holly had cursed at him. "We do not," he said snippily, then rattled off the same options he'd given Alexa.

"The chips, I guess," Holly said with a shrug. "And a Diet Coke."

The waiter cast his eyes up and down Holly, and his lip curled. "I assume you are staying at the Oceania, miss? The pool staff only caters to hotel guests, as I am certain you are aware."

"Uh — me? Staying? Here?" Holly stumbled over her words, glancing frantically from the waiter to Alexa. She'd forgotten that she and Alexa were supposed to be posing as guests.

"Yes, we both are," Alexa leaped in hastily, wanting to murder Holly.

The waiter furrowed his brow and gave a curt nod. As he walked away, Alexa and Holly turned to each other, wide-eyed.

"Could you be any less subtle?" Alexa hissed. "He knows we're faking it. We are so screwed." She wanted to grab Holly and shake some sense into her.

"We shouldn't be lying in the first place!" Holly shot back. She was good and angry now, and she didn't care if it showed. Holly wasn't going to go along with one of Alexa's stupid schemes this time.

"Well, if you hadn't acted like a total hick, we'd be fine," Alexa snapped. She tipped off her float into the water, then bobbed over to the edge of the pool.

"Excuse me for not getting the whole *snob* act down . . ." Holly trailed off, upset. She drew her feet out of the water and hugged her knees to her chest.

Alexa glared up at Holly from the pool. "Just don't say anything when the waiter comes back, okay? Let me handle it." *But what exactly am I going to say?* she wondered.

On cue, the waiter materialized next to Holly. He was holding the chips and soda on a tray, and what looked like an official hotel guest list in his other hand.

"Since you ladies appear to be together, shall I charge both of your orders to the same room?" he asked frostily, throwing a haughty glance at Alexa.

To Alexa's annoyance, Holly sat up straighter, as if she had some sort of idea. "Well," she began, looking right at the waiter, but Alexa coughed loudly, trying to shut her up.

"Please do," Alexa murmured quickly. "Thanks ever so much."

"And what room would that be?" the waiter asked,

flicking his eyes from the guest list back to Alexa. There was an unmistakable snarl of victory forming on his lips.

Alexa's stomach plummeted. They were cornered. How was she going to wriggle her way out of this one?

"Room 201," Holly spoke up promptly. She smiled at the waiter. "We're staying with my aunt, Henrietta von Malhoffer."

The waiter's face fell. He looked down at the list again, then glanced back at Holly, obviously defeated. "Ah, yes."

"She told us the sky's the limit," Holly added with a giggle. "Aunt Henny is so generous!"

The waiter was all graciousness again. "I'm sure she is," he agreed, dipping in a little bow. "Let me know if there is anything else you need."

What? Alexa wanted to shout. What the hell had just happened? Alexa blinked a few times, making sure she hadn't hallucinated the entire exchange.

"We're fine for now," Holly told the waiter, as Alexa watched her, awestruck. As soon as the waiter was out of earshot, Alexa hoisted herself out of the water and sat beside Holly on the pool's edge.

"How did you do that?" Alexa demanded, gripping her old friend's arm. "Are you psychic?"

Holly shook her head, blushing. "Just lucky," she whispered. "When I was in the hotel calling, um, my parents, I overheard this rude woman railing at the concierge about a lost package. And she kept saying, 'I'm Henrietta von Malhoffer, in Room 201!'" Holly giggled as Alexa's eyes grew round. "When the waiter asked for a room number, it all . . . clicked." She looked down, suddenly bashful about her masterful performance.

"Holly Rebecca Jacobson," Alexa whispered, a grin spreading across her face. "I am so impressed. *You* are a rock star!" She regarded Holly as if she were seeing her for the first time.

"Oh, shut up." With her right foot, Holly splashed some water onto Alexa's leg, but she was smiling uncontrollably.

"I'm serious," Alexa went on. "I'm sorry I told you to keep quiet." *Maybe I don't give her enough credit,* Alexa thought, studying Holly's profile.

"Well, you didn't know —" Holly began, reaching for a blue corn chip, but then she stopped abruptly, staring in the direction of the hotel. Her face blanched and her mouth fell open.

"What is it?" Alexa hissed, following Holly's gaze.

Holly couldn't believe her eyes. Henrietta von Malhoffer herself had emerged from the hotel, still wearing the head wrap and choker. Now she had on a ruffly bathing suit under a flowing satin robe and was gliding imperiously toward the pool. Holly watched with mounting horror as the wealthy woman stopped to bark at a passing waiter.

"That's her," Holly muttered under her breath.

"Harriet von Whatever-hoffer?" Alexa gasped, squeezing Holly's arm. "Oh God, Hol. What if she —"

"Let's get out of here," Holly said, standing up slowly. "Now."

Without wasting another second, Alexa sprang to her feet and raced for her tote bag. Holly was right behind her, hurriedly putting on her flip-flops. They were zooming toward the fence door, when they nearly collided with their mustachioed waiter.

"Leaving so soon?" he asked, raising his eyebrows and giving them a tight-lipped smile.

Holly froze. Her earlier composure was quickly fading. "Uh — yeah. We — um . . ." She looked urgently at Alexa.

"We remembered we have an appointment," Alexa said, her natural fibbing abilities kicking in. "Salsa lessons."

"Say 'hi' to Aunt Henny!" Holly added, in a final burst of inspiration. They smiled brightly at the waiter, then darted around him.

They walked briskly out of the pool area, still trying to play it cool, but when they made it the other side of the fence, Alexa whispered, "Go, go, go!" and they broke into a mad sprint. Holly instantly took the lead. *I'm getting my exercise after all,* she thought as they dashed out onto the boardwalk. They jogged along side by side for a few seconds until Alexa had to stop, leaning forward and catching her breath.

"We did it!" Holly exclaimed in shock. She and Alexa exchanged a relieved glance, then burst out laughing.

"And think of it," Alexa gasped. "Now that bitchy *grande dame* has to pay for *our* food and drinks!" She smiled triumphantly, then linked her arm through Holly's. "It was all you, babe. You saved our asses. Big-time."

"Well, you rescued me last night with that bouncer. . . ." Holly shot Alexa a grateful look. "I guess we're even now." Their earlier bickering about lack of sleep and their hostile silences yesterday seemed far away. Holly wondered if the whole trip would be like this — hating Alexa one minute, then having fun with her the next.

"Let's celebrate by calling Ida and asking about that set of wheels," Alexa declared as they started off down the boardwalk once more. "Little Havana, here we come!"

CHAPTER SEVEN
Esta Noche

The sizzling beats of a salsa band pulsed through Esta Noche, a dark, cavernous club with mirrored ceilings. It was half past midnight and Holly was getting the hang of salsa as her partner, a patient, pudgy Colombian guy, demonstrated the quick back-and-forth steps.

She, Alexa, Daisy, and Kaitlin had arrived at Esta Noche around ten. They ate a quick, spicy dinner of *arroz con pollo* on the club's top level, watching as the bottom floor transformed into a hot nightspot. Now, the girls were scattered around the dance floor, each of them having been swept away by a different guy. That was the way it worked here, Holly had noticed as soon as her partner began leading her across the floor;

everybody danced in pairs. All around her, dapper men shimmied with women in shiny, low-backed dresses.

Meanwhile, Alexa was swiveling her hips in time with *her* partner, who'd introduced himself as Pedro. Alexa knew how to salsa fairly well from her brief visit to Cuba. She was having a blast dancing with Pedro, but when he pulled her in closer and tilted his head toward hers, Alexa drew away. He was passably attractive, and kissing him would be a cinch. But for some weird reason, Alexa wasn't in the mood. She waited until the band finished their song, then thanked her disappointed partner and headed to the bar, where Kaitlin and Daisy were cooling off with minty mojitos.

What's my problem? Alexa wondered. Rejecting Pedro was so unlike her. After last night's body-shot debacle, not to mention her gaffe at the pool this morning, Alexa was starting to wonder if her usual boy mojo was running out.

When Holly noticed the other girls gathering, she excused herself from her partner and elbowed her way to the bar. She wanted to make sure the group wasn't planning to leave without her.

"What's going on?" she asked Alexa, brushing her bangs off her sweaty forehead.

"I'm thinking it's time to blow this joint," Alexa said. "*¿Vámonos, chicas?*" She was still disturbed by her moment with Pedro, and wanted to clear her head. Esta Noche had its charms, but the clientele was much older than Alexa had expected — lots of thirty-somethings who mostly seemed interested in honing their dance technique. Alexa needed an encounter with someone suave and sexy, somebody worth her time. And there didn't seem to be any such offerings here.

Already? Holly thought. She was still holding out hope that Diego would magically appear. She could so picture him here, speaking his elegant Spanish to the bartender or sipping a café cubano upstairs. She loved soaking up the Cuban rhythms, knowing that this was Diego's heritage. But she didn't want to argue with the other girls if they were all ready to head out.

"I say we go back to Ocean Drive," Daisy suggested. It was obvious that this mature, sophisticated club was not quite her or Kaitlin's scene.

"But not back to Ohio's," Kaitlin added, crunching on a cube of ice.

Holly nodded emphatically. The Flamingo boys, according to Daisy, had returned to Ohio's tonight. Alexa and Holly had both managed to avoid seeing the twins at the motel all day, and weren't about to push their luck. Kaitlin and Daisy didn't seem remorseful about their makeout sessions the night before, but had still happily accepted Alexa's invitation to a girls' night out when she'd run into them at the motel that afternoon.

Alexa led the group out of Esta Noche, smiling ruefully as Ken-doll and Luis waved to her from the far end of the bar. She walked past the long line in front of the club, to the silver Pontiac parked on the next corner. Ida had dropped the car off with her and Holly that afternoon, encouraging them to keep it for as long as they liked, since she had Miles's car at her disposal. Alexa unlocked the door and the girls slid inside — Holly riding shotgun, with Daisy and Kaitlin in the backseat.

The Pontiac was hardly the glitziest ride in SoBe, Alexa reflected as she turned the keys in the ignition and put one white stiletto on the gas pedal. But it got the job done. And Alexa didn't even mind being the designated driver for the night. She needed a break from alcohol, anyway. Tonight, she was all about understatement. She was wearing a V-cut, shimmery white sleeveless top from a SoHo boutique and a BCBG denim pencil skirt with a thin, silver chain-link belt slung casually around her hips. She'd stained her lips with pink gloss, and that was all.

Holly, on the other hand, had felt so tame and plain at Ohio's that, tonight, she'd decided to go all-out — with a little help from the other Flamingo girls.

From Alexa, she'd borrowed a plum-colored halter top and black hip-huggers. Kaitlin had lent her a pair of strappy black heels, and Daisy had donated an armload of silver bangle bracelets and silver hoops. A double coat of mascara, a couple swipes of blusher, and a little berry lip liner — courtesy of Alexa — completed the ensemble.

Getting dressed in the room that night, Holly had barely noticed the cramped quarters. She and Alexa had navigated around each other effortlessly, and they'd giggled when Alexa overdid the blusher on Holly's cheekbones. There was something intimate and easy about their rapport, Holly realized — almost as if they were back to being good friends.

Now, as they cruised down Little Havana's Southwest 8th Street, Holly felt like an elaborately petaled flower that was starting to wilt. She was sweaty from dancing, so the halter top clung to her curves — she and Alexa were far from the same size on top. And she could feel a blister blooming on her heel from Kaitlin's sandals. Holly gazed out the window at the Spanish street signs and inhaled the rich scents of paella and garlic, wafting over from a corner café. Suddenly, a feeling of resignation settled over her. *Good-bye, Little Havana,* she thought sadly. *And good-bye, Diego.* Her search had proven fruitless.

Diego was somewhere in this big city, but she wasn't going to find him. She had to give up the dream.

"So where to next?" Alexa asked, interrupting Holly's musings. By now they were driving across the MacArthur Causeway, which connected Miami proper to South Beach. "You *mamacitas* still in the mood to *bailar?*" she teased. Alexa, like the rest of the girls, didn't speak much Spanish, but she'd picked up a little here and there. The language was similar enough to French that she felt comfortable throwing a few words around. Especially in Miami, where using Spanish felt so natural, so necessary.

Daisy and Kaitlin were bickering over Alexa's guidebook in the backseat. Kaitlin wanted to check out Crobar, while Daisy insisted they go to Automatic Slims. Meanwhile, Holly wondered how she could gracefully dodge out of going to another club at all. Finally, Daisy suggested Mango's Tropical Café. "They have Latin music, too, but it sounds much more casual than Esta Noche. And it's right near the Flamingo," she said.

"Perfection," Alexa said, turning the car onto Ocean Drive. The traffic was insane. Miles of cars were crunched together, and everybody was honking their horns while people tumbled out of clubs into the streets, adding to the neon-bright chaos. Alexa normally loathed driving in traffic, but this was intoxicating. She managed to squeeze the car into a tiny parking spot, unbuckled her seat belt, and reached into her white clutch. She needed to freshen up before the second phase of the night, so she carefully applied more pink gloss to her bow-shaped lips while looking in the rearview mirror.

"Uh, Alexa? Are you sure this is a legal parking spot?" Holly asked worriedly. "It's really tight." The last thing she needed was for them to get a ticket while using Grandma Ida's car. She could just imagine her parents' reaction to *that*.

Alexa ignored her. Holly didn't even have her license! Who was she to —

Suddenly, their car was tapped lightly from behind by a dark blue Honda. The girls lurched forward in their seats. Holly gasped. Kaitlin screamed.

"Someone hit us!" Daisy yelled. Nobody was hurt, but everyone was getting their drama on.

Furious, Alexa glanced into her rearview mirror and saw the Honda come to a full stop behind them. The driver emerged — a tall, bespectacled Latino guy in a baseball cap. "Bastard," Alexa muttered. He'd most likely dented Ida's car and, worse, caused Alexa to smudge her lip gloss. She was so taking this jerk down.

Alexa burst out of the car, slammed the door, and stormed over to look at the back fender. As she'd feared, it was slightly dented. Mr. Crash Test Dummy was standing in front of his own car, which was unscathed. He looked to be about twenty. His Florida Marlins hat was pulled down low over his eyes, and his chin was shadowy with stubble. He wore a stained gray T-shirt, baggy cargo shorts, and Tevas. Alexa marched right up to him.

"Thanks, asshole," she spat. "This isn't even my car. Now I'm going to have to explain to the owner how it got destroyed." She was exaggerating a little, sure, but that had never failed her before.

The driver set his jaw. "I didn't intend to hit you," he shot back. "You're parked in an illegal spot. Trying to maneuver around you was a nightmare."

"It's not *my* fault!" Alexa retorted, narrowing her eyes at him. "I was sitting there innocently and *you* rammed into —"

"Stop bullshitting me," the guy cut her off, crossing his arms over his chest. "Your car is barely scratched. I'll pay you for whatever damage —"

"Keep your money," Alexa spat. "That's not the point. You could have *killed* me and my friends!"

She looked quickly behind her. Holly, Daisy, and Kaitlin had emerged from the car and were standing on the sidewalk a few feet away. Kaitlin and Daisy were huddled together, shooting murderous looks at the driver. Holly's head hung miserably; she was probably imagining her parents' wrath. The girls all appeared shaken up enough to support Alexa's wild claim. Alexa faced the driver again, smug.

"They seem fine to me —" the driver began, glancing over at the other girls. Then he paused, and lifted the brim of his cap. Behind his wire-rim glasses, his dark eyes grew round.

"What?" Alexa snapped. She shot a look over her shoulder. Who was he staring at? When she turned back to the driver, he was smiling and shaking his head.

"Holly?" he asked, taking a step forward. "Holly Jacobson?"

Holly had been pondering how she could explain this mess to her parents. Then she looked up, startled. Had the guy who'd hit them said her *name*? She stared at him blankly, taking in his wrinkled clothes, baseball hat, and glasses. She must have heard wrong. Holly had never seen this guy before in her life.

But now he was coming toward her and smiling, his arms extended, as if he planned to give her a hug. Holly took a few steps back, bewildered.

"Holly, it's me!" the guy exclaimed. "Diego. Diego Mendieta." He stopped before he reached her, and tilted his head quizzically. "Hey, come on, Holly. I know it's been a while. But don't you remember me?"

Holly wondered if she might pass out. Ocean Drive swam around her, a mass of colors and sounds. She reached out and grabbed onto Kaitlin to steady herself. She opened her mouth but couldn't recall how to speak.

Diego? Could it be? All this time she'd been searching for him, and now, here he was, in the middle of the street, within arm's reach?

Holly gazed up at him incredulously. He looked kind of scruffy. Not as picture-perfect as she remembered him. The baseball cap was shielding his face, and she wasn't used to seeing him in glasses. But now that he was standing close to her, she noticed familiar features — the big black eyes and long lashes, the full lips, the deep dimples that appeared in his cheeks when he smiled. Holly's heart melted. Underneath the scruff, he was still as beautiful as ever.

"I didn't recognize you," she finally said. Her voice came out hoarse.

"I knew it was you right away — you haven't changed at all," Diego said, laughing as he dropped his arms. Then he paused and glanced at his feet. "Well, your face is the same, anyway," he added hastily.

Oh, God. Holly tried not to blush. At thirteen, she'd been scrawny and flat-chested, but had definitely developed since then. Suddenly, she was half-glad to be wearing the clingy halter.

"What are you doing in South Beach?" Diego asked. "Are you staying with your grandmother?"

"Spring break. In a motel." That was all Holly could manage.

"Well . . . it's great to see you again." Diego grinned. Then he stepped forward and wrapped Holly in a hug. Holly wondered if she was having an out-of-body experience. But, no, this was real — her, Diego, their arms around each other. Together again.

Daisy and Kaitlin looked at each other, shrugging in confusion. Alexa, who was still standing in front of the Honda, stomped one stiletto regally. What was happening here? How did Holly know this creep? She walked over to Holly and Diego and tapped Holly on the shoulder, breaking up the friendly embrace.

"Hol, why you are hugging the guy who almost killed us?" Alexa demanded.

Holly pulled away awkwardly from Diego. "He's . . . an old friend," she explained, still having some difficulty with the talking thing.

"I used to live in the same building as Holly's grandmother, in Miami Beach," Diego chimed in. He smiled at Holly again. "How *is* Ida?"

"Fine . . . oh, God!" Holly giggled nervously, suddenly remembering where they were. Ocean Drive. The car. Grandma Ida. "Actually, this is her car — we borrowed it for the night." She gestured to the silver Pontiac.

Diego's expression filled with regret. "Oh, Holly, I'm really sorry. Should I give Ida a call to explain?"

"That won't be necessary," Alexa butted in, seething. *Now* he was apologizing! "Just give me your insurance information. I'll call Ida tomorrow and figure it out." Ida had entrusted the car to her; Alexa was going to be adult and responsible about this fiasco.

Diego turned to face Alexa soberly. "Okay," he said. "I apologize, really. I know I acted like a jerk before." He stuck out his hand. "I'm Diego Mendieta."

Alexa didn't bother to meet his gaze or take his hand. "Alexandria St. Laurent. Incidentally, I'm *also* an old friend of Holly's." She gave him a frosty smile. "But just because we have that in common does *not* mean I'm suddenly cool with this. Ida will be absolutely crushed." She wasn't certain that last part was true, but, again, it sounded good. "I'm going to look at the fender again," she told Holly, then turned on her heel and walked off the sidewalk, back toward the Pontiac.

Holly wanted to crawl into the gutter. She and Diego were finally having their reunion, and Alexa was ruining it by acting like a bitch.

But Diego didn't seem bothered by Alexa's attitude. He continued to study Holly warmly. "Are you okay?" he asked, his dark brows furrowing in concern. "You're not hurt or anything?" He gently touched her bare shoulder.

"I'm fine," Holly whispered. "You barely bumped

us." But she wasn't fine. Not as long as his fingers were on her skin.

"Were you heading out for the night?" he asked, taking his hand away.

Holly looked down, conscious of her outfit again. "Uh — we were — but I don't know now," she said. She glanced over her shoulder at Daisy and Kaitlin.

"We're gonna walk to Mango's," Daisy announced. She and Kaitlin were clearly freaked out by the whole incident. They didn't ask Holly to meet them there, only scampered off into the night.

"I guess not." Holly smiled up at Diego.

He gestured to his T-shirt and shorts. "I'm not hitting any clubs tonight, either," he said, flashing his dimples. "I spent all day helping my buddy Andres and his girlfriend move into their new place — they go to the University of Miami."

"Oh," Holly said, calculating the time that had passed. That made sense. Diego was seventeen going on eighteen — a senior in high school. If he had any older friends, they were already in college. For an instant, he seemed very mature to Holly.

"So I'm ready to go home and crash," Diego continued, reaching into his shorts pocket and pulling out a silver Moto Razr. "But give me your cell number. I'm on break this week, too. Maybe we can hang out tomorrow."

Holly's heart skipped. Everything she'd imagined was coming true. She was going to spend spring break with Diego!

Once they'd exchanged numbers, Diego headed back to his Honda to get his insurance information. As soon as he was out of earshot, Alexa approached Holly again.

"So what's the deal with you two?" Alexa asked, motioning to Diego. "He seems like a total dweeb."

Holly glanced at Alexa. Should she tell her the truth? Holly was so wound-up and trembly, she wanted to broadcast her news to the world: *I found Diego!* Holly shook her head. *Don't*, she told herself. Considering Alexa's foul mood, she'd most likely trample all over Holly's excitement. And Alexa would never understand Holly's feelings, anyway — she'd dismiss her connection with Diego as a childhood crush. Better for Holly to wait until tomorrow and text-message Meghan and Jess instead.

"Nothing," Holly replied, her voice shaking slightly. "I kind of hung out with him the last time I stayed at Grandma Ida's. But I totally wasn't expecting to see him again." She was astonished at how easily the blatant lies rolled off her tongue.

Alexa rolled her eyes. "Well, I wasn't expecting this crap, either. I cannot *wait* to get back to the motel. I'm exhausted." She was brooding over the fact that the car accident had cut her night short. If stupid Diego hadn't crashed into them, she might be hooking up with some cutie in Mango's right now. If that was what she really wanted.

Diego returned, handing Alexa a slip of paper with his insurance information written on it. He seemed about to say something else, but Alexa gave a short nod and marched back toward the Pontiac, dragging Holly with her.

"Wait — I — Diego —" Holly called over her shoulder, but Alexa was hurriedly depositing her in the passenger seat and slamming the door. Holly thought she heard Diego yell "I'll call you tomorrow!" a second before Alexa sped away.

They drove to the Flamingo in silence, Alexa still stewing in anger, and Holly too delirious to think of anything to say.

Back in the motel, they headed to the bathroom to wash up. Alexa brushed her teeth and washed her face in a minute flat, then flounced out of the bathroom in a huff, leaving Holly there alone. Holly was splashing water on her face when the bathroom door opened and Aaron walked in, wearing only his boxers. He looked tired and drunk, but when he saw Holly his expression brightened. Holly immediately faced the sink again, her heart pounding. Aaron was the last person she wanted to see right now.

"Hey," he said, standing at the sink next to her. "Have a good night?"

You have no idea, Holly thought, patting her face with the towel. "It was all right," she answered.

"Yeah, mine blew, too," Aaron replied, watching her in the mirror. "What are you doing tomorrow?"

Seeing a boy who puts you to shame, Holly thought. But she only shrugged, and floated back to her room.

Alexa, wearing her silk nightie, was in bed, lying flat on her stomach. Holly locked the door, sat on the edge of her bed, and changed into her PJs. She slipped a soft cotton tank over her head, and slowly pulled on her plaid boxers. She noticed how the tank top rode up her belly, revealing a sliver of freckled skin. She suddenly felt so aware of her own body — where it curved, and where it lay flat. Usually, Holly thought of her body only in terms of exercise: whether or not she had stretched properly, if her breathing rhythms were correct. But now, even the texture of her skin felt different. Lightly, Holly caressed the spot on her arm where Diego had rested his fingers.

Maybe we can hang out, Diego had said. Holly imagined meeting him on the beach. Would she want him to see her in that boring old Speedo? Holly curled up on the orange bedspread. Meghan had her tankini, so Holly could probably use some extra swimwear. And perhaps it was time to start playing up her assets.

Alexa rolled onto her back and squeezed her eyes shut, trying to block out the glare of the overhead bulb. She wished she'd remembered to pack her sleep mask.

"Hol, are you going to turn off the light?" she asked.

"In a minute," Holly replied faintly.

Alexa opened her eyes and saw her friend tucked into a ball on the bed, wide awake and staring into space dreamily.

"What are you thinking about?" Alexa asked.

Holly paused. "I want to get a bikini," she replied, surprising Alexa. She sat up straight, as if she'd surprised herself, too.

Alexa propped herself up on one elbow. "Why didn't you tell me before, silly?" she asked, laughing. "We'll go shopping first thing tomorrow." Alexa remembered spotting a trendy-looking bikini shop on Collins that afternoon.

"Okay," Holly said, hiding her grin as she slid off the bed and walked over to the light switch. As the room sank into darkness, Holly felt a shiver of anticipation. If only this night were over already. Morning would bring more Diego. And Holly could hardly stand the wait.

CHAPTER EIGHT
Surprises

The insistent ringing of Holly's cell phone woke the girls at ten the next morning.

"Damn it," Alexa groaned, pulling the sheet up over her head. It was probably Holly's obsessive-compulsive parents doing their daily check-in.

Rubbing her eyes, Holly stumbled out of bed and yanked the phone from her little black bag, where she'd left it the night before.

"'Lo?" she mumbled, blinking herself awake.

"Holly? Am I calling too early?"

That voice. Much deeper than she'd remembered it from three years back, but with the same smooth timbre and hint of a Spanish accent. Now, she was completely alert.

"Hi, Diego," Holly said, trying to remain composed. "No, we were up."

Of course it's Diego! Alexa fumed silently from her bed. *First he ruins my night — and now my morning.*

"Cool," Diego was saying. "You took off so fast last night. I didn't even get a chance to say 'bye.'"

"I know," Holly said, shooting a death glare at Alexa's shape under the sheet.

"Anyway, I wanted to check in and make sure Ida was okay about the car," Diego added.

"My grandmother?" Holly replied. She'd almost forgotten about the car; in the harsh light of morning, last night's events seemed hazy. "I didn't call her yet. I haven't really started my day," she admitted sheepishly.

She heard a smile in Diego's voice. "What were your plans for today?" he asked.

"Oh, this and that," Holly replied. *Calm,* she told herself. *Zen-like calm.*

"I'm around this morning," Diego said casually. "Would you want to meet up?"

Holly wanted to throw down the phone and turn cartwheels across the small room. But that wouldn't exactly be too smooth, considering Alexa wasn't supposed to know how she felt about Diego.

"Sure," Holly replied lightly, as if she made dates with boys every day. "What do you want to do?"

"There's this new exhibit at the Latin American Art Museum in Little Havana that I've been wanting to check out," Diego said. "We could drive over there."

Holly bit her lip, hesitating. She wasn't much for museums. And if she and Diego were going to hang out, she wanted to be able to really *talk* to him. To tell him about her life now, and find out about his. It would be hard for them to reconnect while whispering in a sterile gallery.

"Or we could just grab some coffee," Diego offered after Holly had been silent for several seconds.

"Well," Holly replied, feeling torn. Having coffee with Diego seemed almost *too* intimate and chatty; sitting across from him at a small table meant they'd be forced to make constant conversation. Holly wanted to do something in-between — something that felt neutral and safe. Something that would keep her in motion.

"Do you feel like going for a bike ride?" Holly suggested, sitting up straighter. She loved biking: her strong legs working the pedals, the sun warming her hair, the sense of control as she steered the handlebars. Plus, she and Diego had gone bike-riding a few times during that week in June; it might be kind of sweet to recreate their shared activity.

Diego agreed to the biking plan, and they decided to meet at the Bicycle Center on 5th street at eleven o'clock. Holly shut her cell phone and flopped back on her pillow, in a daze.

"Why are you seeing him today?" Alexa asked disgustedly, her voice muffled by the sheet over her head.

"Oh, just to catch up on old times," Holly replied blithely, as if Diego were nothing more than a childhood chum. Just like she and Alexa were.

"Well, don't forget our shopping date," Alexa said, scooting farther under the sheet.

Right, Holly thought. Darn. She'd planned to be decked out in a tiny bikini when she saw Diego again. But she wouldn't have time to get one in the next hour. It was fine, she assured herself. Bikinis weren't really right for bike-riding, anyway. She'd simply have to wear the cutest shorts and tank top she owned.

An hour later, Holly and Diego were biking down the cement promenade that ran along the beach. Holly had decided on a red tank and camouflage short shorts, and dabbed on a bit of her own sheer lip gloss. *I've never given so much thought to my clothes before,* Holly realized as she looked down to examine her berry-red Adidas.

"Hey, slow down, okay?" Diego said, laughing. "This isn't a race, girl."

Holly noticed how fast and hard she'd been pedaling. She couldn't help it; her normal pace was practically warp speed. She slowed down to match Diego's and gave him an apologetic smile.

Diego didn't have his glasses on this morning — contacts, he'd explained when they'd met at the bike rental place — so Holly could admire his soulful, night-colored eyes. His straight black hair was boyishly tousled, and his caramel-colored skin looked even darker against his white T-shirt. He was more than six feet tall now, and his arms and legs were nicely toned. *He's all grown up,* Holly thought, her heart fluttering.

Almost gingerly, with the politeness of near strangers, she and Diego began talking as they pedaled, catching each other up on the missing years. Diego told Holly that his older sister, Marta, whom Holly remembered as intimidatingly beautiful, was now a sophomore at Wesleyan, and then he asked about Holly's own family. Holly recounted to Diego the chaos at Grandma Ida's apartment, including Miles's run-in with Alexa, and received the gift of Diego's warm laugh, and the sight of his dimples.

"I'm sure your friend didn't take that well," Diego observed. "She seems like a real spitfire."

"You could say that," Holly agreed, relaxing. Things were starting to feel more natural between them.

They exchanged a few benign comments on the weather — Diego agreed that it was insanely humid for March — but Holly was quickly noticing that it was hard to carry on an actual conversation while biking. The ocean wind was ruthless against their faces, and other cyclists kept zooming past, sometimes rudely cutting right between them. Holly was relieved when Diego suggested breaking for ice cream. They biked to a stand on Ocean Drive, then rolled their bicycles north to the boardwalk.

"This feels familiar, huh?" Holly asked as she and Diego settled on a bench with their cups of chocolate chip. There was a space between them, almost as if they were leaving room for a third party. Holly considered shifting closer to him, but that would probably seem too forward. She had no idea how things were supposed to go when one was alone with a boy. She didn't exactly have much practice.

"Does it?" Diego asked with a smile, inclining his head.

Holly nodded, nervously digging her spoon into the ice cream. "Don't you remember? Bike-riding and eating ice cream. That was, like, all we did that week . . . you know . . ." She trailed off, suddenly embarrassed by where this topic might lead. *Bike-riding, eating ice cream . . . kissing.*

"Right." Diego shook his head and laughed. "That feels like such a long time ago, doesn't it?"

"Mmm," Holly lied, busy with her ice cream.

"And didn't we go surfing?" Diego asked. Holly nodded as Diego set his empty cup down between them. Then he leaned back against the bench, staring pensively out at the ocean. "Yeah, I remember that," he went on with a grin, clearly enjoying their reminiscing. "We were both such amateurs, but you were braver than me. You'd ride those swells like they were nothing."

"You were scared?" Holly asked, surprised. "You seemed so . . . whatever."

Diego ducked his head. "You think I'd have let on if I was scared? I was trying to impress you, Holly."

Holly felt her cheeks redden. What did *that* mean? Was he admitting that he'd had a crush on her back then? And what about now? She studied Diego's profile expectantly, but he offered nothing more.

Later, when Holly had finished her ice cream and they were walking their bikes back to 5th street, Diego reached over and playfully pulled her ponytail. Holly tensed up; she'd read an article in *Seventeen* that said boys tried to find ways to touch you if they were interested in you.

"Hey," Diego said. "Are you free tonight? Some friends of mine will be going to this hotel bar. Maybe you could bring your friend Alexandria and those other girls from last night. I'd kind of like to apologize to them again," he added with a sheepish smile.

Holly's felt a surge of hope. Up until that moment, she'd been unsure about how things stood with her and Diego. He'd seemed halfway flirtatious, yet somehow also cautious. But his invitation to the hotel bar held all sorts of promise. Of course they hadn't completely clicked *now*, Holly reasoned — how sexy could things feel on a bright Monday morning? But, that evening . . . over drinks, under the stars . . . Holly barely listened as Diego filled her in on the location of the bar. She was too busy watching his full lips. Of course. All she and Diego needed was a more seductive setting, and then they'd pick up right where they'd left off that summer night.

"*He* invited us to the Rose Bar at the Delano?" Alexa asked as she and Holly walked into the bikini shop that afternoon. "It's only the trendiest hotel bar in Miami." Alexa had been hoping for a chance to go to the Delano this week, though hanging out there with Holly's dorky friend seemed less than ideal.

She wants to come? Holly worried as she checked the price tag on an orange bandeau bikini. Holly had been hoping that Alexa would turn down the option so Holly could slink out to meet Diego alone. But now she was realizing that it might not hurt to have some other people with her tonight. She'd feel more secure surrounded by her Flamingo friends. She and

Diego could always ditch the others if things got hot and heavy.

"Yeah, it'll be fun," Holly said casually, joining Alexa at a colorful rack. "And we can bring Daisy and Kaitlin, too."

"But we won't have to actually talk to Car Crash Boy, will we?" Alexa asked, rolling her eyes.

"Of course not," Holly said, feigning interest in a burgundy tankini.

"Good," Alexa said. "Because I guarantee you that there will be *lots* of delicious boys there and we won't want to be associated with someone like Diego." She shuddered, then held up a bright, lime-green halter bikini. "Try this on, Hol. The color will look pretty with your eyes."

"I don't know," Holly said. The bikini wasn't her style at all. The bottoms were cut high up the leg, there were ribbons on each of the hips, and the top half looked like no more than two little triangles of fabric.

But when Holly tried on the bikini in the dressing room, she had to admit it fit her well. The summery color was eye-catching, and the price was right for her tight budget. *Would Diego like it?* she wondered, then chided herself for being such a girly-girl. It shouldn't matter what Diego thought. She was buying the bikini for herself.

Right?

Feeling bold, Holly asked the saleswoman to cut the tags off after she'd paid. She wore the bikini out of the store, under her tank and shorts. She and Alexa drove to Lummus Park Beach. The beach was within walking distance from the shop, but the girls were savoring the privilege of the car. They had called Grandma Ida earlier that afternoon; to Holly's immense relief — and as Alexa had secretly expected — Ida was low-key about the minor fender bender, and told the girls that they could still keep the car for the week.

The beach was crowded at this hour — people were packed together on the sand, towels vying for space with beach chairs. There was a volleyball game going on down near the shore. As Alexa and Holly crossed the sand, Holly thought she noticed a gaggle of teenage guys ogling her. *No, they're looking at Alexa,* she told herself, tucking her hair behind her ears.

They set their towels down in a narrow space between a large family and a canoodling couple. Alexa watched as Holly took off her shorts and settled down on the towel. Holly was totally working the new bikini — but seemed unaware of the effect she was having on the guys around her. Even the boy next to them, who was kissing his girlfriend, paused to gape at Holly. Alexa grinned.

The girls were reaching for their respective sunscreens when a volleyball bounced onto Alexa's towel, and rolled to a stop at Holly's feet. Alexa was miffed. She didn't like it when sports-type people invaded her personal space. A girl in a flowered two-piece jogged toward them, her long dark braid swinging from side to side. "Sorry," she said as she bent to retrieve the ball. "Hey, are either of you up for a game?"

"No, thanks," Alexa said, lying back on her towel. She was heinous at volleyball. Plus, all that grunting and jumping around was so inappropriate for the beach — the whole point of sunbathing was to lie still for as long as possible.

Normally, Holly might have shied away from a stranger's invitation, but her date with Diego that morning, combined with the new bikini, was making her feel bizarrely confident. And next to track, volleyball was her favorite sport.

"I am," Holly said, getting to her feet. She asked Alexa to watch her stuff, and followed the girl down to the volleyball net. There was a nice mix of guys and girls on both sides, and Holly spotted some eye candy on the opposite team: a boy with shoulder-length brown hair and the lanky, fit shape of a surfer. When everyone went around and said his or her name, the guy introduced himself as Shane.

Holly dove into the game, spiking and serving with verve. There was hot sand beneath her feet, surf just inches away, and seagulls sailing overhead. Holly could feel the muscles working in her legs. The sweat trickling down her bare back felt good and healthy. What a day she'd had already — Diego, this game, and, possibly, kisses to look forward to tonight. Holly couldn't remember feeling this satisfied in a long time.

Her team was rotating when a bearded guy in his fifties, wearing a sun visor and carrying a megaphone, walked smack into the middle of the game, followed by another guy holding a television camera. Holly's teammates looked at one another, surprised at the interruption.

The guy with the sun visor spoke into the megaphone. "Good afternoon, all. I'm Mike Koch from the Pulse Network and we're filming our annual spring break special here in South Beach."

A buzz rippled through the crowd and Holly glanced at her teammates excitedly. Pulse was a trendy new cable network that showed music videos, documentaries about teens, and reality shows set in high schools. Pretty much everyone at Oakridge High watched Pulse. Holly had seen some of last year's spring break special, which they'd filmed in Fort Lauderdale.

"We're holding a bikini contest over there," the

man continued. He pointed toward the other end of the beach, where Holly saw a television crew assembling lights and cameras. "Would any of you ladies care to volunteer? The first-place winner gets two free passes to a new nightclub."

The girls on Holly's team pushed forward, chattering eagerly. Holly hung back, studying her toes. She didn't like to volunteer for anything, and the idea of a bikini contest seemed ridiculous to her. She just wanted to go back to playing volleyball. Suddenly, she heard the Pulse guy say, "What about you, miss?" When Holly glanced up, he was pointing straight at her.

"Me?" Holly stammered. She'd almost forgotten that she was even *wearing* a bikini. She looked back up the beach, wanting to ask Alexa what she should do, but couldn't find her friend in the sea of sunbathers.

"Yeah, you," Mike grinned, waving her over. "Come this way. We'll just need you to sign some release forms —"

Holly took a few steps forward. They wanted *her*? Through her fog of disbelief, she felt a shiver of pleasure. She — bland, stay-at-home Holly Jacobson — was going to be on TV!

*   *   *

Alexa was sitting on her towel and fiddling with her tiny digital camera — she'd packed it in her tote, hoping she'd be inspired to take some photos today — when she heard a commotion from the other end of the beach. She squinted into the distance. A makeshift catwalk had been constructed on an elevated platform, and there was a huge television crew. Swarms of people were gathering around the set, and Jay-Z was blaring out of tall speakers.

"What's going on?" Alexa asked the couple next to her, who had stopped feeling each other up long enough to check out the action.

"I think it's Pulse TV," the girl said. "They're filming some kind of contest."

"Really?" Her curiosity piqued, Alexa stood and picked up her tote. This she had to see. She lifted Holly's tote, too, then glanced down to the volleyball net. There were no longer any players in sight. Alexa shrugged. Maybe they had all gone down to watch the contest, though it was weird Holly hadn't come by beforehand. And Alexa was mildly annoyed that she was saddled with Holly's beach gear.

Alexa looped Holly's bag over her other shoulder and trudged across the sand to the catwalk. She had to push past hordes of curious spectators in order to get a good view of the stage. There were cameras everywhere, trained on the catwalk. Clearly, a bikini contest was under way. The girl with the long braid who'd invited Holly to play volleyball was strutting her stuff across the catwalk, holding a small cardboard sign bearing the number 3 out in front of her. There were whistles and catcalls from the crowd. The girl paused on the edge, thrust out her hip, and pouted at the three judges who were seated at a table right off the catwalk. Alexa recognized the judges: one was a famous swimsuit model, the other was a hip-hop producer, and the last was a B-list sitcom star. *It's a real show!* Alexa thought, looking around the crowd for Holly. This would be a great story to tell the kids in Oakridge when they were back home.

The guy standing next to Alexa nudged his buddy and pointed to the catwalk. "That one's on fire!" he commented. Alexa turned back to the catwalk. And there was Holly.

Alexa's mouth fell open in shock as she watched her friend walk across the elevated platform. Holly looked a little tentative, taking small steps and hesitantly holding out her "Number 4" sign. But, as the cheers and whistles around her grew in volume, Alexa could see Holly relax and become more confident. She tossed her shoulders back and put one hand on her hip, striding along in time to the thumping hip-hop beat. She looked from side to side, her face breaking into a wide smile, her gray-green eyes shining. She looked like a girl who was realizing for the first time how attractive she could be.

Alexa felt a sudden burst of jealousy. *She* wanted to be up there, working it for the judges in her red-and-white checked bikini. *Am I actually envious of* Holly? Alexa wondered. She never would have expected feeling like that. But it was as if the girl strutting across the catwalk wasn't Holly at all — at least not the same Holly who'd clutched Alexa's arm on the airplane two days ago. Alexa smiled as Holly stopped in front of the judges and gave a little curtsy. She had to admit that her friend looked pretty adorable up there.

Holly stepped off the catwalk and went to rejoin the other contestants, and Alexa could hear everyone buzzing about the girl in the lime bikini. Alexa felt a flash of pride. *She'd* told Holly to get that green two-piece. Alexa was nothing if not a fashion connoisseur.

Another girl, a voluptuous redhead in a tiger-print bikini, wiggled across the catwalk. She was definitely hot, Alexa thought, but she had nothing on Holly's genuine vibe. After Tiger Girl had descended, a baby-faced, spiky-haired guy wearing shades got up on the catwalk with a microphone. Alexa recognized him as Zack Ferguson, the crushworthy host of Pulse's music video hour.

"Very nice!" Zack exclaimed. "This is a tough call. Let's have all our lovely contestants back onstage while the judges make their decision."

Tiger Girl, Volleyball Girl, Holly, and two others filed onto the catwalk as the judges huddled. Holly was chewing on her lip, Alexa noticed. She had to be beyond nervous up there. Imagining how her supremely shy friend must be feeling in front of this crowd and all the cameras, Alexa felt a rush of sympathetic butterflies.

"It's time for our judges to tell us who our first-, second-, and third-place winners are," Zack announced. "Delilah, let's start with you. Who did you guys pick for third place?"

The swimsuit model stood up and held up a cardboard sign with "Number 1" on it. Cheers erupted from the crowd as one of the girls Alexa hadn't seen walk leaped up and down in excitement.

"Congrats to Kelli from Chicago," Zack said. "You win a free beach ball! And who's in second place?"

Alexa realized she was wringing her hands. She watched with bated breath as the hip-hop producer held his sign aloft. "Contestant Number five," he announced.

Tiger Girl smiled with her lips closed. It was clear she'd expected to win first place. Zack congratulated her on winning a year's supply of suntan lotion. Then a loud drumroll came over the speakers.

"All our contestants are extremely smoking," Zack called into the microphone. "But we can have only one winner. This lucky girl will win two free passes to Yacht — the hottest new club in town. Bob, can you tell us who that winner is?"

The sitcom star flipped over his sign and held it up to the crowd. Number 4. Everyone burst into wild cheers and applause.

Alexa didn't register that Number 4 meant Holly until she saw the expression on her friend's face. Holly looked dumbstruck and her cheeks turned crimson. Every camera in the vicinity zoomed in on her. The host took her hand and pumped it in the air.

"Yes, Holly!" Alexa cried. All her earlier jealousy had vanished, and was replaced with pure excitement. She tapped the guy next to her on the shoulder. "That's my oldest friend up there!" she exclaimed, bursting with pride.

"Go congratulate her," the guy replied, gesturing toward the catwalk.

Alexa elbowed bystanders out of the way, and leaped onto the catwalk, not caring if she was allowed up there or not. She set down the two tote bags, then tore toward Holly and enveloped her in a huge hug.

"Alexa!" Holly cried. She was surprised at how happy she was to see her old friend on the catwalk. "I won!" They hugged each other and jumped up and down, an act they'd perfected back when they were ten years old.

The other contestants were milling about on the catwalk, casting envious glances in Holly's direction. Some of the kids from the volleyball game had climbed onto the stage, dancing to the music while the cameras continued to film.

Alexa squeezed Holly's hand. "This is unreal, Hol," she whispered, then drifted off to dance.

Holly shook her head dazedly. Unreal was right. If she told anybody back home, they wouldn't believe her. But home was so far away — and so were her parents. They had no idea what she was doing down here.

And for the first time in her life, Holly Jacobson felt blissfully, completely and simply . . . free.

A warm hand on her back made her spin around. Shane from the volleyball game was grinning at her.

"Hey, Holly. Congrats!" he exclaimed. "You were incredible." Without warning, he leaned over to give her a hug and kiss her cheek. Holly, panicked by the sudden attention, turned her head to the side and accidentally brushed her lips against Shane's. She immediately stepped back, mortified, her hands flying to her mouth.

"Whoa, relax," Shane said, smiling. "It's cool. We're all sharing the love here." Then he winked and loped off, utterly unruffled by the encounter.

"Did that guy try to make out with you?" Alexa asked, sidling up to Holly. She'd been flirting with Zack Ferguson — who'd turned out to be totally dense — when she'd seen Holly sort-of kissing a boy. *Was that her first kiss?* Alexa wondered, curious. But she knew she couldn't ask Holly that type of question in public.

"It was an accident," Holly mumbled, overcome. Suddenly it was all too much. The blinding sun and the cameras and the roar of the crowd. Holly wanted to escape from the beach and unwind somewhere, but she knew she had to talk to the Pulse producers and pick up her prize. She made her way off the catwalk toward Mike and the people from Pulse, with Alexa at her side.

Mike handed Holly the two passes to Yacht and told her that the bikini contest would be airing that night at ten o'clock.

"Too bad there's no TV at the Flamingo," Alexa said to Holly. "I'll call my dad and have him TiVo the show so we can watch it when we're back home."

"Okay," Holly said slowly, unsure if she wanted to see herself on-screen.

"Besides," Alexa added, "we'll be at the Delano by ten tonight, won't we?"

The Delano, Holly thought, remembering Diego. She drew a breath. As much as she was looking forward to the night ahead, she hoped it would be a laid-back evening. After everything that had happened today, she couldn't handle any more surprises.

CHAPTER NINE
Under the Stars

At a quarter to ten that night, Alexa and Holly glided into the lobby of the Delano hotel, looking their most glam. Holly was wearing a brand-new white lace dress, with flutter sleeves and a black sash cinching the waist — definitely the girliest article of clothing she had ever owned. Holly had bought the dress that afternoon, with Alexa's help, at the Intermix on Collins, deciding she needed something special for her big night out. The dress had been on sale, but as Holly had handed over the cash, she'd felt mildly worried; her funds were rapidly dwindling.

But money was the last thing on Holly's mind as she strode across the Delano's cherrywood floor in Kaitlin's strappy black sandals. She had gotten a slight sunburn from her long day at the beach, but Alexa had assured

Holly that the color gave her a healthy glow. With Daisy's faux diamond studs in her ears, and makeup expertly applied by Alexa, Holly felt like an impostor — but a desirable impostor. She was anxious for Diego to see her. In her black bag, she'd secretly tucked her two free passes to Yacht. She figured that if she and Diego wanted to make their escape from the others, the two of them could sneak off to the nightclub alone.

"We look so much hotter than those girls," Alexa whispered to Holly with a devilish grin, motioning to a cluster of Prada-clad models who stood in line for the bathroom. Holly grinned in return; she did think she looked pretty good, but she wished she could carry off Alexa's complete confidence.

Alexa had decided that a visit to the Delano was the ideal occasion to debut her floaty, ethereal Laundry strapless dress; its dusty rose color perfectly set off her tan. Her hair was done up in a loose bun and she'd lined her eyes to make them look smokey, but left her lips pale, with just a hint of gloss. It had taken her a while to get ready that night, but the effort was worthwhile. The Delano's lobby was just as luxe in real life as it had appeared in the *Elle* photo.

Flowing, gauzy white drapes cascaded down from the high ceiling and white columns lined the main corridor. There was a sushi bar and the fancy Blue Door restaurant, and on Alexa's immediate right, the crowded, dimly lit Rose Bar. At the very end of the lobby was a set of a doors leading out to the lush back orchard and pool.

Suddenly, Alexa felt a hand on her shoulder and she gave a start.

"Hey," Thomas said to her. "Wanna come grab drinks with us?"

Oh, right. Alexa had been so caught up in her Delano reverie that she'd momentarily forgotten about the Flamingo crew. The boys in Number 5 had learned about her and Holly's Rose Bar plans from Kaitlin and Daisy, and they'd eagerly tagged along with the girls. Now, Thomas was leering at Alexa, while Aaron was mooning over Holly. Meanwhile, Daisy, Jonathan, and Kaitlin were holding a whispered discussion about a possibly famous person they'd seen walk by.

"We'll catch up with you guys in a few," Alexa told Thomas, stepping out of his reach. She sighed with relief as he led the others over to the Rose Bar.

"Whew," Alexa said. She faced Holly again, but her friend was busy waving to someone at the end of the lobby.

Holly's eyes were dancing. "There he is!" she murmured, more to herself than to Alexa.

Alexa made a face. Was Holly actually *that* excited to see Car Crash Boy? Alexa turned around, following Holly's expectant gaze. She saw the Prada girls again, walking in a tight pack. Then, one of them stepped aside.

And there he was.

Alexa stared at the tall, olive-skinned boy making his way toward them. Surely this wasn't the same Diego from last night. This Diego was so polished and put-together that he could have been cast in *The OC*. His dark hair was combed back neatly, revealing his large, jet-black eyes. He'd clearly shaved; his well-defined cheekbones stood out prominently. He wore a striped, collared Thomas Pink shirt that enhanced his broad shoulders, and simple, classy black pants and shoes. He held a gin and tonic in one hand, and waved the other in Holly's direction.

Oh . . . my . . . God, Alexa thought. Her entire body flushed so deeply that she wondered if she was getting a fever. She was unable to take her eyes off Diego as he neared.

Maybe it had been the baseball cap and glasses, or maybe her own anger but, last night, Alexa had utterly failed to notice what this guy looked like. But now, she was noticing. Big-time.

Diego was absolutely, devastatingly gorgeous.

Alexa took a deep breath to steady her nerves. *You hate him, remember?* she reminded herself sternly. *He's the jerk who ruined your night.* Alexa could hold on to her grudges with impressive will. She wasn't going to forgive Car Crash Boy so easily, even if the sight of him was making her stomach feel funny. Trying to still her thumping heart, she watched as Diego leaned over to kiss Holly's cheek.

Does Holly even notice how sexy this guy is? Alexa wondered, observing her friend. Holly hadn't mentioned anything about finding Diego cute last night or this morning. *Holly is generally oblivious to boy matters,* Alexa thought with a smile.

Holly, meanwhile, was having heart palpitations of her own. She'd never seen Diego look so grown-up and well-groomed. As he kissed her cheek, she breathed in the scent of his heavenly cologne. He was clearly in his element at this chic hotel bar. Holly couldn't believe that the Diego standing before her was the same boy she'd gone for a bike ride with that morning, let alone the same boy she'd known three years ago. She felt even more tongue-tied in his presence now than she had upon first seeing him last night.

"I'm glad you could make it tonight," Diego told Holly, flashing his dimples. "You look really nice."

"Thanks," Holly replied, unable to meet his gaze. She wasn't sure what else to say. "I got a little too much sun this afternoon," she finally added, pointing to her pink arms.

"Be careful," Diego said. "You can really get burned in South Beach."

Again, Holly found herself at a loss for words, and was relieved when Diego turned his attention to Alexa.

"Hello, Alexandria," he said, his expression serious.

Alexa nodded coolly, barely looking at him. Holly's stomach clenched. Couldn't Alexa at least attempt to act friendly toward Diego?

"Look, I —" Diego began, but he stopped when two other well-dressed guys appeared at his side, both carrying drinks. One was short and wiry; he had a dark complexion, a shaved head, and a goatee. The other was almost as tall as Diego; he had a mop of straw-colored hair and hazel eyes behind round glasses.

"Hey, D, introduce us to these two beauties," the blond boy said, smiling at Alexa and Holly.

Alexa smiled back, glad for the distraction. She was finding it increasingly difficult to keep up the ice-queen act toward Diego.

"These are my boys, Andres and Ian," Diego said, gesturing to, respectively, the bald guy and the blond guy. "This is Holly, who I was telling you guys about, and her friend, Alexandria," he said to his friends.

Who I was telling you guys about. Holly smiled, flustered and flattered by those few words.

Just then, a tiny, dark-haired girl wiggled up to Andres, taking his hand and whispering something into his ear. Andres hardly glanced back at his friends as the girl led him away. Holly was relieved the seductive siren hadn't hung around to talk to Diego.

"You have to excuse Andres." Diego grinned. "He and our friend Marisol finally got together this past winter after, like, years of sexual tension. Now they're so into each other they couldn't care less about being polite."

Alexa was cursing the blush that had warmed her cheeks when Diego spoke the words "sexual tension." *What's wrong with me?* she thought, tugging on one of her dangly pearl earrings. She couldn't remember the last time a boy had thrown her so off-kilter. Luckily, Ian sidled up to her then and asked how she knew Holly. Ian was cute in a completely nonthreatening way, which restored Alexa's sense of balance.

With Ian and Alexa engaged, Holly and Diego regarded each other again. There was a moment of awkward silence.

Holly shifted her weight from one foot to another, Kaitlin's shoes biting into her ankles. Her mind was completely blank. She and Diego had had plenty to say to each other over ice cream that morning, Holly mused. But now the vibe between them felt stilted. *Can we only connect when we're reminiscing?* Holly wondered, with a sinking sense of dread. *Maybe all we have in common is our shared past.* She shook her head, dismissing the thought, and she gazed desperately around the lobby, searching for a conversation starter.

"Is that J. Lo?" Holly asked at last, pointing toward a curvaceous woman who was walking out to the back garden, surrounded by two bodyguards.

"There'd probably be a bigger crowd around her," Diego replied, his dimples showing. "But who knows? You can sometimes see celebrities in this place."

"Right." Holly nodded, playing with her silver ring. "So . . . do you come here often?" *I did* not *just ask that,* she thought, horrified.

"Mostly on weeknights, when it's not overrun with tourists," Diego said. He flashed her an apologetic grin. "Not that tourists are bad."

"Oh, I wasn't offended," Holly said, too quickly, her words overlapping his. *Stop,* she told herself. *You're making it worse.*

Diego rubbed his chin, looking pensive. "It's funny. The Delano's great, but I kind of feel over the South Beach scene. I'm definitely ready for college. I need a change, you know?"

Holly didn't know. College was still a while away; she wasn't even taking her SATs until senior year. Her parents had driven her to look at Rutgers back in January — naturally, they wanted Holly to stay close to home. But Holly herself had no idea what *she* wanted yet. She felt, as she had last night, that Diego was somehow far ahead of her — beyond her.

"I guess," Holly replied after a minute. "Do you know where you want to go?"

Diego glanced down modestly. "Actually, I was accepted early-decision to Princeton. They have a really good premed program."

Princeton? Premed? Jeez. Holly had never realized how smart Diego was. She was racking her brain for a response to his grand announcement when she felt her cell phone vibrating in her bag.

"Excuse me," Holly said, taking out her T-Mobile. When she saw the caller ID on the screen, her stomach sank. Why were her parents calling now? She'd spoken to them that morning, in between biking with Diego and bikini shopping with Alexa. Holly had avoided mentioning the car accident, but now she wondered if they'd found out from Grandma Ida. That was the only reason she could think of that they'd be bothering her at night.

"Do you need to get that?" Diego asked. Holly glanced up at him.

This is the perfect metaphor for my life, she realized. *I'm talking to an older boy about college and* Mom and Dad *check in.*

"No," Holly said, turning off her cell and dumping

it back into her bag. She'd talk to her parents tomorrow. She couldn't let them interrupt her good time.

But am I really having a good time? she asked herself. When she noticed a stylish woman slink by with a frosty Cosmopolitan, Holly decided she could use a drink, too. That Cuba Libre had relaxed her in Ohio's. With a drink in hand, maybe she'd feel more on even footing with Diego.

"I'm going to check out the bar," she told Diego casually. She glanced at Alexa, who was still talking to Ian. "Alexa, do you want to come?" Holly asked her friend.

Before Alexa could respond, Ian raised his empty glass, rattling the ice. "I'll join you," he said to Holly. "I need another Jameson on the rocks."

Thank God, Alexa thought. Ian was boring her into a state of utter numbness — their well of small talk was running dangerously dry.

"I'll be back, okay?" Holly told Alexa and Diego as she followed Ian to the Rose Bar. She hoped Alexa would behave herself somewhat with Diego. It was clear the two of them didn't get along, and Holly could do without *that* tension ruining an already awkward night.

Alexa watched Holly and Ian walk off, and realized she was alone with Diego. He was standing to her left, silently examining his gin and tonic. Alexa dug around in her clutch, pretending not to notice him. Of course, it would help if her fingers would stop trembling.

"What I meant to say before," Diego spoke up, as if they had been in the middle of a conversation, "was that I'm sorry about last night. I hope you won't hold it against me until the end of time." His voice was solemn, but when Alexa looked up at him, she saw a teasing glint in his dark eyes.

Is he making fun of me? Alexa wondered. But instead of feeling defensive, she suddenly wanted to laugh, too. Maybe she did take herself too seriously sometimes.

"Do I act like I might?" Alexa teased in return, raising one eyebrow and meeting his gaze. When their eyes locked, her cheeks burned.

"Well, you still seem kind of . . . pissed," Diego said. He was trying not to smile, but his dimples gave him away.

Alexa glanced in the other direction, looking at the chandelier that hung above the Rose Bar. She *could* be a bit bullheaded now and then. It was something that she had always disliked about herself.

"*Petit taureau,*" she said, remembering out loud. "Little bull. That's what my father used to call me when I was younger." She looked back at Diego, and gave him a half smile. "I guess I am pretty stubborn."

Diego was studying her with interest. "Stubborn . . . and French?" he asked.

"Half. I was born in Paris," Alexa explained, slightly flustered by the intensity of Diego's gaze. She suddenly felt self-conscious — a rare sensation for her.

Diego tilted his head thoughtfully. "I've been to Paris only once, but I really want to go back. They have the most incredible museums there — The Louvre, the Musée d' Orsay . . . And the city itself is like a work of art, isn't it? The way the light falls on the stone cathedrals and the bridges over the Seine . . ." He gestured with his hands, as if he wanted to conjure up the city. "It's beautiful."

Something about the way Diego emphasized the word "beautiful" made Alexa think, for one heart-pounding instant, that he actually meant *she* was beautiful.

Don't be conceited, Alexa admonished herself, remembering the incident at the Oceania. Not every boy who paid attention to her was hitting on her. She hadn't been very nice to Diego; she couldn't even expect him to like her as a *person.* Still, Alexa wished that Diego did think she was beautiful. It was sort of hard not to fall for a boy who spoke so poetically about Paris.

"Isn't it gorgeous?" Alexa replied, focusing on him again. "I suppose I'm biased, but I've traveled to lots of other cities, and I still love Paris the most."

"Where else have you traveled recently?" Diego asked. The two of them began slowly walking away from the Rose Bar, toward the double doors that led to the garden. Alexa thought fleetingly of Holly; she'd wonder where they were when she returned from the bar. But when Alexa felt the back of Diego's hand lightly brush against her arm, her concern evaporated. Holly would find them somehow.

"Cuba," Alexa answered, after a moment. "I went with my dad when he was studying the architecture in Havana. We had to fly through Canada to get there. The trip was so eye-opening. Like nothing I've ever experienced."

Diego's face lit up and Alexa felt a rush of pleasure, knowing she'd made him happy somehow. "My parents are from Havana," he said. "But I've never been. Neither has my sister — we were both born here in Miami."

They had reached the double doors but stood still for a moment, facing each other.

"I feel really close to my Cuban background," Diego went on. "But since I've never seen Havana . . . it's like this essential piece of me is still missing."

Alexa stared into Diego's dark eyes, feeling a sharp tug on her heart. He was killing her.

"What was Havana like?" he asked. "I've only seen my parents' old photos, but it must look different now . . ."

"I took a lot of pictures," Alexa told him. "Maybe I can . . . send them to you." She'd almost said *show them to you.* But that would mean she expected — hoped — to see him again.

"I'd like that," Diego said. He held one of the doors open for her. The humid night air blew in, lifting the hem of Alexa's dress. "Are you an aspiring photographer?" he asked.

Alexa smiled, pleased that he'd so insightfully picked up on her passion. "I like to document all my travels, when I can," Alexa replied as they walked out onto the back patio. She realized then that she hadn't yet taken any pictures in South Beach. And if there was any place that deserved to be captured on film, it was the back orchard of the Delano.

Lazy hammocks were strung up between giant tree trunks, and indoor lamps swung from branches, casting a warm glow. A row of cozy white cabanas, each containing a white sofa with a white gauze curtain, caught Alexa's eye. A few of the cabanas were occupied by couples, hidden in their own private cocoon. Palm and ficus trees were everywhere, creating a dense canopy through which moonlight filtered dreamily.

"Wow," Alexa said, breathless.

"I know," Diego said. "The pool is even better." He

put a hand on the small of her back as he guided her down the steps. Alexa was tempted to sink back against him, so he would encircle her waist with his arms. She wanted to feel his lips against the nape of her neck. But she resisted. She still wasn't sure what he thought of her.

They walked to the infinity pool — a flat sheet of clear, blue water. People lay around on white lounges, sipping drinks. Beyond the grounds lay the beach, and Alexa caught a glimpse of the ocean behind the palms. She and Diego stood side by side, their shoulders rubbing lightly as they admired the pool. Then Alexa tipped her head back. It was a sticky, too-warm night, and the sky was cloudy, but she could make out a brilliant sprinkling of stars, glinting in the blackness.

"What sort of photographs do you take, Alexandria?" Diego asked.

Alexa looked away from the stars, back at Diego. She loved how he spoke her full name, pronouncing certain vowels with a lilting Spanish accent. But hardly anybody called her Alexandria, especially not her friends. And she did want Diego to be her friend.

"Will you call me Alexa?" she replied softly. The wind blew tendrils of hair into her face. She thought she heard the distant rumble of thunder.

"Alexa," Diego echoed. He reached over and brushed the hair away from her eyes. For a minute, Alexa forgot what they had been talking about.

"I . . . I like to capture people in public places," Alexa said, coming to. "On street corners, or in cafés. Actually, I was hoping to take pictures of Lincoln Road one night this week."

They drifted toward one of the unoccupied, white-draped cabanas, their conversation unspooling naturally, fluidly. Alexa sat down on the soft white sofa, and her rose-colored skirt spilled out around her, princesslike. She felt incredibly elegant, being here with Diego. He sat next to her, setting his drink down on the glass table in front of them, and she inhaled his spicy Cool Water cologne. She was dying to find out what his lips tasted like, felt like. Was it the humidity that was making her feel so sensual? she wondered, watching as people paraded past.

Alexa noticed a brown-haired girl in a lace dress go by. "I wonder if Holly's still inside," Alexa mused aloud. Of course, she had no intention of going back in to find Holly; she felt deliciously languorous sitting right where she was.

"I bet Ian's hitting on her." Diego's eyes flashed mischievously. "I guess it's pretty obvious he's on the make, huh?"

"No kidding." Alexa rolled her eyes, then smiled at

Diego. "Poor Holly. She's not very good at handling advances from boys." Alexa remembered how antsy Holly had been on the beach after kissing the surfer dude. "I think she just needs some experience," Alexa added thoughtfully. "With the right guy."

There was a moment of silence, and Diego moved closer to Alexa on the sofa. When he spoke, his breath tickled her ear.

"How about you?" he asked, his voice suddenly husky. "Have you found the right guy?"

Alexa turned to look at him. His dark eyes were fixed on her intently.

"You mean am I seeing anyone?" she asked. Suddenly, her palms were clammy and her heart was thumping like mad. "No," she said. "I just came out of a relationship. And he wasn't the right guy. He didn't get me the way —" *You do,* she wanted to say. *The way you do.*

Very gently, Diego traced his fingers up and down her arm. *Yes,* Alexa thought. Her entire body tingled, responding to the feel of his warm fingertips on her skin. She couldn't believe he was touching her so deliberately. Was something going to happen between them?

"I broke up with my girlfriend this past year," he said. "And it was the same thing. I felt like we never really connected." He paused, then let his hand float up her arm over to her back, tickling her ever so slightly. Alexa closed her eyes. His touch was setting her skin on fire.

"You know when you have that connection with someone," Diego whispered. "You just feel it."

When Alexa opened her eyes, Diego's face was very close to hers.

"Do you feel it now?" Alexa asked him, her lips brushing against his. She was heady with lust.

Diego didn't answer. Instead, he leaned in and kissed her.

It was a serious kiss. Deep, and slow, and full of longing. Diego's full mouth felt sublime pressed against hers. Alexa was already greedy for the next kiss. She couldn't get enough of him.

The humidity that had lingered all evening exploded in a clap of thunder. Fat, heavy drops of rain began to fall, splashing on Alexa's bare arms, and legs. She was disappointed when Diego pulled away, stood, and drew the gauzy white drape across the cabana, shielding them from the rain. But then he returned to the sofa and resumed kissing her, even more passionately this time. Alexa twined her arms around his neck, drinking in his kisses. Then, she drew back to catch her breath. Her mouth felt wonderfully tender. Alexa realized she didn't want to kiss five guys in one night. Kissing Diego, and only Diego, was almost more than she could take.

Diego slowly stroked the back of her neck, his lips

teasing her earlobe. Then he reached up and undid her loose bun, so her hair spilled around her shoulders.

"*Qué linda*," he murmured, gazing at her. "You are so pretty."

"Say something else in Spanish," Alexa whispered, nuzzling his neck.

Diego smiled. "Do you like that?" he asked. "There *is* something sexy about speaking a foreign language. You really got me back there when you spoke French."

"I did?" Alexa asked in surprise. "Up until, like, two seconds ago, I didn't even think you *liked* me."

Diego shook his head, his dimples deepening. "No way. As soon as you got out of that car last night —"

"Oh, stop." Alexa put her fingers on his lips.

"I'm serious," Diego went on, caressing her arm. "It's wasn't only how you looked. You had this fire and energy that I've never seen in anyone, except . . ."

"Yourself?" Alexa finished for him.

"I guess," he said with a slow smile. He slid his arms around her waist, pulling her in closer. "I wanted to see you again, but I thought you hated *me*. I didn't expect you to come tonight."

"But I did," Alexa whispered, leaning in to kiss him again. "And I'm happy I did. So happy."

I'm miserable, Holly thought as she stood in the Rose Bar, having failed at her attempt to order a drink.

183

When she'd managed to flag down a bartender, she had hesitated, then ordered an apple martini, which was what she'd overheard the girls beside her order. But the bartender had asked to see Holly's ID, promptly ending their exchange. Ian had offered to buy Holly a drink — he looked old enough that nobody thought to card him — but Holly had refused. She'd read in *Cosmo Girl* that boys expected something from you if they bought you alcohol. And Holly did not want to go down that road with, of all people, Diego's friend.

But why did talking to Diego *feel so lackluster?* Holly wondered as she stood there, drinkless and boyless. She watched as Ian chatted up a girl at the other end of the bar; he seemed to have no problem making conversation. Holly remembered her awkward silences with Alexa on the plane ride to Miami. *It's me,* she thought. *I must be socially inept.*

"Why so blue, Holly?"

Holly turned to see Aaron standing very close. He smiled, his aquamarine eyes boring into her.

Holly looked around. Thomas, Kaitlin, Daisy, and Jonathan were nowhere to be seen.

"Oh, I'm not blue," Holly lied, annoyed that Aaron had cornered her.

"Promise?" he asked "Are you okay? I mean, I feel like you've been avoiding me or something."

"That's because I am avoiding you," Holly retorted.

She paused, startled by her own response. Maybe it was her frustration both over being carded and the way things were going with Diego, but suddenly she felt a lot more gutsy than usual.

Aaron looked surprised, but he didn't back down. "Well, maybe we could hang out sometime," he continued. "You seem like a really special girl."

That rattled Holly for a minute. Aaron was definitely adorable and he did seem kind of into her. Perhaps she was being foolish, pining for Diego, when another guy was willing and available.

Then Holly remembered being with Diego that morning — the easy way they'd laughed over their memories. And the tantalizing, unspoken promise that more memories were waiting to be made. Holly couldn't just throw that promise away. It was for *Diego* that she'd come to Miami in the first place. Not Aaron.

"Someone's waiting for me," Holly told Aaron. She stepped around him, and walked back into the lobby with a burst of determination. This time, she wasn't going to make lame small talk. She was going to walk right up to Diego . . . and kiss him. That would certainly loosen things up, she decided boldly.

But, as Holly scanned all the fabulous people milling about, she couldn't spot Diego. Maybe he'd gone outside. Alexa wasn't around, either, but Holly figured she was off somewhere with the other Flamingo kids.

Not wanting to lose her nerve, Holly hurried out the double doors into the back garden. The night air was thick with moisture. There were ominous sounds of thunder overhead and the palm trees were swaying wildly in a gathering wind. Holly cut across the lawn, threading past couples snuggling in hammocks. She checked out the pool, deflated. No Diego.

It felt all too fitting when the skies opened up and it started to rain: a sudden, violent thunderstorm. Everyone started running for cover, girls shrieking and using their designer cardigans as makeshift umbrellas. Holly was wearing white — not a good plan in a downpour. She lowered her head and began hurrying back to the hotel. She was sprinting past the row of romantic cabanas when she heard the unmistakable sound of Alexa's laugh coming from one of the white-curtained booths.

Holly paused, suddenly seized with the desire to talk to her old friend. Holly hadn't fully realized until now how much closer she'd felt to Alexa in the past couple days. Alexa probably suspected Holly's crush on Diego, anyway — it was silly for her to keep that secret. And Holly hadn't had time to text Meghan or Jess that day, so she was dying to indulge in some good girl talk. Now would be the perfect time to unburden herself to Alexa.

She'll probably have some good advice, Holly reasoned, trying to peer through the gauzy white curtain. She could make out Alexa's pink dress and a boy's striped shirt. Holly wondered if Alexa was with Thomas, or some other guy she'd picked up in the lobby. Holly didn't want to burst in and interrupt if they were making out or something.

"Alexa?" Holly asked tentatively, stepping closer to the curtain.

"Holly?" she heard Alexa respond, sounding surprised.

"Alexa, I'm sorry, but there's something I really need to tell —" Holly began apologetically, drawing back the curtain. She stopped talking when she saw the couple on the sofa. Alexa had her arms around the boy's neck, and was cuddled close to him, as if they were about to kiss. Or already had. Holly saw the boy's caramel-colored hand on Alexa's arm, then recognized his black pants and shoes. Her eyes moved disbelievingly up to his face, to the jet-black eyes that widened as he looked back at her.

It was Diego.

Diego and Alexa. Together.

CHAPTER TEN
Betrayal

Holly hugged her arms to her chest, suddenly aware that she was drenched to the bone. She should have been freezing, but instead she was burning hot — her skin boiling with hurt and shock. Something Diego had said to her earlier that night sprung unbidden into her mind: *You can really get burned in South Beach.*

"No shit," Holly muttered, glaring at Diego. She wished she had been able to get a drink at the bar — just so she could fling it into his stupid, I-swear-I'm-innocent face.

"Holly, what's wrong?" Alexa asked, watching as her friend's eyes darkened with anger. Was Holly just freaked to see her making out with someone? Alexa looked at Diego in confusion, but he was glancing anxiously from her to Holly, his expression tinged with guilt.

Holly felt the deep, familiar ache of tears building in her throat as she struggled to make sense of it all. When she'd left Alexa and Diego in the lobby, they clearly still hated each other. How could they have gone from that blatant hostility to getting it on in a private cabana?

Alexa, Holly realized with a shiver of fury. Seductive, devious, *slutty* Alexa. Holly flashed to an image of her friend grinding with the twins back at Ohio's. Alexa just *had* to make sure every boy in the universe was drooling all over her, didn't she? *And Diego must be an extra-special treat*, Holly thought, trembling. Alexa had pursued him on purpose. Just to have in her clutches the one boy Holly really wanted.

"I — I can't believe you," Holly hissed at Alexa, once she found her voice. "How could you do this to me?" Her eyes filled with tears.

"What are you talking about?" Alexa cried, suddenly scared. Why was Holly looking at her with pure hatred?

Diego got to his feet, running a hand nervously through his dark hair. "Holly, please calm down —" he began, approaching her.

"Don't," Holly whispered. She took a big step away from him and burst into tears. Then she turned and ran back into the heavy rain. Holly was so flustered that she dashed in the direction of the beach instead of the hotel. But she didn't care where she went, as long as it was away from the two people who had betrayed her.

Alexa watched Holly dash off, sobbing, and suddenly she understood. Of course. Holly and Diego had something going on. It all added up: their seemingly innocent date that morning. Holly wanting to buy a bikini — and a new dress. Holly's eagerness to see him tonight. . . .

Alexa stood abruptly, studying Diego with a new set of eyes. He'd played her. All his thoughtful words, and the intense way he'd looked at her, had been bullshit. And he'd even had the nerve to talk about Holly, mentioning that Ian might be hitting on her. As if *Ian* were the creep! *It figures, doesn't it?* Alexa thought bitterly. The only guy she'd met in a long time whom she'd instantly clicked with had turned out to be a two-faced liar.

"Alexa, wait. I can explain," Diego said, accurately reading the stony look on her face. He reached for her hand. "It's not what it seems like."

"Oh, *that's* original," Alexa snapped, rolling her eyes. "Please, Diego. Save your lies for some other girl."

She shoved past him and stormed away from the cabana. She had to find Holly. The wind whipped

Alexa's hair, and the rain soaked her thin dress. Alexa spotted Holly sprinting toward the pool. *Why isn't she running back toward the hotel?* Alexa thought in alarm. Slipping off her sling-backs, she quickly followed Holly across the lawn.

Holly reached the infinity pool, shivering and limping. The rain was coming at her sideways. *Damn Kaitlin's shoes,* she thought, resting against a table and unbuckling the strappy sandals. She wiped her teary face with her hand, then stared helplessly at her mascara-blackened fingers. All she wanted to do was collapse on a bed, and wallow in a long, shuddering sob session. Holly was wondering if she could walk back to the Flamingo barefoot before she realized Alexa had the room key. And then, without warning, Alexa was there, beside her, rain streaming down her face.

"Holly, what are you doing?" Alexa cried, breathless. "Come on, let's just go inside." She gestured back toward the hotel.

"Get away from me," Holly spat. She never wanted to see Alexa again. She spun around and fled off the Delano's grounds and onto the beach. She clutched Kaitlin's shoes to her chest as she trudged across the sand. To Holly, the ocean looked as furious as she felt — a roiling mass of blue-black waves. A zigzag of lightning split the charcoal sky.

"Holly, I didn't know!" Alexa called through the wind and rain. "He didn't tell me." She ran up behind Holly and spun her around so that they were facing each other. "*You* didn't tell me."

And why *didn't she say anything?* Alexa wondered, studying Holly's mascara-stained face. She knew she and Holly weren't remotely as close as they had once been. But did Holly have such little regard for her that she'd keep secret something that had happened on this very trip? So Holly *had* noticed how sexy Diego really was, Alexa realized with a wry smile. She simply hadn't trusted Alexa enough to share that knowledge with her.

At the sight of Alexa's smile, Holly felt another burst of rage. Did Alexa find this all funny? She was acting so innocent, but Holly wasn't buying it. So what if Holly hadn't told her the full truth about Diego? Alexa *knew* that Holly and Diego had some sort of history. But she'd still jumped him the minute Holly's back was turned.

"You expect me to believe that Alexandria St. Laurent, boy expert, couldn't have figured it out?" Holly asked Alexa through clenched teeth. "Give me a break. You knew what you were doing. You probably *pretended* to hate him so I wouldn't catch on, right? And then you just threw yourself at him like . . . like a *slut.*"

Alexa recoiled, as if Holly had slapped her. *Slut.*

The word sounded as sharp as a weapon. Alexa remembered how she'd almost let those frat boys do body shots off her in Ohio's, and that seeing Holly across the bar had stopped her. *But what gives Holly the right to pass judgment on me?* Alexa fumed. She made her own decisions when it came to boys. And she'd be damned if anyone — let alone Holly Jacobson — told her how to conduct her love life.

"How dare you talk to me that way?" Alexa shot back, her eyes flashing. "At least I'm not some uptight *prude* who doesn't know what sex is." A violent crash of thunder punctuated Alexa's statement. "I mean, how many times have you even kissed a boy?" she challenged, staring Holly down.

Holly brushed her wet bangs off her forehead. Her hands were shaking. The question cut her to the quick, but she couldn't let Alexa see her cry again. *Besides,* Holly thought, *since when does Alexa care about what I do with boys? Since when does she care about me, period?*

"It's none of your business," Holly spoke quietly. "And you don't know everything about me, Alexa. Things have happened in my life since I was twelve."

"What's that supposed to mean?" Alexa asked, wiping drops of rain out of her eyes. The storm was letting up, slowing down to a drizzle.

"Since I was twelve," Holly repeated, louder this

time. Holly felt her pent-up resentment toward Alexa, which had simmered for so many years now, finally boil over. "You know, back when we stopped being friends?" Holly went on, her voice quavering. "When you decided to *drop* me?"

Alexa bit her lip, ignoring a surge of guilt. "I didn't drop you," she snapped. "We grew apart, Holly. It happens. Deal with it." She tucked her wet hair behind her ears, suddenly worried that they were heading toward dangerous territory.

"Oh, right. We 'grew apart.'" Holly made air quotes with her fingers. "That's code for *you* deciding I wasn't cool enough to be your friend." Holly was on a roll now, her memories resurfacing in a torrent. "Did you conveniently forget everything, Alexa? Like the time in seventh grade when I came to your house, and you told me to go home because you were making out with Eliot Johnson? Or when I called you for a straight week and you never called me back?" Holly crossed her arms over her chest. "You'd already dumped me by then, Alexa. I just didn't realize it." She let out a big breath, feeling drained and shaky.

Alexa stood still, the drizzle drumming on her face and arms. Now that Holly brought it up, Alexa did remember that time — Holly showing up unannounced on Alexa's doorstep, wanting to bake cookies, right when Alexa had been about to get to second base with Eliot. Alexa had promptly sent her away and had also ignored Holly's numerous phone calls the following week; she'd simply been too busy with Eliot.

Alexa thought about how Portia and the girls gave her shit when she ignored them in favor of her boyfriends. Alexa wondered, not for the first time, if she was a bad friend. She swallowed the lump in her throat.

"I'm sorry, okay? But that was forever ago," Alexa told Holly, collecting herself. "And it's not like I set out to hurt your feelings," she added defensively. "Not then, and not now. I'd never have kissed Diego if —"

"You kissed him?" Holly asked, her chin trembling. She'd been secretly hoping that Diego and Alexa hadn't gotten that far in the cabana. Holly shook her head. Diego was supposed to kiss *her* that night. Where had it all gone wrong?

"Yes," Alexa said. "But if I'd *known* that you two were together —"

"We're not *together*," Holly said with a sob. It was true; she had no real claim on Diego. *Was I just being stupid this whole time?* Holly wondered. *I actually believed we had something.* That morning's bike ride had literally been nothing more than two old friends catching up. She and Diego didn't have chemistry anymore; all they had in common was one week, three

195

years ago. Holly didn't even know for sure if Diego remembered their kiss.

The rain had stopped and the clouds began to part. Being out here on a beach, with the moon suddenly shining overhead, Holly was reminded of that long-ago night with Diego. It had been such a perfect memory, but now it was forever tarnished. Holly felt fresh tears spring to her eyes.

Alexa's cheeks were very pink. "You're not seeing him?" she asked, realizing with mounting regret that she should have given Diego a chance to explain himself. She watched in disbelief as Holly shook her head and dissolved into tears. Had Holly thrown a hissy fit because she had some stupid *crush* on Diego? Suddenly, Alexa understood with utmost clarity how different she and Holly were. This whole fight had been pointless. Alexa wondered why she was even wasting her time out here with such nonsense.

"You were *hoping* the two of you would get together, right?" Alexa murmured, sizing Holly up. "Classic, Holly. Absolutely classic. You were the same in grade school. Did you conveniently forget *that*?" Alexa asked, her voice cold. "Getting all excited because, say, some boy you were obsessed with smiled at you in gym class. Remember?" Holly had always been the master of making something out of nothing.

"Why are you bringing that up?" Holly asked through her tears. "That's not the point —"

"You dredged up grade school, too, Holly," Alexa said softly, wanting her words to hit their mark. "And you know what? I guess I did drop you. Because, face it, Holly: You were nothing but a baby then. And you're nothing but a baby now."

Holly put her hands to her cheeks, startled by Alexa's brutal honesty. She had no idea how to retaliate. Alexa had struck the core of Holly's deepest insecurity. She was still the same person she'd been in elementary school: Shy and awkward. Needing her parents' approval. And terrified of everything — especially boys.

When Alexa saw the raw hurt register in Holly's eyes, she felt a wave of regret. But Alexa wasn't one to take back her words. She had accomplished what she'd intended. The fight was over. There was nothing more to say.

Alexa sighed and turned away. Her shoes dangling from her hand, she headed toward the hotel, wishing she had driven to the Delano that night. The hotel was within walking distance from the Flamingo, but Alexa wanted to be back in her motel room *now*. In her bed, under the sheets, dreaming this entire night away.

Holly watched Alexa go, then sank down on the

wet sand. She knew her new dress was getting ruined, but she didn't care. She listened as the ocean, much calmer now, broke against the shore. And she stayed that way for a long time, Alexa's words echoing in her head.

CHAPTER ELEVEN
Girl Goes Wild

When Holly returned to the Flamingo that night, she knocked on Kaitlin's and Daisy's door. A bleary-eyed Kaitlin let her in, and told Holly she could crash in Daisy's mysteriously empty bed. Kaitlin offered no further explanation, but Holly was grateful just to change into a clean pair of Kaitlin's PJs and crawl under the covers.

But sleep wouldn't come. Holly tossed and turned, replaying the evening's events in her head. She finally drifted off after daybreak, only to be awakened a few hours later by Daisy creeping back into the room. Daisy assured Holly it was fine to stay in her bed, but by then Holly was sitting up and stretching. Daisy perched on the dresser, and Kaitlin stirred in the next bed.

Holly expected to feel achy and cotton-mouthed after getting such little sleep. Instead, adrenaline was racing through her body. She felt like she could run a marathon. Waking up in an unfamiliar room, wearing borrowed pajamas, was oddly liberating. Holly swung her legs off the bed, ready to begin her day. Last night suddenly seemed far away.

"Why didn't you sleep in your room?" Daisy asked, looking at Holly with unabashed curiosity.

"Yeah, why?" Kaitlin echoed, climbing out of bed. "Did Alexa bring Thomas over?" she added, a note of bitterness in her voice.

"Doesn't she wish," Holly cracked, and Kaitlin and Daisy burst into giggles.

Where did that come from? Holly wondered. First of all, it wasn't true — Alexa didn't seem to have a thing for Thomas. And Holly rarely made sarcastic comments. But she felt pleasantly reckless this morning, and surprisingly comfortable hanging with Daisy and Kaitlin.

"Nah," Holly went on. "Alexa got all psycho on me last night, so I needed to escape." Again, Holly's choice of words and tone of voice felt unfamiliar to her own ears. In a good way.

"Ooh." Daisy grinned, raising her eyebrows. "Cat fight?"

Holly remembered how furious she'd been at

Alexa last night. Maybe it would have felt invigorating to give those silky blonde locks a good yank.

"Not yet," Holly replied, a wicked grin spreading across her face.

"Holly, you are such a badass!" Kaitlin exclaimed, pulling up the window shade.

"Who knew?" Daisy teased her, which annoyed Holly. She was fed up with everyone thinking she was an angel.

"So where were *you* last night?" Holly asked Daisy, wanting to take the focus off herself.

Daisy's cheeks colored, and she ducked her head.

"Oh, come on," Kaitlin urged, shooting Daisy a glare. "Stop with the false modesty."

"It's not that," Daisy protested. "We're keeping it on the down low. Jonathan doesn't want —" She gasped and put a hand to her mouth, realizing she'd given herself away.

"Jonathan?" Holly repeated. She wasn't too surprised; Daisy and Jonathan had kissed that first night at Ohio's, and were always being flirty with each other. "But wait. You stayed over in his room? What about Thomas and Aaron?" Holly wondered aloud.

Daisy blushed even deeper. "Oh, we went somewhere else. . . ." She trailed off, swinging her legs.

Holly started to blush, too. She couldn't even begin to guess where Daisy and Jonathan had gone, or imagine what they had done. *Why am I so naïve?* Holly thought, frustrated.

"Suffice it to say I need to catch up on my sleep today," Daisy said with a yawn. "Jonathan's taking me to Sushi Samba for dinner, so it'll probably be another late night."

"Poor you." Kaitlin rolled her eyes. "Who cares about sleep when you're getting action on a regular basis? Of course, *I'm* basically living in a convent so I wouldn't know."

Holly looked thoughtfully from Kaitlin to Daisy. She wondered if that issue was a recurring motif in their friendship — cute-but-chubby Kaitlin constantly overlooked by boys, while petite, pretty Daisy got all the attention. Holly's heart went out to Kaitlin; she could relate.

"Hey, Kaitlin," Holly said, suddenly inspired. "If you don't have plans tonight, would you be up for checking out a new club?"

"Which one?" Kaitlin asked sourly, plopping back down on her bed.

"Yacht," Holly said, standing and picking her black bag up off the floor. She'd been hoping to use the free passes with Diego last night. Oh, the irony.

"*Yacht?* Please," Kaitlin said with a sigh. "The bouncers would never let me in. And the cover's supposed to be really high."

"Not if you can get in for free," Holly said. She walked over to Kaitlin's bed and handed her the two still-damp passes.

"You are kidding!" Kaitlin squealed, beaming at Holly. She bounced up and gave Holly a quick hug, while Daisy, announcing she was jealous, flounced off to take a shower.

"Listen," Kaitlin said to Holly. "Do you still not have a fake ID?"

Holly shook her head. "But that shouldn't matter," she said. "I mean, with the passes — "

"Whatever," Kaitlin cut her off. "This is a crisis situation. Go shower and change," Kaitlin commanded, pointing to the door. "We've got a busy day ahead of us."

"Uh, okay," Holly said, realizing she needed clean clothes from the room across the hall. Which would mean confronting Alexa. Hurriedly, Holly asked Kaitlin if she wouldn't mind popping into Number 7 to retrieve some of Holly's stuff. Sending a go-between was a bit immature, Holly knew, but anything was better than facing Alexa again.

Kaitlin didn't seem to mind. But before she headed out the door, she turned to Holly again.

"What were you going to wear tonight?" Kaitlin asked. "I'll bring it in."

"Well . . ." Holly's new dress was gross and

muddy — not to mention stained with bad memories. "Maybe, like, a tank and jeans?"

Kaitlin shook her head. "The bouncers at a place like Yacht will never let you in if you're wearing jeans! Girl, we are going shopping. Let me teach you what spring break is all about. Repeat after me: tube tops, tube tops, tube tops . . ."

"Tube tops . . ." Holly echoed as Kaitlin nodded approvingly. Holly couldn't help but think — with a twinge of irritation — that she'd traded in one Little Miss Bossy for another.

After hitting up Place Vendome for clothes, and securing Holly with a fake ID, Kaitlin, Daisy, and Holly treated themselves to lunch at the Front Porch Café. When the bill arrived, Holly opened her wallet and her stomach sank. The shopping that afternoon had eaten up more of her money, and now she was practically broke. How was she going to pay for her Flamingo stay at the week's end? As Holly reluctantly forked over her share of the bill, the solution came to her: Grandma Ida. Holly's grandmother would gladly lend her cash, especially for the Flamingo. Holly could repay the loan once she was back in New Jersey.

They walked out of the restaurant, and Holly told the girls she needed to make a call. They agreed to meet up at the motel later, and Kaitlin and Daisy headed off for their daily dose of beach dozing. Holly stood in front of the Penguin Hotel, taking her cell phone out of her tote.

When Holly turned on her cell, she saw, to her surprise, that she had three new voice messages. One was probably her parents' from last night, but who else had called since then?

Hesitantly, Holly punched the button for the first message and held the phone to her ear.

"Holly Rebecca." Her mother's voice sounded clipped. Holly could hear her parents' TV blaring in the background. "It's ten fifteen on Monday night and your father and I need to speak to you. We've phoned Grandma Ida but she tells us you're out. Call us back immediately."

Holly felt a pang of fear. This was serious. Something worse than the fender bender. But what? Did her parents know about the Flamingo?

Her stomach in knots, Holly went on to the next message.

"Cookie dough, it's me." Grandma Ida, sounding oddly wired. "It's — what time is it, Miles? — ten thirty. On Monday night." Holly heard Grandma Ida's TV in the background, also on at full volume. "*Bubeleh,* Miles and I just saw you on television! You're a star!"

Holly gasped. The bikini contest! It had aired last

night at ten o'clock. Holly had been too busy dealing with her own untelevised drama to even think of the spring break special. But why had her *grandmother* been watching Pulse?

"The only problem is, your parents saw you, too," Grandma Ida was saying worriedly. "They called and told me to turn on the program. And . . . ah . . . I don't think they were very happy."

Holly stood stock-still, her heart hammering. This had to be a joke. Her *parents* had seen the bikini contest? What were the chances?

"You should call them back," Grandma Ida added. "But it will be fine, my dear. I'm so proud of you! I thought you were shapely, but who knew you had *such* a body on you? What, Miles? Holly, pudding, I have to go, but call me back —" The voice mail system cut her off.

No no no no, Holly thought as she walked quickly down Ocean Drive, the phone pressed to her clammy ear. Her parents were going to *flip out* on her. She could already hear their hysterical voices: "What were you thinking, prancing around half-naked?"; "Do you know that easily a million people must have seen you?"; "Aren't you ashamed of yourself?"

Holly felt like she might throw up. The situation was so typical. Just when she had done something completely unlike herself — while feeling completely sexy in the process — her parents came along to burst her bubble of self-esteem. Calling them back was going to royally suck.

Suddenly, Holly wished that Alexa were there; cool, quick-thinking Alexa would know how to handle this mess. Then, as Holly stopped on the corner outside the Versace Mansion, she shook her head. After last night, Alexa was history.

Holly punched the button on her cell and steeled herself for the next and final message, anticipating her mother's voice again. Instead, a boy spoke into her ear, giving Holly a mini heart attack.

"Holly . . . it's Diego. Hi. It's Tuesday morning. Listen, I know last night was weird." He took a deep breath, sounding much less smooth than usual. "I wanted to apologize for whatever I did wrong. Give me a call, okay? And, um, is your friend Alexa still mad at me? Okay. Bye."

Ugh. Holly rolled her eyes. For someone Princeton-bound, it seemed Diego could be extremely dense. His genuinely bewildered voice infuriated Holly, and his question about Alexa was the icing on the goddamn cake. But his message also confirmed Holly's epiphany from the night before: Diego *had* never wanted anything more than friendship with her. And, Holly realized with a pang, he must have really liked Alexa. Maybe it hadn't even *been* Alexa who'd initiated their hook-up.

Everything was converging on Holly: Diego. Alexa. Her parents. Holly wasn't equipped to handle this insanity. She'd never before had so much going on at once in her life.

Meghan, Holly thought, filled with sudden comfort. She couldn't believe she'd gone this long without talking to her best friend. Meghan would set Holly straight again. Holly opened her phone and punched "2" for Meghan's cell. After several rings, Meghan answered.

"Oh, Holly, I'm so glad you called!" Meghan cried over a loud din. "But you'll have to shout, okay? Jess and I are in line for the Pirates of the Caribbean ride, and it's *nuts.*"

"We miss you, Holly!" Jess hollered in the background. Holly heard little kids yelping and tinny music blasting over a loudspeaker.

Suddenly, Holly felt utterly disconnected from her friends, as if there were more than just miles separating them. Meghan and Jess were off having their safe, happy Disneyland adventure; they'd never understand South Beach.

Numbly, Holly assured Meghan they could catch

up later. Then she pressed END and looked down at her phone as if it were a ticking bomb. Should she call Diego and suffer through a tense, nauseating explanation of how Holly had misread his signals? Hell, no. But her other options — calling her parents, or even Grandma Ida — seemed no better.

Holly felt something snap inside her. Screw it all. She was sick of being Ms. Dutiful — forever returning calls, always apologizing, acting prim and proper. *I'm not that Holly anymore,* she thought fiercely. She wanted to be sassy. Edgy. Kaitlin had called her a badass that morning; maybe it was high time Holly started acting like one.

Holly turned off her cell phone, then slammed it shut with such force it slipped from her hand and landed on the sidewalk, the battery snapping off. Holly grinned. Whatever. She'd fix it later. Or not at all. This way, nobody could reach her; her room in the Flamingo didn't have a phone. Holly gathered up the battery and phone and buried them deep in her tote bag. She'd ask Grandma Ida for a loan another time. And for now she was simply going to pretend she'd never gotten a single message. She was on spring break, and she simply refused to be bothered. Holly Jacobson was overdue for some serious fun.

*   *   *

Around eleven that night, Holly eagerly waited outside Yacht with her fake ID in hand, the afternoon's voice messages long forgotten.

"You look great," Kaitlin assured Holly as they approached the muscle-bound bouncer manning the velvet rope. "Definitely twenty-one."

"That's the plan," Holly said, grinning. She was wearing her new silver-and-pink tube top, a silver miniskirt, and platform sandals. Kaitlin had done her face, so Holly's lids were sparkly with pink eye shadow, and there was glitter on her cheekbones. Her hair was loose, and she wore dangly silver shell earrings. The outfit was borderline trashy, yes, but Holly felt adult and alluring, if a little nervous

Tossing her shoulders back, Holly strutted up to the bouncer and handed him her free pass and, with a flourish, the ID. As the bouncer shone his flashlight on the small card, Holly put one hand on her hip and struck her most mature pose, trying to quell any lingering nerves.

"Go ahead, beautiful," the bouncer told her, motioning toward Yacht's entrance.

Holly's heart soared. *Beautiful!* To think she'd once been that scared, shaky girl stranded outside Ohio's. Holly smirked at the memory as she and Kaitlin headed inside.

Yacht was designed to look like a two-level luxury

ship, complete with porthole windows that overlooked the ocean, and bartenders dressed as sailors.
The bottom level, to Holly's delight, was open-air; tiki
lamps burned around the perimeter of a private boardwalk, and people were grooving to house music under
the sweeping night sky. Next to the wraparound bar
was a hot tub where people were stripping down to
their undies or bikini bottoms and splashing right in.

Still glowing from her velvet rope triumph, Holly
grabbed Kaitlin's hand and led her into the crush of
dancers. Holly threw her arms in the air and moved her
hips to the pulsing beat, giving herself over to the
rhythm. She and Kaitlin had been dancing for a while
when Holly noticed two guys watching her from the bar.
One of them, a tall, slender African American boy with
a wide smile gave Holly a slow, approving once-over.

This time, Holly didn't assume that the boys were
checking out another girl. *They think* I'm *hot,* Holly
thought, feeling a rush of confidence. Boldly, she
winked at the smiling boy, and he nodded back at her,
lifting his drink in apprecation. *Boys are easy,* Holly
realized. *What was I always so nervous about?* Twirling
around, she noticed another boy, right on the dance
floor, who was blatantly checking her out. And when
he sidled up to dance with her for a bit, Holly didn't
stiffen up or shy away. Instead, she danced close to
him, reveling in the attention.

"This place is amazing!" Holly shouted to Kaitlin, after her partner had left her for the bar.

"There's Daisy!" Kaitlin shouted in response, pointing across the boardwalk. Holly looked over in surprise. There *was* Daisy, not only with Jonathan but with Aaron and Thomas as well. Holly noticed that the twins in particular were dressed well; they must have made the extra effort to get into Yacht. The Flamingo kids were admiring their surroundings but hadn't yet noticed Holly or Kaitlin. *What's Alexa doing tonight?* Holly wondered fleetingly. Then she shoved the thought away.

"Let's make fun of them for paying the cover!" Kaitlin cried, bobbing in Daisy's direction. Holly started to follow her, but then she felt a hand on her arm and heard a boy exclaim, "Hey, Bikini Chick!"

Holly turned to see Surfer Guy from the beach. His hair was in a ponytail and he wore a white linen shirt and wide-legged hemp-colored pants. "It's Shane," he reminded her with a smile.

Holly glanced over her shoulder. She couldn't make out Kaitlin's red curls in the sea of people, and she'd also lost sight of the other Flamingo kids. Holly figured she could meet up with them later. Besides, she decided, Shane was much more interesting.

"Tell me your name again?" Shane asked as she turned back to him.

Holly felt a flash of annoyance that he didn't

remember; he'd seemed so focused on her yesterday. She thought back to their accidental kiss, and her pulse quickened. She let her eyes linger over Shane's lips for a minute, wondering what it would be like to kiss him for real. Suddenly, Holly didn't feel so socially inept anymore.

"You've forgotten me already?" she asked with a bubbly laugh, surprised at how much she sounded like Alexa. "I'm so insulted!"

"Oh, come on. At least give me a clue," Shane said, his face breaking into a grin.

"Well, it starts with an 'H'. . . ." Holly murmured, lowering her lashes. *Am I flirting?* she wondered. Having never officially flirted before in her life, she wasn't quite sure. But, in any case, whatever she was doing felt terrific.

"Heidi?" Shane guessed. Holly shook her head. He grinned and kept trying. "Hannah? Heather? Uh, Hepsaba?"

Holly giggled. "Nope, nope, and nope," she purred.

"Oh, dude . . ." Shane said in mock frustration. "Okay. How about I buy you a drink? *Then* will you tell me?"

Holly's knee-jerk reaction was to refuse his offer, but suddenly her whole don't-let-boys-buy-you-drinks plan seemed stupid to her. She was trying to save money, wasn't she?

"I'll see how I feel," Holly teased, but she gave Shane a smile that clearly meant *yes.*

He led her to the bar, where they perched on stools. Shane ordered a frozen strawberry margarita for Holly and a Jack and Coke for himself. Holly took a careful sip of the margarita. Cold, frothy, and sweet, the delicious drink tasted more like candy than alcohol. Holly took a bigger swallow, enjoying the slight burning sensation in her throat.

"Holly," she told Shane, still sipping her margarita. "My name is Holly." She had always felt that her name was too cutesy, better suited to a pigtailed little girl. But revealing her name to Shane breathed new life into it. "Holly" suddenly sounded like the sultriest name in the world.

"Knew it," Shane said, hitting a hand to his forehead.

"*Sure* you did," Holly taunted, downing more of her margarita.

They continued their banter for a while, and soon Holly's glass was empty. When Shane offered to buy her another, Holly hesitated only a moment before accepting. Her cheeks were warm but she wasn't dizzy. *I'm not drunk at all!* she thought. *I must have really high tolerance.*

Her second margarita arrived, and Holly took a giant gulp. Okay, maybe her head was the slightest bit spinny. She and Kaitlin had gone out to dinner that night at the Sushi Rock Café, but Holly, conscious of her cash supply, had only ordered miso soup. Now, she was wondering if she should have had more food in her stomach before she started guzzling margaritas. Wasn't that one of the rules of smart drinking? Holly wasn't sure, but it didn't matter now. She held her glass up, admiring the drink's vibrant pink color.

"It matches my shirt!" she told Shane, exploding into giggles.

"I like your shirt," Shane said softly, running a finger down her midsection. Holly's heart leaped.

A gaggle of rowdy college girls in matching halter tops swarmed the bar, loudly demanding shots. Holly glanced over at the girls, remembering her humiliation at not knowing what body shots — or even tequila shots — were. It was time to redeem herself, she decided, swallowing most of her margarita.

She turned to the girl next to her, whose long, wavy blonde hair made Holly think momentarily of Alexa.

"Are those tequila shots?" Holly asked the girl as the sailor-bartender set several shot glasses filled with amber-colored liquid on the bar.

"Southern Comfort and lime juice," the girl replied, as her face turned an interesting shade of green. "Actually, do you want mine?" she asked Holly with a hiccup. "I feel kind of sick." Without warning, she turned and fled the bar, most likely in search of the nearest bathroom. None of her friends followed her.

Holly felt so loose and carefree from the two margaritas that she didn't think twice about picking up the girl's abandoned shot glass. "Cheers!" the other halter-top girls toasted her. Holly clinked her shot glass against theirs and tipped her head back, swallowing the tangy, sour drink in one go. *Whoa.* Her mouth felt like it was on fire. The bar in front of Holly seemed to tilt, then right itself.

"I can't feel my feet!" she confessed to Shane in a slurred whisper. He chuckled and slowly ran his hand down her back.

The DJ took a break from techno and started spinning vintage Madonna: "Into the Groove" — one of Holly's favorites. The halter-top girls squealed in appreciation, and the ringleader, a busty brunette with a flower tattoo on her arm, cleared the shot glasses away, and promptly hoisted herself up onto the bar. She began dancing in her spiky heels, flinging her curly hair around. Quickly, the other girls followed suit. They all started shaking it on top of the bar, as the other clubbers cheered them on. Holly clapped her hands, watching the girls in awe.

"Get up here, babe!" the brunette shouted to Holly. Holly slid off the stool, flushed with a sense of belonging. As soon as she was on her feet, she felt how insanely drunk she was. But the fuzzy, swaying sensation made her feel as if she could do anything. She handed Shane her little bag and, with his help, climbed up and joined her newfound friends atop the bar.

"*Live out your fantasy, here with me!*" Holly shouted along with the song, dancing wildly. People whose faces she couldn't make out were pointing at her and whistling. *This* is *like a fantasy,* Holly thought foggily. From where she stood, the energetic crowd, the hot tub, and the boardwalk swam together in a happy blur. When the song ended, Holly wobbled in her platforms, suddenly worried she might fall.

Shane, clearly seeing she was in trouble, took Holly's hands, carefully guided her off the bar, and handed her bag to her. Holly, needing all the support she could get, grabbed on to Shane's arm. She was only mildly surprised when he smiled, lowered his face, and kissed her. *So* this *is what it's like to kiss a random boy in a bar,* Holly thought as Shane's tongue touched hers. But it didn't feel cheap or skanky. It felt . . . yummy. Holly stood on her tiptoes, her lips eagerly responding to Shane's.

She heard Shane's breath quicken as his hands roamed around her waist, up under her tube top, along her back, and over to her breasts. Holly gasped, instinctively pushing his hands away and jerking back. Shane had just unwittingly attempted to go where no boy had gone before.

"What's wrong?" Shane asked, confused. "Aren't you up for some fun?"

Abruptly — even through her drunken haze — Holly understood Shane's impression of her. He'd only seen Holly at the volleyball game and bikini contest and, most recently, atop the bar. He simply assumed she was an über-confident girl who had no problem letting boys grope her. He'd never known the *other* Holly.

"I — I don't want us to do more. . . ." Holly mumbled, drawing back from Shane. She could feel some of her old shyness slipping over her.

Suddenly, somebody on Yacht's upper level turned on a giant foam machine, spraying the crowd below with white, frothy bubbles. Holly shrieked as the foam hit her in the face, and then she slipped and almost fell. When she straightened up, she couldn't see Shane anywhere in the soapy madness. Holly felt a stab of panic, and elbowed her way out of the bar area, past people having foam fights and making out. She was maneuvering past the hot tub when a shirtless, obviously plastered guy darted across Holly's path. Before he reached the Jacuzzi, he took off his pants and boxers. Then, totally naked, he plunged into the water with a shout of triumph.

Ew! Holly thought as the others in the hot tub shrieked and whooped. *I have to get out of here.* Desperately, she searched the foam-covered crowd for Kaitlin and Daisy, or any of her Flamingo friends. She felt enormously relieved when she spotted Aaron hovering by one of the tiki lamps, drinking a Sam Adams. He caught Holly's eye and waved her over.

Grateful to see a familiar face, Holly impulsively flung her foamy arms around Aaron as soon as she reached him.

"Where is everyone else?" she cried drunkenly.

"They headed over to Nerve," Aaron replied, returning her embrace. "I told them to wait for you, but . . ." He shrugged and gave her a sympathetic smile.

Holly pouted. Kaitlin had abandoned her? "They could've told me they were leaving," she huffed. "Those . . ." She searched for the perfect word to sum up her frustration. Holly rarely cursed, but now she felt it was necessary for the occasion.

"Assholes," she and Aaron spoke at the exact same instant. Then they glanced at each other in surprise and cracked up.

"Jinx," Aaron told her, linking his pinkie with hers.

Holly grinned, completely forgetting her hostility

toward Aaron from the night before. They suddenly seemed exactly on the same wavelength.

"Should we go catch up with them?" Aaron asked, still hanging onto her pinkie.

Holly closed her eyes against the boardwalk spinning around her. "I want to, but I'm . . ."

"You're . . . ?" Aaron prompted gently.

"Trashed," Holly said, opening her eyes. Once again, she and Aaron burst out laughing.

"If I laugh, I get more dizzier," Holly explained, clinging to Aaron's arm.

"'More dizzier?'" Aaron teased, setting down his beer bottle. "Come on, let me walk you back to the Flamingo. You're in no shape for another club."

Aaron took hold of Holly's hand. As he led her away from the crush, and out of Yacht, Holly felt a rush of gratitude toward him. He was so sweet to have waited for her, and such a gentleman to be walking her home, Holly thought as she swayed along at his side. When they entered the Flamingo lobby, still holding hands, Aaron said to Holly, "I think Kaitlin and those guys didn't want to bother you because they saw you kissing someone."

"They did?" Holly squeaked, her cheeks burning with shame.

"Yeah," Aaron went on, his eyes dancing. "And we *all* saw you up on the bar."

"No!" Holly cried, pulling her hand out of his grasp. "Oh, my God! I'm so embarrassed."

"Why?" Aaron asked. He took a step toward her and put his hands on her hips. "*I* enjoyed watching you. Come on, dance for me again. Right here."

"No!" Holly shrieked. "You can't make me!" Giggling, she turned and tore toward the back exit that led to the pool. Aaron followed her, their laughter echoing through the empty lobby.

The pool's surface shone diamondlike in the bright moonlight. Holly skidded to a stop, then whirled around to see Aaron approaching her.

"Do it, Holly," he teased. "Come on. *Get into the groove,*" he sang, moving his shoulders to the beat.

"You're making fun of me!" Holly exclaimed, blushing madly. She walked backward, holding her hands up and dropping her bag. "Don't . . . come . . . near . . ."

Suddenly, Holly lost her already shaky footing and fell over into the pool. She screamed as she hit the water, and went under. She resurfaced, gasping, her drenched clothes plastered to her body.

"Look what you did, Aaron!" she spluttered, but she was laughing. The pool water was almost cold enough to sober her up. Almost.

"Oh, calm down," Aaron snorted. "It's no big deal. Look, I'll do it, too." He took off his Polo shirt and his pants, carefully removing his wallet from his back pocket and setting it on the nearest chair. Then he kicked off his sandals and dove into the pool wearing only his boxers, sending up a great splash. Holly screamed again, paddling away from him.

"Shh," Aaron said, swimming up behind her and putting his hands on her shoulders.

"Get off me," Holly said, but she didn't really mean it. Aaron had big hands and long, tapered fingers that felt so nice against her skin.

"I wasn't making fun of you," Aaron murmured into her ear. His breath was hot on her neck. "I think you are so sexy, Holly."

"You do?" Holly asked giddily, floating around to face Aaron. Sure, she'd suspected that those boys at Yacht tonight — and Shane — thought she looked good. But to actually *hear* a boy say it was something else entirely.

She and Aaron bobbed up and down, their legs brushing underwater. Anticipation made Holly's skin quiver. She wanted him to touch her again.

"Uh-huh," Aaron replied, his voice velvety. "I thought that from the first minute I saw you."

Holly smiled, remembering how she'd opened the door in her bathing suit to see Aaron and Thomas.

"You have the prettiest smile," Aaron whispered, tracing his thumb over Holly's lower lip. Holly held her breath as he leaned over and lightly touched his mouth to hers.

"I — I thought, maybe, you liked me," Holly said, the alcohol loosening her tongue. "But I wasn't sure."

"Oh, come on," Aaron murmured, his fingers grazing her collarbone. "It wasn't exactly an accident that I walked in on you in the shower over there." He motioned with his head.

"You planned that?" Holly gasped, getting water in her mouth. "But you — you acted all surprised and shy. . . ." She trailed off, remembering that night.

Aaron laughed softly. "I could tell you were a good girl, so I figured I'd play nice."

A good girl. Holly felt a rush of anger, mixed with desire. She was *not* a good girl anymore. And, to prove her point, she put her arms around Aaron's neck and kissed him hard on the mouth.

"Wow," Aaron whispered, drawing his head back to look at Holly. "All *right.*"

He kissed her deeply, sliding his muscular arms tight around her waist. Holly pressed close to him, and they both submerged. Kissing underwater felt so sensual, the cool water enveloping their bodies. When they came up for air, Holly shook out her sopping hair and laughed, gesturing down to her soaked tube top.

"I'm all wet," she complained.

"Let me help you," Aaron said, reaching down and sliding Holly's tube top up over her head. He tossed it out of the pool, and it landed on a beach chair.

Holly bit her lip, as Aaron smoothly reached behind her and unhooked her strapless bra. She remembered how Shane had tried to go up under her shirt at Yacht, and she'd stopped him in a panic. Things felt different now; she was still a little hesitant, but Aaron seemed safer. Familiar. He was literally the boy next door — at the Flamingo, anyway. As Aaron drew her close again, she thrilled at the new sensation of skin on skin. His hard chest felt so warm and smooth against her own silky softness that it sent tingles through Holly's whole body. She smiled as she wrapped her legs around Aaron's underwater.

"I've got condoms in my wallet," Aaron told her. His teeth were very white in the darkness. "Just in case."

Is that where this is leading? Holly wondered. She hoped Aaron couldn't feel the mad pounding of her heart. "That's good," she said lazily, as if she'd done this a thousand times before. To mask her nerves, she leaned in and started kissing Aaron's neck.

"Hey, Holly?" Aaron murmured.

"Mmm?"

"You know this is just for fun, right?" he asked. "Like, I'm not planning on breakfast or some shit tomorrow morning."

Holly glanced up. Aaron's face floated above the water, serious.

"Oh, sure," Holly replied tremulously. She hadn't really thought about tomorrow. She guessed she didn't want any strings attached, either. That would get too complicated.

"I mean, you can't really stay over tonight," Aaron went on. "My brother and Jon and I have this thing about girls sleeping over. It's too weird if one of us guys is in the room. You know what I'm saying?"

Holly nodded, remembering what Daisy had told her that morning. So would she and Aaron, like, go all the way . . . and then trek back to their separate beds? Holly shivered in the cold water.

Back in Oakridge, whenever she thought about sex, she always imagined her first time would be with her first real boyfriend. Someone Holly would feel absolutely comfortable with. Someone who knew how to kiss her and touch her just the way she liked, and who'd want her to sleep in his arms all night. Someone she'd love, and who'd love her, too. Had she been naïve to hope for all that — just as she'd foolishly hoped for a chance with Diego?

"I just thought we'd lay down some ground rules first," Aaron explained, squeezing Holly's waist underwater and kissing the side of her neck. "I generally like to do that."

Holly stomach turned. *How many girls has he been with?* she wondered.

Suddenly, being here with Aaron felt all wrong. And it wasn't because Holly was thinking she should have been with Diego, or with any other boy. She was thinking about herself. Just because she was being naughtier and wilder tonight did *not* mean she had to give it up to some loser. No, Holly realized. She wasn't being naïve this time. She simply knew, with absolute certainty, that she deserved better.

"Here's a ground rule for you, Aaron," Holly said, pushing him off her. "Next time you want to get lucky, try not to be such a slimy *bastard*."

Aaron's jaw dropped. "You're turning me down?" he asked incredulously.

Holly rolled her eyes. "Get over yourself, Aaron," she replied. Grabbing her bra, she climbed out of the pool and pulled on her wet tube top. Then she snatched up her bag, and, without looking back at him, hurried out of the pool area as quickly as her waterlogged platforms could carry her.

It was almost three in the morning as she shot through the Flamingo lobby and up the stairs. Out of habit, Holly headed toward Room Number 7, and paused in front of the door. Though Holly felt much more sober, she still needed a dose of clarity. *I need to talk to Alexa,* Holly realized. But Holly was still sore about last night. She wasn't about to apologize to Alexa yet.

Still, Holly didn't want to spend another night in Kaitlin and Daisy's room. She wanted to change into *her* own pajamas, and climb into the narrow bed that had become familiar to her since Saturday. She just craved some sense of normalcy. So Holly hesitated, then braced herself, and knocked on the door.

CHAPTER TWELVE
Temptation Times Two

There's nothing like the sight of drag queens to cheer you up, Alexa reflected as she peered through the lens of her digital camera. It was Tuesday night, around ten, and Alexa was taking pictures of people on Lincoln Road. After nibbling on a slice at Pizza Rustica, she emerged in time to see three drag queens in high heels and tight, sequined dresses sashaying down the strip. Alexa grinned as she snapped the picture. Then she settled down on a nearby bench to review the images in her camera, but soon she was stifling a yawn. Alexa couldn't concentrate on photography tonight. Her eyes stung from lack of sleep, and she had plenty of other things on her mind.

Alexa had left her door unlocked last night on the off chance that Holly decided to come back to the room. But she had been so paranoid about the possibility of intruders sneaking in — and so haunted by her exchange with Holly on the beach — that she didn't fall asleep until after dawn. She was rudely awakened a few hours later by Kaitlin, who barged in to retrieve Holly's necessities for the day. Alexa had rolled her eyes, supremely annoyed. The fact that Holly clearly didn't have the guts to confront Alexa only deepened Alexa's aggravation toward her former friend.

But as Alexa showered and changed, she found that she was kind of missing the company of said former friend. Alexa drove to the Miami Art Museum, hoping a dash of culture and beauty would revive her. After wandering the galleries for the afternoon, however, her argument with Holly still gnawed at her like a persistent toothache. Even a phone call to Portia from the car didn't help; Portia couldn't talk because she and the other girls were on a private cruise with boys they'd met the night before. When Alexa returned to the Flamingo, she ran into Thomas and brusquely turned down his invitation to join him later that night at some outdoor club he'd forgotten the name of.

So that was how Alexa found herself with her camera on bustling Lincoln Road, wearing a simple, peach-colored cotton sundress, her hair in a low braid, and no makeup. It was the first time in years that Alexa St. Laurent was out after sundown . . . and not *going out.*

But she craved time alone tonight — time away from the whirling circus of bars and clubs and alcohol. And, mostly, she needed time away from boys. Because, out of all the unpleasant memories Alexa couldn't shake from last night's fight, the most persistent one was Holly calling her a slut.

In the heat of the moment, Alexa had been more than ready to defend herself. But after the argument, doubts began to brew in Alexa's mind. *Was* she sort of a slut? Did she move from boy to boy mindlessly, using their affections to fill some sort of void in herself? Alexa had to admit that this concern had been plaguing her since that night at Ohio's. And that was why she'd grown so enraged at Holly's accusation last night. The truth always bit sharpest, didn't it?

But with Diego, it felt different, Alexa mused, gazing off at the bright lights of the Colony Theater. Though she'd been totally sober, Diego had made her feel drunk with possibility — with the sense that she'd finally found a boy who understood her. And Alexa hadn't aggressively flirted with him, as she'd done with hot boys in the past. Their coming together had felt fluid, elegant, inevitable.

Forget him, Alexa chided herself, turning her attention back to the camera. Diego was too confusing.

Even though Holly had said that she and Diego weren't together, Alexa still wasn't sure what their history *had* been. It was impossible for Alexa not to feel a little guilty for kissing Diego — even if he was technically available.

"Excuse me, but I'm looking for a professional photographer." A deep male voice interrupted her thoughts.

Alexa glanced over, irritated that some creep was ruining her moment of self-reflection.

But the boy beside her on the bench was none other than the very focus of her thoughts. Alexa gave a start. It was as if she'd been thinking about Diego so much he'd sprung, fully formed, from her head.

"I'm hoping you can help me," Diego continued, a smile tugging at his full lips. "I'm looking for someone smart and beautiful who likes to take candid shots of people in public places." He reached over and gently tucked a strand of hair behind Alexa's ear. "Do you know anyone who fits that description?"

Alexa inched away from him, trying not to notice how her whole body responded to even his slightest touch. She was also doing her best to ignore how good he looked in a long-sleeved black shirt and Sean John jeans. She could smell his Cool Water, and wished she could lean over and rest her head in the crook of his neck.

"What are you doing here?" she finally asked, taking her gaze off him. She pretended to watch a musician performing in the street.

"You told me you wanted to take pictures of Lincoln Road at night," Diego said. Out of the corner of her eye she saw him lift his hand as if he wanted to touch her again, but then he dropped it back into his lap. "I figured I would see you if I walked up and down the strip enough times." He paused and she could tell he was smiling. "I hope that doesn't make me a total stalker."

Alexa shook her head, suppressing her own smile. A group of drunken spring breakers wove past, arguing noisily about which bar to hit next.

"It's just that I really wanted to talk to you about what happened at the Delano," Diego explained, his voice impassioned. "I called Holly today, too, hoping I'd get in touch with you through her. But she never called me back."

"I haven't even *seen* Holly since last night," Alexa replied. "But I'm guessing she's still pretty upset." Then Alexa turned her head and looked straight at Diego, her heart aching at the sight of him. "Did *anything* ever happen between you guys?" she asked plainly.

This time Diego was the one to look away, glancing down at his hands. "Back when we were kids," he said. "When I still lived in Miami Beach. I was like, fourteen, and we spent a week hanging out together. We had a lot of fun and on her last night . . . I kissed her." Diego glanced briefly at Alexa, smiling his frustratingly adorable smile. "But that was three years ago. And when I met her again this week —" Diego shook his head. "It just felt like we were old buddies, and that was all. I mean, Holly's a sweetheart, and she's a really good-looking girl but . . ." Diego looked back up, his dark eyes sweeping over Alexa's face. "She's not the girl for me."

Alexa bit her lip, unable to tear her gaze away from his. She held her breath as he leaned close and cupped her face in his hands.

"*You're* the girl for me," Diego said softly.

Alexa was dying to melt into his arms and kiss him with all the tenderness she was feeling. But everything was still so jumbled in her mind — the fight with Holly, and Alexa's own feelings of guilt and uncertainty. She'd resolved to take a break from boys and had to stick to that plan. It would give her the space and time she needed to sort herself out.

"Diego . . ." Alexa began. Even saying his name was painful. "Diego, I think you're so wonderful. But I can't be with you right now." She tried to turn away again but Diego kept his hands gently on her face.

"Alexa," he pleaded. "Maybe Holly thought she and I had something more than we did, and I guess that's why she got so mad last night. But I swear to you that there's nothing between us. I never lied to you, Alexa."

"I know," Alexa whispered, choking up. How could she have ever doubted the burning sincerity in Diego's eyes? She hadn't imagined the intensity of his feelings last night; they'd been as real and powerful as her own. His honesty was so seductive, but Alexa couldn't give into him now.

"It's not only about Holly," Alexa said as she slowly removed Diego's hands from her face. "It's about me." She felt her eyes grow hot, and she blinked back tears. "Maybe it's because I just got out of a relationship, or because of what happened at the Delano. But I need to, I don't know, make peace with *myself* before I can be with someone else again." She dabbed at her eyes with the back of her hand and gave Diego a small smile. "Does that make sense?"

Diego nodded, swallowing hard. "It does. But I wish you'd . . . you'd still give me a chance." He suddenly sounded so lost, like a little boy. Gone was the suave gentleman he'd been last night.

Alexa knew that if she sat there any longer, she'd lose it and start weeping into Diego's shirt. She *hated* crying in front of anyone. So she stood and dropped her camera back into her tote.

"I should go," she told Diego, her voice breaking.

He stood quickly and took her hands in his. "Alexa,

wait — will I see you again? When are you leaving Miami?"

"On Friday," Alexa whispered. "But please don't try to find me, Diego." She gazed into his beautiful eyes one last time. "Maybe . . ." she added thoughtfully. "Maybe if we're meant to be together, we will be. Someday."

Then she raised her mouth to his and let herself kiss him quickly. If the kiss had lasted a second longer, she knew she wouldn't have been able to leave him. She pulled back just in time, ran her finger along his sharp cheekbone, and walked off into the night, half hoping he would follow her. But he didn't. As Alexa crossed Washington Avenue, she told herself she'd done the right thing. If only the right thing didn't feel like utter heartbreak.

Back in her room at the Flamingo, Alexa locked the door and settled on the carpet. She'd stopped at the drugstore on the way back and purchased new nail polish. Mani–pedis were Alexa's favorite form of therapy, after shopping and boys. She didn't have the energy to try on clothes now, and boys, of course, were out of the question.

Alexa rubbed nail polish remover on her nails, thankful for the quiet around her. It was eleven o'clock, and everyone on her floor was most likely already out for the night, lining up for some club or another. For an instant, Alexa wondered what Holly was doing, but then she dismissed the thought entirely.

Alexa was unscrewing the cap on her jar of Mystique Pink when somebody rapped on the door. She glanced up, irritated at the interruption. Was it Holly? Or, more likely, Kaitlin, acting as Holly's proxy again? Alexa wasn't sure which would be worse. Then the person knocked again and tried the doorknob.

"Come in!" Alexa called imperiously.

There was no response at first. Finally, a male voice asked, "Alexa?"

Alexa caught her breath. No. It couldn't be. How would he know to find her *here*?

She stood and walked slowly to the door. Her imagination was playing tricks on her. It was probably Thomas, still hoping she'd be up for clubbing tonight.

But when she unlocked the door and eased it open, she learned that her first guess had been accurate.

"Tyler?" she whispered. She wanted to pinch herself. Was she actually looking at her ex-boyfriend? Here? In Florida?

Tyler ran a hand through his thick, dark-blond hair and gave Alexa a sheepish half smile. He had his black messenger bag slung across his chest and was carrying a Puma duffle. He wore jeans, a hooded sweatshirt and Timberlands. He must have just flown in from New Jersey. But how? And why?

"Hey," he said awkwardly. "Surprise."

Alexa stared at him, speechless.

"Can I come in?" Tyler asked, gesturing to his bags.

"I — why — why are you here?" Alexa spluttered. "I never told you I was going to South Beach." Dazed, she moved aside to let him enter, then shut the door and turned to face him as he set his duffle and messenger bag on the floor.

Seeing Tyler in the middle of her room at the Flamingo felt no less bizarre than if a spaceship had suddenly crash-landed on the beach. Alexa shook her head, then sank onto the edge of Holly's bed.

"I know," Tyler said, cracking his knuckles. "At first I figured you were spending the break in Oakridge, like me."

"So, wait, you didn't go to Aspen?" Alexa asked.

Tyler shook his head and smiled sadly. "Of course not, Alexa. Who was I going to go with at the last minute?"

Alexa stared down at her bare toenails. That made sense. It also made her feel beyond guilty.

"So I'm at home this week, watching, like, way too much TV," Tyler continued, as if he'd rehearsed just how to tell Alexa his story. "And on Monday night, I start watching Pulse's spring break special. Just to torture myself, I guess, because they're showing all these guys on a beach having a great time."

"Why don't you twist the knife a little deeper, Tyler?" Alexa sighed. "I get it. I suck."

"Let me finish," Tyler said. "Then they start showing this insane bikini contest. And then I see Holly Jacobson up there! Random, right? And I'm remembering how you once told me you and Holly used to be good friends, and *then . . .*" He shrugged, as if he still couldn't believe it. "Then I see you. Up on the stage with Holly. I thought I was dreaming."

"You *saw* the bikini contest?" Alexa cried. She was surprised by the coincidence, but also thrilled by the fact she'd actually been on TV. She'd always secretly suspected she might become famous one day. "I didn't think anybody I know saw it! I mean, I *did* ask my dad to TiVo it but —"

"Yeah," Tyler said. "I called him as soon as I saw it. He told me everything. That you'd gone down to South Beach with Holly. Where you were staying. All that."

I'm going to kill my father, Alexa thought. She'd described the location of the Flamingo to him when she had called him after the bikini contest on Monday afternoon. He'd told Alexa to enjoy herself, and that he'd see her on Friday. Alexa had never suspected he would betray her by giving all the details to *Tyler.* And couldn't he have even called Alexa to let her know

Tyler was on his way down? Alexa could picture her dad, chain-smoking on the phone while flipping through the latest issue of *ARTnews* and half-listening as Tyler rambled on. He'd probably found Tyler's phone call romantic, and had been happy to play the part of Cupid.

"I got tickets online. The only available flight to Miami arrived at ten tonight," Tyler finished with another shrug. "So here I am."

"How was the flight?" Alexa asked, remembering that Tyler had never flown before.

"Whatever." Tyler shrugged, but Alexa knew him well enough to know what that meant: He'd been completely terrified. She thought of Holly, and smiled to herself.

A tense silence settled over the room as Alexa and Tyler studied each other. Alexa remained on Holly's bed while Tyler stood by the dresser, and Alexa was acutely aware of the gulf between them. She was reminded of their last encounter, back in her bedroom on that gloomy Thursday afternoon. Had it really been less than a week? So much had changed between then and now.

As if he were thinking the same thing, Tyler said, "You seem kind of different."

"How so?" Alexa asked, tugging on her braid and feeling mildly self-conscious.

"Just . . ." He angled his head. "More laid-back or something."

"Oh," Alexa said. She looked at Tyler, trying to surmise if he seemed different in any way. Tyler was so handsome that, sometimes, if Alexa hadn't seen him for a while, his classic good looks were almost startling. She'd forgotten how chiseled his features were. In spite of herself, Alexa couldn't help but feel flattered that Tyler had rushed down from New Jersey expressly to see her. To try and win her back.

"Anyway," Tyler said, clearing his throat. "We need to talk." He folded his arms across his chest and looked at Alexa somberly. "I came down here because —"

"I know," Alexa cut him off gently. "You don't have to explain. I'm blown away that you made this big trip for me, Tyler, but . . ." She shook her head. "We can't get back together." She lowered her lashes, hoping Tyler would take the rejection fairly well. She couldn't believe she had turned down two boys over the course of one night. That had to be some kind of record, albeit one that was very different from the record she'd set in Cannes.

Tyler shook his head. "That's not why I'm here, Alexa," he said.

Alexa blinked in surprise. "It's not?"

Tyler's golden-brown eyes were thoughtful. "Well,

when I first decided to fly to Miami, it was because I wanted to get back with you. I thought I'd pick up a bottle of wine, and roses, and tell you all the reasons we should be together."

Alexa pouted. Why *hadn't* he brought her wine and roses? She was a total sucker for sappy gestures.

"But . . ." Tyler continued. "Then I started thinking about things a lot on the plane. And I guess I actually came down here because I wanted a better answer."

"A better answer for what?" Alexa asked nervously.

"For why you dropped me so suddenly," Tyler said. "Like you'd made this split-second decision that I wasn't good enough for you."

Alexa remembered Holly's words from the night before: *When you decided to drop me . . .* Alexa's throat tightened.

"Tyler, the last thing I ever wanted was to hurt you," she began, her voice shaking. *Oh, God.* She couldn't be about to cry *again*.

"I was more confused than hurt," Tyler said, drumming his fingers on the dresser behind him. "I spent the past five days trying to figure out what the hell happened in your bedroom, but I couldn't. So I thought I'd go to the source." His smile was tinged with sadness again.

Alexa thought back to last Thursday, and how she'd closed the door on Tyler. Shame flooded through her. Then, she'd been so pleased with how she'd gotten rid of Tyler. Now, she felt terrible.

"I was so callous," Alexa finally spoke, her vision blurred with unshed tears. "I handled the situation all wrong."

Tyler crossed his arms over his chest again. "Well, you certainly did take me by surprise," he admitted, addressing the carpet.

Alexa sniffled. "I'd been thinking of ending things for a while, but I always put off saying something to you. There was never anything specific you did wrong." She gave Tyler a teary smile. "I know it's such a cliché, but it's wasn't you. It was —"

Tyler groaned. "Alexa. Come on."

Alexa shook her head. She had to set this straight. "Tyler, you are . . ." She groped for the right word. "Awesome," she said with another smile. "Really. You're thoughtful and considerate and, well, you're not bad to look at." Tyler colored slightly. Alexa tried to laugh but she was too close to tears.

"But I didn't appreciate your good qualities," she continued. "I was always hung up on how we weren't right for each other. How different we were." The lump in her throat that had lingered since her conversation with Diego grew larger. Alexa felt as if everything was hitting her at once: Tyler. Diego. Holly. Even her father, so wrapped up in his work back home that he hadn't thought to warn her that Tyler was coming. And Alexa thought of her mother, who was so consumed by *her* fashionable New York existence that she didn't even *know* Alexa had gone to South Beach in the first place. All the pain Alexa had worked so hard to bottle up threatened to overflow. She didn't think she'd be able to hold back her tears this time.

Tyler nodded. "When I was with you, I always felt as if I couldn't . . . measure up. I couldn't give you what you wanted." He regarded her seriously "We *are* so different, Alexa. I think I realize that now."

"I just don't think we were ever destined to be together," Alexa whispered to him. Then, hot salty tears coursed down her cheeks and she began to sob, burying her face in her hands. "And when I told you that you'd find a better girl for you, I—I meant it. . . ."

Tyler immediately walked over to the bed and sat beside Alexa, wrapping his arm around her shoulder.

"Shhh," he murmured. "Don't cry, Alexa. I can't stand seeing you this upset."

"Really?" Alexa sobbed, looking up at him. "You don't hate me?"

Tyler reached into his back pocket and pulled out a folded tissue. He handed it to Alexa and she blew her nose. "I was good and pissed at you," he said. "I deleted all the pictures of you from my cell phone, and I wrote you this e-mail full of swear words that I never even sent. But I don't think I could ever hate you, Alexa." Gently, he pressed his lips to her cheek.

Through her tears, Alexa thought about how cute it was that Tyler had used the phrase "swear words." Only Tyler. . . . It was so reassuring to have a pair of masculine arms around her, and so comforting to smell Tyler's fresh, soapy scent that Alexa forgot all about her taking-a-break-from-boys plan. Tyler being here was bizarre, but at the same time, familiar. Easy. Alexa didn't think twice before she turned her face and put her mouth on Tyler's.

She felt him hesitate, and start to draw back, but then he returned her kiss. Alexa leaned back on the bed, drawing Tyler along with her until they were both lying down. Alexa arched her back, pressing up close to Tyler. Kissing him wasn't as electric as kissing Diego, but, God, he felt so good. She realized with a smile that, this time, her father *wasn't* downstairs; Tyler would let her take this as far as she liked.

But before Alexa reached down to tug off Tyler's sweatshirt, she realized how wrong their sleeping together would be. It would confuse everything between them. And it would mess up Alexa's state of mind even more.

Alexa broke off their kiss, turning her head away. Tyler paused, studying her face, then he pulled back. They both sat up and faced each other sheepishly.

"We shouldn't," Alexa said.

Tyler nodded. "Yeah," he said after a minute. "That would be a bad plan. I mean, you're pretty hard to resist, Alexa. But I need to move on."

"Are you going back to Oakridge tonight?" Alexa asked, blotting her cheeks with her tissue. The way he said *move on* had sounded sort of literal.

"I don't think so," Tyler said. "My flight back isn't until Saturday. And the guy downstairs told me there are lots of vacancies here. He's gonna put me in a single upstairs."

"Of course there are lots of vacancies," Alexa said, giggling. "This place is a total dive."

Tyler laughed. "I didn't even notice. Seems cool to me."

It felt good to be laughing and talking with Tyler, Alexa thought. He gathered his bags, and they agreed to meet for brunch sometime during the week. *Maybe I'll do the impossible and actually be friends with an ex,* Alexa thought incredulously as she hugged Tyler good-bye. *That would be a first.*

But as Alexa closed her door and confronted her empty room, her feeling of contentment vanished. Seeing Tyler had been so surreal that now she was dying to share the news with someone. She thought of picking up her cell to call Portia, but then Alexa realized whom she really wanted to talk to: Holly. Telling

Holly would be so much fun — she would get all big-eyed, and would be hilariously freaked by the fact that Alexa and Tyler had almost gotten busy on *her* bed. But even if Holly walked into the room that minute, Alexa knew she still couldn't bring herself to confide in her. After last night, things were bound to feel awkward between them, and as much as Alexa hated to admit it, she was much too proud to apologize yet.

Alexa returned to her nails with a sigh. She *did* have to acknowledge that Holly's reaction made more sense now that Alexa had heard the backstory from Diego. At the thought of him, Alexa felt her chest seize up. Her encounter with Tyler had somehow only enhanced her longing for Diego.

After Alexa finished her nails, she went to bed, but, again, she was too on edge to sleep. She stared up at the ceiling for hours, watching the patterns cast by passing headlights. She was considering turning on the light and finishing her copy of *Confessions of a Shopaholic* when a knock on the door made her jump. It couldn't be Tyler again; he was too polite to disturb anyone at three in the morning. Hesitantly, Alexa opened the door and found herself staring at Holly, who looked pissed, soaking wet, and possibly drunk, in an over-the-top pink-and-silver outfit.

"Are you okay?" Alexa asked. She knew she and

Holly weren't supposed to be speaking, but she was too curious to keep quiet.

For a second, Holly's expression softened, and she looked as if she wanted to tell Alexa a hundred different things. Alexa bit her lip, hoping Holly would be the one to break the ice. She knew that if Holly spoke first, she'd readily reciprocate.

But the moment passed. Holly's face closed again. "What do you care?" she asked Alexa. Then Holly stormed past her and pulled her duffle bag from beneath her bed, digging around for a towel.

Alexa shrugged and shut the door. She got back into bed, pretending to sleep as Holly dried off, changed, and collapsed into her bed. Neither girl let on how much she wanted to talk to the other. Instead, they remained silent, their unspoken words hovering in the muggy room all night.

CHAPTER THIRTEEN

Payback

Holly and Alexa still didn't speak the next morning, skirting around each other in silence as they got dressed for the beach. Holly dropped in on Kaitlin and Daisy to pick up the tote she'd left in their room yesterday, and then emerged just as Alexa was locking the door to Number 7 behind her. The two girls tramped down the stairs, with Alexa in the lead, each one careful to keep a few feet away from the other. As they cut through the lobby, Holly — worried about seeing Aaron — put on a burst of speed and tried to overtake Alexa, who was also speeding up since she was a little anxious about running into Tyler.

Outside the Flamingo, Holly pulled ahead of Alexa, then crossed the street. Alexa followed suit, but her spirits fell when she saw Holly turn onto a particular beach. That was right where Alexa had planned to sunbathe today. She wasn't about to change her plans, though. Alexa stomped onto the beach, and saw Holly laying out her towel in the perfect spot — close enough to the shore to feel the ocean's light spray, but with the sun directly overhead.

How dare she? Alexa thought.

She marched over and defiantly laid her towel directly beside Holly. Then she plunked down her tote, sat on the towel, and began squirting sunscreen onto her calves and arms, glaring at Holly, who was doing the same.

Both girls finished applying sunscreen, then silently stretched out on their backs and pointed their faces toward the sun.

Very slowly, Holly turned her head to look at Alexa, and saw that Alexa was looking back at her. At the same instant, she and Alexa both reached up and took off their sunglasses. Holly could see Alexa's mouth twitching, and Holly felt her own laugh bubbling inside her. It was ridiculous how they were each pretending to be alone while spending their morning together.

In unison, the girls burst out laughing.

Holly sat up on her towel, clutching her belly. Alexa was sitting up, too, her shoulders shaking with silent laughter.

"I'm gonna pee my pants!" Alexa threatened, getting to her feet.

"Do you always have to pee when we're on the beach?" Holly asked with a snort.

Alexa flung her hair back, trying in vain to keep a straight face. "Well, maybe we can sneak into a hotel and you can pretend to be somebody's niece."

"Ooh, where did you get *that* idea?" Holly grinned.

Suddenly, they both became aware that they were behaving as if nothing had changed over the past two days. They grew silent, Alexa poking at the sand with her big toe, and Holly staring out at a cruise liner gliding across the horizon.

"Okay, this is ludicrous," Alexa spoke finally. "I'm absolutely sick of not talking to you."

"Oh, God. I am *so* glad you said that!" Holly confessed. She stood, and regarded Alexa sheepishly. Then, the girls threw their arms around each other.

"I've *missed* you, you freak," Alexa admitted, squeezing Holly tight, and feeling choked up. What was with her crying jags lately? She was on an emotional roller coaster.

"I've missed you, too," Holly said as she hugged Alexa tightly.

Holly was startled by how true her admission was; though she'd been mad at Alexa — and was maybe still a little mad at her — Holly had really felt her friend's absence yesterday. It was almost as if going wild last night had been Holly's way of channeling Alexa. At the fuzzy memory of her drunken escapades, Holly shook her head and pulled away. "And I have so much to tell you," she added with a smile.

"Me, too!" Alexa exclaimed. "You wouldn't *believe* what's happened —"

"You go first." Holly waved her hand at Alexa.

"No, you." Alexa grinned. Then, she thoroughly surprised Holly by crossing her big blue eyes. And the silly gesture still reduced Holly to laughter — just as it had when the girls were little.

They sat down on their towels, facing each other. Neither Alexa nor Holly was quite ready to offer any actual apologies yet, but they were both relieved to be speaking — and joking — again.

Holly reached for her sunglasses. Standing and sitting so quickly had given her a head rush. "I need these puppies," she told Alexa as she slipped on the shades. "I think I'm a little hung over."

"Holly Jacobson!" Alexa cried in mock horror. "What did you *do* last night?" She scooted closer to Holly, eager for an explanation.

Breathlessly, Holly divulged the details she could recall from her surreal experience at Yacht, and her skeevy moment with Aaron in the pool.

"That *sleaze*," Alexa said of Aaron when Holly had

finished. She shuddered. "Ugh. Didn't I say he wanted you from the beginning?"

Holly nodded, hugging her Neutrogena-slick knees to her chest. "You did. I guess I should listen to you when it comes to boys."

At the mention of boys, the girls fell silent again, each one thinking of — but not bringing up — the boy who had come between them.

"So, speaking of boys," Alexa said, struggling for a semi-smooth segue. "Guess who showed up unannounced at the Flamingo last night? *Tyler.*"

"Tyler . . . Davis?" Holly asked, surprised but relieved that they weren't steering near Diego. Yet.

"Yup. My ex," Alexa said, rolling her eyes. Holly frowned sympathetically, and Alexa added, "It's fine, though. We kind of got . . . closure on our relationship."

"Wait. He came all the way down here just to find you?" Holly was confused.

Alexa laughed. "Yeah, get this, Hol. He saw the bikini contest on Pulse! That's how he knew —"

"Him, too?" Holly gasped. Had everyone in Oakridge seen her on TV? How humiliating.

"Why? Who else saw it?" Alexa asked, excitedly.

To Alexa's astonishment, Holly's face turned pale and her lips trembled. "My *parents,*" she whispered. When she removed her sunglasses, Alexa saw that Holly's eyes were bright with tears. "My parents!"

Holly repeated, in a near wail. The sunbathers near them cast glances at Holly, but she carried on. "Oh, Alexa — my mom left me this mean voice message yesterday, and then Grandma Ida told me — and they're so angry. . . . They're definitely going to ground me. . . ." She paused for a shaky breath. "And then I kind of broke my cell phone so I haven't called them back yet, and I don't know what to *do*. . . ." She put her head on her knees, and let out a sob.

"You broke your cell phone?" Alexa asked, taken aback by Holly's freak-out. "Is that why you didn't return Diego's call?" The question slipped out before she was able to stop herself.

Holly looked up, squinting at Alexa. "How did you know he called me?" she demanded suspiciously.

Alexa took a deep, fortifying breath. Quickly, she told Holly about seeing him — and leaving him — on Lincoln Road. Alexa didn't offer the details of their conversation, or describe the heart-wrenching effect Diego had on her. But she was careful to mention that Diego told her about kissing Holly, back in the day.

Holly's face flamed, and she studied her knees. So Diego *did* remember their kiss. That knowledge suddenly filled Holly with a degree of comfort, and she felt some of her bitterness melt away.

"He was my first kiss," Holly admitted bashfully, looking down at the striped pattern on her towel. "It was . . . pretty meaningful." Diego would always be her first kiss, but he was no longer her only kiss, Holly reflected. And, she realized, there were probably more kisses, from other boys, for her to look forward to.

Holly raised her head to meet Alexa's gaze. "I think I hoped for something more with him this time around." She shrugged. "And that's why I got all psycho when I saw you guys together." As she was speaking, Holly understood how greatly she'd overreacted at the Delano. Her perspective had been so skewed. "I'm sorry," Holly finished, looking at Alexa sincerely.

"No, *I'm* sorry," Alexa said softly. "I acted like a complete bitch to you."

"But I *was* sort of being a baby," Holly said, with a short laugh. "When Diego and I were talking at the Delano I should have known the score. It was pathetic — we had nothing to say to each other." Holly shook her head at the memory, then studied Alexa. "But it wasn't like that with you and him, right?" she forced herself to ask. Alexa and Diego's connection might have been painful to acknowledge, but Holly knew she had to face reality. "You guys had, like, stuff to talk about?"

Alexa rolled a few grains of sand between her thumb and forefinger. "I guess we have a lot in common," Alexa said quietly. She was trying to sound nonchalant, but she knew her flushed cheeks betrayed her true emotions. She could feel Holly studying her. "But it doesn't matter," Alexa went on, looking up to smile at Holly. "I'm off boys. All boys. You were right, Hol. I go through guys like crazy. It's not *healthy* or something."

"Did I say that?" Holly asked, knitting her brows together. "Oh, you mean when I called you a —" Her eyes grew round and she clapped a hand to her mouth, looking embarrassed. "Alexa, I was so mad I didn't know what I was saying. . . ."

"Well, I didn't mean to say all that horrible stuff about — why we stopped being friends," Alexa said guiltily, her face still warm.

"It was pretty upsetting." Holly shrugged. "But what you said was also this total wake-up call. That's why I ignored the parent issue yesterday. When my parents get all overprotective, it makes me feel like a two-year-old. I don't want them to have that *hold* on me anymore."

"But, you know what?" Alexa said thoughtfully. "I think if you called them back today, and actually confronted the issue . . . *that* would be the most mature thing you could ever do."

"You think?" Holly gave a sigh, but she knew Alexa was right. She couldn't hide from them forever. "Is it stupid that I'm scared?" she asked, fiddling with her silver ring.

Alexa smiled. "Nah. I mean, your parents are pretty . . ."

"Scary?" Holly offered, rolling her eyes.

"Intense," Alexa said, remembering Mr. and Mrs. Jacobson with a dash of fondness. She'd always half-envied the attention they lavished on Holly. "Listen, would it help if I stuck around while you made the call? Or would you rather have some privacy?"

Holly thought back to how she'd missed Alexa's comforting presence yesterday during the voice mail debacle, and she shook her head. "Privacy? Are you crazy? I'll need all the support I can get."

The girls headed to the News Café on Ocean Drive for a big lunch — which, to Holly's relief, Alexa insisted on paying for. Over burgers and salads, they filled each other in on more missing details from their day apart. When the girls had finished their meal and their gossip, Holly slid her battery back into her cell phone. Alexa patted her hand across the small table.

"I think you should call them now," Alexa suggested gently.

Holly glanced around; the outdoor café was crowded with other diners, but thankfully the tables immediately around her were empty. Holly didn't want anybody to hear her in case she started to cry.

Before she punched "1" for her home number, she looked at Alexa.

"What should I say?" Holly asked nervously.

"Tell them that you're sixteen years old and responsible and you can take care —" Alexa stopped. When they were younger, she had loved telling Holly what to say and do. Now, that dynamic felt wrong to her; Holly had to figure this one out for herself. "Hol, you know just what to say," Alexa amended. "You don't need me."

"We'll see about that," Holly muttered, holding the phone to her ear. She listened to the line ring. She bet her dad was cleaning out the hall closet, while her mom was in the kitchen, paying bills. Josh was probably holed up in his bedroom, practicing his Torah portion.

"Jacobsons," Holly's father chirped, picking up on the second ring.

Holly tensed up. *This is it*, she thought. Instinctively, she reached across the table and took hold of Alexa's hand.

"Dad?" Holly asked tentatively.

"Holly? My goodness, Holly, where have you *been?*" her father demanded, managing to sound angry and relieved at the same time. "Your cell phone keeps going to voice mail, and every time we call your grandmother, she tells us you're out."

"I've been, um, busy," Holly began, instantly flashing on an image of herself dancing on the bar at Yacht.

"I'll say," her father replied. "Mr. Berger from down the street called us on Monday night, swearing his daughter saw you on television. When your mother and I turned on the TV, we couldn't believe our eyes. Lynn!" he called, and Holly heard a loud crash in the background. "Oh, darn it. Lynn! Pick up in the kitchen. It's Holly!" There was another crash.

"What's going on?" Holly asked, making an anxious face at Alexa.

"I'm cleaning out the hall closet," Holly's father explained. "The vacuum cleaner almost fell on me." Then Holly heard the click of her mother picking up the extension in the kitchen. Holly rolled her eyes at how accurate her image of her parents had been. She was positive this conversation was going to be a nightmare.

"Well, well," Holly's mother was saying. "Look who decides to finally check in."

"I meant to call sooner —" Holly tried to explain as Alexa nodded encouragingly.

"But let me guess," her mother cut in. "You were having too much fun prancing around on television half-naked."

"Easily a million people must have seen you," her father added before Holly could respond.

"You should be ashamed of yourself," her mother insisted.

Check, check, and check, Holly thought wryly. Her parents were, once again, acting exactly as she'd predicted. She always felt so defenseless when they ganged up on her, two against one. But when Holly looked across the table at Alexa, she felt newly confident. She *wasn't* alone.

"I'm sorry you're upset," Holly replied at last. "But I didn't do anything wrong." She couldn't believe how calm and articulate she sounded. "I wasn't actually *naked.* And besides — " Holly gave Alexa's hand a fast squeeze. "A lot of people, um, said I looked good." Holly's heart was hammering as Alexa gave her the thumbs-up sign with her free hand.

"We don't care what 'a lot of people' say," her mother retorted. "We're worried about you, Holly. We saw you kiss that boy. What were you thinking?"

"I — I didn't really mean to kiss him," Holly protested, blushing, as Alexa grinned at her. *At least, not then,* Holly thought.

"Then who put you up to it?" her father asked, misunderstanding. "Was this whole thing Alexa's idea?"

"That girl is pure trouble, Stan," her mother said. "Who knows what kinds of other dangerous activities she's making Holly do down there?"

"This all seems so unlike you, Holly," her father said. "How are we supposed to trust you again?"

Suddenly, Holly understood. Her parents still saw her as the skittish, scrawny Holly she'd been when she was little. And when they'd seen her up on that catwalk, that old image had disappeared. The new Holly — sassy and self-assured — had taken its place. And they were freaking out.

But Holly liked who she'd been on the catwalk. It wasn't the wild girl she'd become at Yacht, and it wasn't the hesitant Holly of Oakridge. It was something in between. Something that felt just right.

"Mom? Dad?" Holly cut in. She took a deep breath, and forged ahead. "Nobody made me do anything. *I* decided to be in that bikini contest. I can think for myself, you know." She felt bold. After arguing with Alexa, and getting rid of Aaron last night, Holly was starting to suspect she could stand up to people better than she'd anticipated.

"Holly!" Alexa squealed, completely impressed.

There was silence on the other end. Holly was positive her mother had stormed into the hall with the cordless phone so her parents could stare at each other in horror.

"And I'm not doing anything stupid," Holly went on, remembering how she'd pushed Aaron away from her in the pool. "You *have* to trust me. You've always taught me to be responsible, right? Besides," Holly added defiantly, "it's spring break. I'm just having fun."

Alexa nodded emphatically. "Tell them you're *supposed* to go crazy on spring break," she whispered. Of course, Alexa couldn't help thinking that the only crazy thing she herself had done on spring break was . . . be less crazy.

Holly shook her head at Alexa. She knew that would be pushing it with her parents.

Holly's mom and dad were still silent on the other end. Finally, her mother spoke. "I drove to Myrtle Beach with some friends for spring break when I was in college," she said thoughtfully. "But we were twenty, not sixteen."

Did she have a few spring break adventures of her own? Holly wondered, suddenly a little curious about her mother's past.

"We don't want you to *not* enjoy yourself," Holly's father was saying, sounding less angry than before. "We only want to know that you're being safe and smart." He cleared this throat. "Actually, Holly, would you mind putting Grandma Ida on the phone? I just want to make sure she's okay with all this."

Holly froze. Had she survived the showdown with her parents only to get busted for the Grandma Ida lie?

"Grandma Ida?" she mouthed to Alexa in desperation.

Alexa didn't miss a beat. "Mah-jongg," she mouthed back.

"She's playing mah-jongg with friends," Holly told her parents. She gave Alexa a big smile. "I'll tell her to call you when she gets in." Holly was so thankful to have Alexa there with her.

Holly's parents confirmed that they'd be meeting her at Newark on Friday morning, and that they'd continue their discussion then. Holly said good-bye and clicked off, triumphant. Her parents might still decide to ground her when she was back home, but that didn't matter. The point was, Holly had faced her fear head-on. And talking to the 'rents hadn't been a nightmare at all. *Maybe things always seem scarier in your head*, Holly thought.

Alexa leaned across the table and planted a kiss on Holly's cheek. "See? You did it, Hol. And you were so inspiring." Alexa had never seen her old friend pull herself together so well; over the course of these past few days, she seemed to have blossomed.

"I literally could not have done it without you," Holly replied truthfully.

"All I did was let you crush the feeling out of my hand," Alexa teased, sliding her fingers out of Holly's grip.

Holly giggled. "*And* you came up with that last-minute mah-jongg save."

"Well, you were, like, on a roll, being so honest!" Alexa exclaimed. "I was terrified you were going to spill the beans about the Flamingo."

"Please," Holly said, shaking her head. "These are my parents we're talking about! One thing at a time."

After the girls left the News Café, they strolled back to the beach with their arms lightly linked, enjoying the mellow afternoon sunshine on their shoulders and faces. Holly was reluctant to interrupt their moment of silent bonding by reaching for her cell phone again. But she had to call Grandma Ida to relay the latest about her parents, and ask for that loan.

Fortunately, Holly's chat with her grandmother was a brief one. They made plans to have dinner in South Beach that evening so Grandma Ida could pick up her Pontiac, lend Holly the money, and hear all about the girls' week. Holly shut her phone with a satisfied sigh.

"Where are we meeting Ida?" Alexa asked as they meandered down the promenade.

"Puerto Sagua, a Cuban place," Holly replied. At the same instant, both she and Alexa made the mental leap to Diego. And Holly realized there was still one more call to make. But this time, she decided, she shouldn't be the one making it.

"But I don't think you should come with us," Holly said.

"Why not?" Alexa asked, startled.

"Because there's someone else you should probably see," Holly explained, finding Diego's number in her cell. "Alexa, I want you to call Señor Mendieta. You know he called me yesterday, but I think it's pretty obvious who he really wanted to talk to."

Alexa shook her head as a blush slowly warmed her face. "Holly, can we both just forget about Diego? It's too messy —"

Holly gave Alexa a long, steady look. "Alexa, *I* am on my way to forgetting about Diego. But I don't think you are, no matter what you say about being 'off boys.'"

Alexa didn't respond. She *did* want to see Diego again. She wanted to stay in touch with him in some capacity — even just as a friend.

At the sight of Alexa's scarlet cheeks, Holly felt even more confident that she was right. She could always talk to Diego another time. But, judging by the look on Alexa's face, she needed to be in touch with him — the sooner the better. Diego and Alexa — her two old friends — together made sense to Holly now, even if that realization was tinged with a bit of sadness.

"Look," Holly said, pushing her cell phone into

Alexa's hand. "You convinced *me* to make a scary phone call today, right? So . . . consider this payback." Holly held her friend's gaze, serious, for a long moment. "Okay?"

A smile of comprehension bloomed on Alexa's face. On the beach that morning, she and Holly had each said that they were sorry. But Alexa supporting Holly during the talk with her parents, and Holly now encouraging Alexa to call the boy she'd once loved, were their *true* ways of apologizing.

"Okay," Alexa said softly, accepting the cell phone. She hoped her expression conveyed the depth of gratitude that she felt toward Holly for showing such maturity.

"I think I'll give *you* some privacy now," Holly said over her shoulder, starting off down the promenade. "Meet me back on the beach, okay?"

Alexa clutched the cell phone, insanely nervous. Last night, she'd told Diego that they shouldn't see each other again, but now here she was, calling him up. What would he make of that? What would *she* make of that? *Friends,* Alexa told herself firmly. *I'll say we should be friends.*

Alexa wasn't quite sure if she was acting wisely, but it was too late to stop now. She was already clicking on Diego's name and holding Holly's phone to her ear. It was as if Alexa were being driven forward by an irresistible and irrational force. Because, even though she still felt a little confused about the whole boy issue, Alexa was absolutely clear on one thing: She couldn't go back home without seeing Diego Mendieta one more time. She only hoped he'd want to see her, too.

CHAPTER FOURTEEN

Meant to Be

That night, after Holly left to meet Ida, Alexa stood waiting outside the Flamingo, fiddling with the gold bangles around her wrist. Her nervous hands had to play with *something*, and the bracelets were her only accessories. Alexa was deliberately keeping her look simple that night; she wore a silky, daffodil Betsey Johnson slip dress and gold ballet flats, and her freshly washed hair spilled down her back.

During her slightly stiff conversation with Diego on the phone that afternoon, Alexa made it clear to him that she wanted nothing more than friendship, but mentioned that she wouldn't mind seeing him again — just for coffee or whatever. Diego had suggested a casual dinner, and offered to pick Alexa up at the Flamingo, since the café he had in mind was driving distance from the motel. Ida was taking back her car that night, leaving Alexa without a set of wheels, so she had agreed.

And now she stood on the corner, her stomach in knots, as she saw the familiar dark-blue Honda make its way toward her.

Diego pulled to a stop at the curb. Alexa walked toward him, watching through the passenger window as he put the car in park and ran his fingers through his dark hair. He looked a little nervous, but also more breathtakingly hot than ever.

"Good Lord," Alexa muttered to herself. Suddenly, she wanted to get into that car, slide her arms around his neck, and run *her* fingers through his hair. *Friends,* she reminded herself sternly as she stepped off the curb. To settle the butterflies in her stomach, Alexa mentally ticked off all the reasons she shouldn't be lusting after Diego: There was her need to be single for a while. Her lingering worries about Holly's feelings. And the fact that it was simply silly to get invested in a boy who lived all the way down in Miami. The whole long-distance thing was *so* not Alexa's style.

She was reaching for the handle on the car door when Diego emerged from the driver's side. Their eyes met. He smiled, and Alexa felt her knees weaken at the sight of his delicious dimples. Diego walked around the car, over to where she stood, one hand behind his back, the other in his pocket.

They faced each other on the street, just as they had on that fateful Sunday night. Then, there had been fiery anger between them; now, there was just palpable, almost excruciating tension. Diego's dark, soulful eyes lingered on Alexa's face, and she wondered if he was feeling as she had felt about him two seconds ago: dying to touch her, but knowing he shouldn't.

"Hi," Alexa said, sliding the bangles up and down her wrist.

"Hi," Diego said. He moved his hand from behind his back and held it out to Alexa. He was holding a single, perfect white orchid.

"For me?" Alexa asked, her heart jumping. Orchids were her favorite flower — exotic, rare, wild.

But not exactly "friendly."

"Diego, you shouldn't have —" she began, her voice quivering, but he shook his head and smiled.

"Blame my mom," he said. "She taught me to always bring a girl flowers. Even girls who are just friends," he added, his expression slightly teasing.

"Well . . . thank you," Alexa relented, taking the orchid. Diego opened the car door for her, and she slid inside with a smile. There was something funny about getting into the very car that had brought her and Diego together in the first place, Alexa reflected as Diego returned to the driver's seat. She longed to share her thoughts with him, but she held back. She could bring it up over dinner, when she was feeling less on edge. She set the orchid in her lap and took a deep breath.

"So where's this café?" Alexa asked as Diego turned the key in the ignition and steered the car into the traffic.

"Hmm. Not too far," Diego replied mysteriously, his eyes on the road. He was an amazing driver, Alexa noticed: Smooth and slow when he needed to be, fast and almost reckless when he could be. *I bet he's good at everything else, too,* Alexa thought, her skin flushing hot.

"What kind of food is it?" Alexa asked, forcing herself to think chaste thoughts.

"Oh, you know," Diego said, changing lanes, and flashing her an incredibly sexy smile.

"Italian?" Alexa guessed, suddenly intrigued. She loved going out to eat, and had practically memorized the "Eating & Drinking" section of her Miami guidebook. "Is it Caffe Abbracci in Coral Gables?" she asked excitedly.

"Not exactly," Diego said.

"Well . . . so is it sushi, then?" Alexa asked.

Diego shook his head, his dimples showing. "Stop guessing, Ms. Impatient."

Alexa laughed, feeling some of the tension between

them ease. As Diego drove through the shimmering South Beach streets, they talked easily about movies they'd seen that year, songs they'd recently downloaded onto their respective iPods, and the big bonfire and concert that was taking place at Lummus Park Beach the following night.

We work well as friends, Alexa thought as Diego parked the car in front of a tall apartment building. But she couldn't ignore the fact that even talking about everyday things with Diego felt somehow electrifying to her.

Diego opened the door for her, and Alexa got out of the car, still clutching her orchid. She looked around in confusion. They were in a tree-lined residential area of South Beach that was unfamiliar to her, and there didn't seem to be any cafés nearby.

"Are we going to walk from here?" she asked Diego, who was, inexplicably, guiding her toward the front door of the apartment building. Alexa was about to ask him where they were going when she saw three slender ivory orchids, tied with a piece of twine, propped up against the door. Tucked into the twine was a folded piece of white paper with ALEXA written in bold, blocky handwriting. Her breath caught. The flowers were meant for *her*. Disbelieving, she walked toward the doorway and scooped up the orchids, their heady scent dizzying her. Diego was holding the door open, and Alexa, too confused to ask any more questions, stepped through it into a gleaming lobby. This was clearly a swankier building than Grandma Ida's, with tall mirrors and shiny floors.

"Where *are* we?" she asked Diego at last, turning to him, her arms full of orchids.

"This is where I live," Diego explained, his eyes dancing.

"We're going to have dinner at your house?" Alexa exclaimed anxiously. Her mind was racing. Did Diego want her to meet his parents? Or were his parents not even home? Either setup would be *way* too serious.

Diego shook his head, grinning. "Not unless you want to spend the evening watching *CSI* with my mom or helping my dad organize his medical journals."

"So then where are we . . ." Alexa trailed off, catching sight of another bouquet of orchids resting delicately in front of a nearby bank of elevators, also bearing a note with her name on it. Once again, her heart skipped, and she looked at Diego, confused but curious. "Am I supposed to follow the orchids?" she asked with a slow smile of understanding.

Diego tilted his head to one side, saying nothing. Instead, he gently took her elbow and led her toward the elevators. Alexa picked up the flowers, and they stepped inside. Diego pressed a button marked R and the elevator swept them up. Alexa realized she was trembling with anticipation. *What about the café?* she wanted to ask, but she was too overcome by the flowers, and Diego's nearness, and a wonderful sense of bewilderment.

The elevator doors slid open, and they walked out into a narrow corridor. They stopped in front of an unmarked door, where another bunch of orchids lay waiting. Diego took a key out of his pocket, and unlocked the door. Alexa followed him outside into the night air.

She gasped. They were standing in a spectacular roof garden, looking out on a sweeping nighttime view of South Beach. The city was aglow with thousands of sparkling lights, and the full moon rose above the vista, round and plump as a peach. Alexa took it all in, her eyes scanning the bright, seemingly infinite panorama.

"Oh, Diego," she whispered. "It's amazing." She turned to study his beautiful profile.

"I thought you should get another look at South Beach before you leave," Diego said, gazing out at the view. "And I reserved the roof for the night, so it's all ours to admire."

And then Alexa noticed that the roof garden itself was aglow. Small white candles flickered all along the wide ledge, and everywhere she looked, there were bouquets of white orchids. Her eyes followed the trail of glorious flowers to a picnic blanket, strewn with pillows. On the blanket was a bottle of Merlot, two full wine glasses, a basket overflowing with French bread, cheeses, olives, and grapes, and two white plates, carefully laid with napkins and silverware. Next to the blanket rested a sleek silver CD player, and the classic sixties song "My Cherie Amour" was playing softly. For the first time in her life, Alexa St. Laurent found herself flustered beyond words. No boy had ever done anything this romantic for her before.

"Do you like it?" Diego asked, taking a step closer to her. She turned to him. His big black eyes were hopeful.

Alexa managed to nod, and then she tried speaking. "I — why did — you shouldn't —"

Diego grinned, putting a finger to her lips. Then he placed his hand on her waist and pulled her in. "Let's not talk yet, okay? Let's just dance."

Alexa let the orchids fall from her arms as she drew close to Diego. She twined her arms around his neck, breathing in his warm, spicy scent. His full lips were tantalizingly near hers, and, as they danced to the slow, jazzy music, Alexa felt their bodies melding together perfectly. They moved exactly in sync with each other. The music shifted fluidly into one of Alexa's favorite Bob Marley songs, "Turn Your Lights Down Low." *He must have made a mix this afternoon, after we talked,* Alexa thought dreamily. He'd planned all this — the flowers, the food, the rooftop. Every-thing.

"You didn't listen to me at all," Alexa finally said.

"What do you mean?" Diego asked innocently, but the mischievous sparkle in his eyes gave him away. He twirled her around, then pulled her back in, wrapping his arms around her waist.

Alexa drew back a little and gestured to the swoon-worthy roof garden. "I said we should have a friendly dinner, and you played along. . . . But this is not very *friendly*, you know." She tried to sound firm, but Alexa knew her words were pointless. She couldn't be Diego's friend. She was head over heels for this boy.

"Friendly." Diego furrowed his brow and tipped his head to one side, as if he were deep in thought. "Hmm. I might have some problems with the exact definition of 'friendly.'" He stopped dancing and studied her, his hands on her arms. "For instance, can you tell me if this is friendly?" He leaned forward and planted a quick kiss on her cheek.

Alexa nodded slowly. If only that friendly kiss wasn't making her body ache for some more not-so-friendly kisses.

"Then how about this?" Diego whispered, putting one hand behind Alexa's neck and touching his full lips to the corner of her mouth.

"That was a little questionable," Alexa responded shakily. Her lips were tingling.

With agonizing slowness, Diego kissed the divot above Alexa's upper lip, then her chin, her forehead, and both her cheeks, deliberately avoiding her lips. Alexa closed her eyes, half-delirious from this delicious torment. When she opened them again, Diego was gazing at her with that familiar teasing look. He traced the delicate shape of Alexa's mouth with his finger.

"Alexa, I hope you won't take this the wrong way," he murmured. "But I don't think we should be friends anymore."

"Me, neither," Alexa sighed, and, at last, Diego kissed her on the lips. Fully and deeply. Alexa clung to him, returning his kiss with all the pent-up longing she'd borne since that night at the Delano. Then, abruptly, she remembered her list of reasons from earlier, about why they shouldn't be together, and she snapped back to reality.

"No," she mumbled, pulling away from him entirely. "I want this so badly . . . but . . . like I said before . . ." She was having trouble forming the words. She had told Diego, last night, that she needed to make peace with herself. But maybe she already had. Her talks with Tyler and with Holly had helped Alexa start to untangle some of her own issues. *And*

Holly is *over Diego,* Alexa reasoned. *She's the one who made this date happen tonight, right?*

"I'm so confused, Diego," Alexa finally said, putting her hands to her cheeks.

"Come here," he responded softly, taking Alexa's hand and leading her to the picnic blanket. They knelt down on the pillows, and Diego pulled a dangling bunch of grapes and a triangle of cheese from the basket. The food looked delicious, but Alexa wasn't sure she could eat. The scent of the orchids, and the music melding with the hum of the night breeze was making her feel light-headed.

"After we talked on Lincoln Road last night, I also thought I was confused," Diego began. He took a sip from his wineglass. "But then I realized how simple it all was." He reached for Alexa's hand, his expression serious. "Alexa, I just want to be with you."

When Alexa shook her head, Diego added, "I understand that you might need space now. I get that *logically.* But I can't stop thinking about you — and thinking that we should be together." Diego shrugged. "Maybe it's irrational, but . . ."

"I feel exactly the same way," Alexa confessed in a whisper, threading her fingers through Diego's. She remembered how she'd been unable to stop herself from calling him that afternoon. *Maybe,* Alexa thought, *it's your irrational feelings that tell you the truth.* She picked up her wineglass, too, taking a sip and savoring the sweet, oaky taste.

"But," Alexa added reluctantly, putting her glass down. "How would it even work? I mean, you're here in Florida and I'm in New Jersey and . . ."

Diego shook his head, his face breaking into an irresistible smile. He squeezed her hand. "Alexa, I'm in New Jersey, too. Or I will be."

"What are you talking about?" Alexa asked incredulously.

"I'm starting Princeton in the fall," Diego told her.

"You are?" Alexa cried. Somehow, in all their conversations, the topic of college had never come up. But this news changed everything: Princeton was only twenty minutes from Oakridge. Alexa's mind leaped ahead, considering the sumptuous possibilities: She could drive to Diego's dorm after school; he could come to her house; they could take weekend trips. . . . They could be together whenever they wanted.

Boyfriends aren't *overrated,* Alexa realized with a burst of joy. Not when you found someone who was so absolutely right for you.

"What are you thinking?" Diego asked, staring at Alexa with undisguised affection. He set down his wine, then reached over and stroked her cheek.

"I'm thinking . . . that I can't wait until the fall,"

Alexa whispered, slipping her hand under the collar of Diego's shirt, feeling the heat of his skin.

Diego's face lit up as he took in the full meaning of Alexa's words. "Neither can I," he murmured. He reached down and plucked a burgundy grape off the cluster, then held it to Alexa lips. "But we still have some time in South Beach," he added. "We should make the most of it, don't you think?"

Slowly, Alexa opened her mouth and ate the grape, her tongue brushing against his fingers. "Sounds like a plan," she said, her eyes never leaving his.

Diego swallowed hard, then put his arm around Alexa, drawing her very close. "I can't believe you're here with me right now," he told her. "If you hadn't called this afternoon, I'd be having dinner with some friends at Puerto Sagua and moping over you."

"Puerto Sagua?" Alexa repeated. "I was supposed to go there with Holly and Ida tonight."

Diego shook his head, smiling in disbelief. "You mean we would've seen each other, anyway?"

"Remember when we said good-bye on Lincoln Road?" Alexa asked, burying her head in Diego's warm neck. "And I told you we'd find each other again if we were meant to be?" She looked up at him tenderly. "So I guess we *are*. You can't argue with destiny, right?"

In response, Diego kissed her again. And again. Each kiss was deeper and more burning than the last.

Wordlessly, Alexa and Diego fell back against the pillows, their lips and hands exploring, searching. The candles glimmered around them, and the city shimmered below them, but Alexa was only aware of Diego's breath as it joined with hers, his lips at her throat, the smooth feel of his cinnamon-colored skin. . . .

Feverishly, Alexa undid several buttons on Diego's shirt, kissing his neck and chest. Diego carefully slid down Alexa's yellow spaghetti straps. He stroked her bare shoulders and planted purposeful kisses all the way down her collarbone, while gently moving his hands along her body, and playfully toying with the hem of her skirt. Alexa gave a murmur of pleasure, and Diego looked up at her with a smile.

"You tell me how far you want to go," he whispered.

Alexa buried her hands in his smooth dark hair and guided Diego's face back down toward her neck.

"I will," she sighed. She stretched luxuriously up against him, utterly losing herself in the moment.

And Alexa's last coherent thought, before she sank into a haze of desire, was that she wished this for Holly. This feeling of sensual satisfaction, this breathtaking romantic intensity . . . and this pure joy, knowing the person you were falling in love with was falling in love with you, too.

CHAPTER FIFTEEN

Completely Real

Holly walked up Ocean Drive, swinging her little black bag, pleasantly flushed from the mojito she'd had with dinner. Over a long Cuban meal, Holly had filled Grandma Ida in on the past week's events, and her grandmother had, predictably, been supportive about everything. The only slightly sour part of the evening had been when Diego's friend, Ian, along with a bunch of other guys and girls, sauntered into the restaurant. *This town is too small,* Holly had thought, reluctantly returning Ian's wave. She finished the rest of her mojito quickly, Grandma Ida paid the bill, and Holly walked her grandmother to the street where Alexa had parked the Pontiac.

Before taking off in the car, Grandma Ida gave Holly the necessary cash, wished her luck with her parents, and insisted that Holly have as much fun as possible during her last two nights in South Beach.

Now, as Holly approached the Flamingo, she wondered what sort of fun she'd have between tonight and Friday. After last night's misadventures — a few of which were still foggy in Holly's head — she was done with clubbing for a while. Holly felt comfortable in her own skin tonight, happy not to be dolled up and tottering around in strappy sandals. She was wearing a floral A-line skirt that came to just above her knees, her black Urban Outfitters tank, and black flip-flops. Holly remembered her pink-and-silver getup from the night before with a shudder. She should probably donate it to Kaitlin or Daisy, either of whom would get more use out of it than Holly ever would.

Holly stopped in front of the Flamingo, and gazed up toward the small, darkened window of Number 7. Should she go upstairs? When she and Alexa had parted ways in the lobby that evening, they'd decided that Holly should take the room key for the night. Holly had agreed to leave the door unlocked if she got home before Alexa, and Alexa had assured Holly she wouldn't be back late. *I wonder what Alexa and Diego are doing*, Holly thought, feeling the faintest prickle of jealousy.

Holly began walking under the Flamingo's arch, reaching inside her bag for the key. This was good.

She'd get to bed at a decent hour, wake up early, and go for a jog on the promenade. Despite her best intentions, Holly realized, she hadn't gone running once during her time here.

But it was a balmy, breezy night, and something about the full moon and the sway of the palm trees felt so seductive. Holly closed her bag, turned, and walked away from the Flamingo. She wasn't sure what she wanted to do, but she wasn't quite ready for bed yet.

Aimlessly, Holly crossed the street and wandered out onto the beach, slipping off her flip-flops and letting her bare feet sink into the cool sand. There were a few couples cuddling in the darkness. Holly walked past a group of kids in a circle, passing around what she guessed was a joint, but for the most part the beach was empty. Holly drifted toward the ocean and walked briskly along the shore, the cold, foamy water licking her toes. The full moon hung overhead, casting a hazy white glow over the waves.

Up ahead, Holly saw a boy jogging along the shore. He was tall and trim, with wavy, dark-blond hair, and he wore a hooded sweatshirt over track pants. He was running at a steady, rhythmic pace, and his movements were graceful.

Why didn't I think of that? Holly wondered. A moonlight run on the shore would have been the perfect way to cap off her evening. *He must be a dedicated ath-lete,* Holly thought. *And,* she couldn't help but notice with a grin, *he has a pretty cute butt.*

Curious about the mystery jogger, Holly put on a burst of speed, walking quickly until she was directly behind him. Suddenly, he seemed to sense someone was following him. He stopped abruptly and wheeled around, locking eyes with Holly. She gasped, ready to apologize for acting like a stalker, when she recognized the jogger. It was Tyler Davis — the lacrosse guy from Oakridge. Alexa's ex.

Right, Holly realized, remembering Alexa's story.

Tyler's face broke into a wide smile. "Holly," he said, almost as if he'd been expecting to see her.

"Hey, Tyler," Holly said shyly. "Fancy meeting you here."

Back in Oakridge, the mere idea of talking to Tyler Davis would have totally intimidated Holly. He was the school's golden boy: gorgeous and gifted. There was even a rumor that he'd modeled for American Eagle. Holly had had a few classes with him, she'd seen him in the stands at a couple of track meets, and she knew he was dating Alexa. But she couldn't remember ever speaking to him. Boys like Tyler usually made her way too nervous.

But now, standing on this familiar stretch of sand, Holly was utterly at ease. The wind was blowing her sun-streaked hair back, and she felt tanned and lithe and relaxed. She had reconciled with Alexa, she wasn't worrying about her parents anymore, and the Diego drama was finally behind her. All that was on Holly's mind was the ocean and the moon and the sultry spring night. Here, none of the rules and hierarchies of high school applied.

Tyler was only slightly out of breath. *He must be in good shape,* Holly thought. He pulled off his sweatshirt and tucked it under his arm, his shoulders broad in a white Oakridge Lacrosse T-shirt. He rested his hands on his hips as he and Holly stood facing each other at the water's edge. He had the most interesting eyes, Holly noticed — light brown, with flecks of amber.

"I thought I might run into you at some point," Tyler said. "No pun intended."

Holly grinned at his lame joke. She'd always imagined Tyler as sophisticated, but he seemed sort of boyish now.

"It does make sense," Holly agreed. "Alexa told me you're also crashing at the ever-so-glamorous Flamingo." She giggled.

The moonlight was bright enough that she could make out Tyler blushing.

"You guys are rooming together, right?" he asked. The unspoken sentiment was: *So you know everything.*

Holly nodded, remembering the details Alexa had

told her over lunch. Tyler had been in her room. On her bed, in fact. Weird.

There was a pause, and Tyler looked down at the sand. There was something endearing about his embarrassment, Holly thought.

"I think it's really romantic, what you did," Holly said truthfully. She had been bowled over by Alexa's story. What Holly wouldn't give for a guy to hop on a plane just for her.

Now Tyler was definitely blushing. "Nah," he said. "Try impulsive. I just saw that show on Pulse, and boom — decided to come down."

Oh, yeah. Now Holly felt herself blushing. Tyler had seen the bikini contest. He'd seen *her.*

Tyler seemed to sense what she was thinking. "Was it cool being on TV?" he asked.

"I guess," Holly replied, feeling some of her earlier confidence ebb away. "Was it weird seeing me?"

Tyler shrugged. "I was surprised at first. But you, um, you looked good."

"Did you even recognize me?" Holly laughed nervously. She thought of herself back home in Oakridge — usually in a hoodie and jeans.

"Totally," Tyler replied. "You looked exactly like yourself. Just more . . ."

"More of me?" Holly cut him off. She giggled and Tyler laughed, too.

"More confident or something," he said. "Not that you don't seem confident in school and stuff — it's just —" He was stammering, and now *he* seemed kind of nervous. *He must still feel awkward about the Alexa thing,* Holly realized. She probably should leave him alone for the night.

"Did you want to keep running?" Holly asked, turning to head back up the beach. "I'm sorry I was trailing you. I like to run myself, so I wanted to see if I could keep up with you."

"No, that's cool," Tyler said. "I'm kind of due for a break, anyway." He lifted the bottom of his T-shirt and wiped his face with it. Holly caught a glimpse of his toned six-pack. "Do you want to sit down?" he asked her. "My towel's over there." He pointed back up the beach.

"That sounds nice," Holly said. She could hang with Tyler for a little while and then go back to her room. It would make for a funny story to tell Alexa later on.

She followed Tyler to his New Jersey Nets towel, which was big enough for both of them to sit on comfortably. He had a cooler with two bottles of vitamin water, which he opened for each of them. He and Holly sat side by side, sipping their water.

"Have you ever gone running at night?" Tyler asked. "It's awesome. I bet you'd like it."

Holly liked the way Tyler said "awesome" — with

so much energy and verve. She was surprised at how nice he was to be around. She'd never have guessed he was so down-to-earth.

"I actually haven't been very disciplined about going for runs since I've been down here," Holly admitted with a smile.

"You run track at Oakridge, right?" Tyler asked.

As they sat there, finishing their waters, Holly told Tyler about the team, and he told her about lacrosse. They discussed their respective plans to go to sports camps that summer. Holly always loved talking about sports with Meghan and Jess, but she'd never imagined she could have the same sort of conversation with a boy. She and Tyler seemed to have so much in common that Holly forgot to feel even remotely tense around him. She didn't notice the time passing, until she looked up at the moon. The sky was very dark, and a hush had settled over the beach. It must have been pretty late now, but Holly didn't care. She gazed contentedly out at the moonlit sand and water.

"It's so pretty here," Holly whispered, almost to herself. She didn't want to go back to boring old Oakridge. How could she leave this tropical oasis?

"I know," Tyler said. "Makes me not want to go back to New Jersey."

Holly grinned. "My thoughts exactly."

"I've only been here a day, but I think I've figured out what makes South Beach so awesome," Tyler said. "It has this feeling of possibility. Like the most unpredictable thing in the world could happen, and it would seem normal."

The most unpredictable thing in the world. Holly smiled. A week ago, she never would have predicted that she'd be sitting on the beach at night, having a great conversation with Tyler Davis. Which, now that it was happening, felt perfectly normal.

"So what's happened to you so far?" Holly asked, a teasing lilt to her voice. "Did you have, like, a crazy night or do something really wild?"

Tyler smiled sweetly, shaking his head from side to side. "I like to go out now and then, but the whole clubbing vibe can be too intense. Besides, I'm not big into . . ." He blushed again. "You know, random hook-ups or whatever."

"Me, neither," Holly said, also blushing and banishing all thoughts of Shane and Aaron from her mind. There was a moment of silence so she rushed to fill it. "Anyway," she added, trying to sound understanding, "you're probably still thinking about Alexa." Holly didn't want to break it to Tyler that his lost love was most likely getting it on with another guy at that very moment.

"Actually, I'm not, anymore," Tyler admitted. "Alexa's great, but we didn't fit well together. I only saw that after she ended things."

"But sometimes you can't help who you fall for," Holly said, remembering herself with Diego. "Even if it's not the right person for you."

"That's true." Tyler smiled at her. "But sometimes, if you're lucky, you *do* fall for the right person. The one you *should* be with."

Holly felt her pulse flutter in her throat and at her wrists. Was it her imagination or did Tyler's voice suddenly seem different — deeper, more serious? Why did she sense this crackling energy between them? Was she just sleep-deprived? Maybe she was still buzzed from the mojito.

"But how do you know?" Holly asked carefully. "I mean, is there any way to be sure that a person is . . . *fated*, for you or . . . whatever?" She laughed to cover her embarrassment, but Tyler was studying her intently.

"I'm not sure," he said, his warm brown eyes searching her face. "You almost have to believe in destiny, I guess."

"Do you believe in destiny?" Holly asked Tyler, before she could stop herself.

"Maybe." She saw his Adam's apple bob up and down. "Sometimes stuff is too strange for it to be a coincidence."

"Like what?"

"Well . . ." Tyler gave her a shy smile. "Like if some guy came down to Florida to find a girl . . . but ended up falling for her friend."

Holly thought about how she'd come down to Florida to find Diego. But he'd ended up falling for *her* friend. She shook her head, but then, with a jolt, realized what Tyler had just said. It almost seemed as if he were talking about himself.

Am I *that friend?* Holly wondered. It couldn't be. This was all in her head — again. She had to be careful not to blow things out of proportion. She gave a little shiver, suddenly feeling the nip in the night air.

"Are you cold?" Tyler asked. He handed her his sweatshirt, and she wrapped it around her shoulders, inhaling the clean, crisp scent. His scent. With his sweatshirt against her skin, Holly felt suddenly safe and, at the same time, brave. She didn't know what Tyler had meant with that friend comment, but she was too curious to let it go.

"But what if . . ." Holly said, continuing Tyler's earlier train of thought. "What if the guy who came down to Florida didn't even *know* the girl's friend? How could he like her?" She bit her lip, waiting for his response.

Tyler moved his hand so that his fingers were

lightly grazing the back of Holly's hand. Holly felt a shiver of pleasure at his touch. "Well, maybe this guy *sort of* knows this friend, since they go to the same school and all. Maybe he'd always secretly thought she was cute, but then he ran into her outside of school and knew it for sure."

Holly's face flamed as she glanced away. Okay. He definitely meant her. She couldn't *believe* this moment. But it wasn't in Holly's imagination. This was completely real.

"Maybe the guy met this girl on the beach at night, and they started talking," Tyler went on. His fingers continued caressing Holly's hand. "Would that be destiny or coincidence?"

Oh, my God, Holly thought as his words fully sunk in. *Tyler Davis . . . and* me?

She turned to look at Tyler. Maybe it was a combination of the sultry night air, the confidence Holly had gained during the past several days, or the intensity in Tyler's eyes, but suddenly Holly Jacobson decided to take the plunge. She wasn't feeling reckless the way she had last night; she knew she just had to follow what her intuition was telling her to do.

"Hmm," Holly said softly, returning Tyler's gaze. "Maybe there's only one way for the guy to find out."

"What way would that be?" Tyler murmured, taking Holly's hand in his.

"Well . . . let's say he kissed her or something," Holly whispered, trembling.

Tyler's eyes widened, and then he grinned in surprise, as if he couldn't believe his good fortune. He lifted Holly's hand to his lips and kissed it, very gently. Holly wanted to die. She'd never seen anyone do that, except in Jane Austen movies.

Then, Tyler gently put his hand under Holly's chin and inclined his head, bringing his lips to hers. His kiss was slow and soft, almost teasing. Electric. Holly felt a spark race down her body. It was the smoothest, most delectable kiss she'd received in her short history of kissing.

Tyler slowly ended the kiss, and rested his forehead against Holly's, his expression rapt. Boldly, Holly slipped her arms around Tyler's neck, and pressed her lips against his, and they were kissing again, seriously kissing, Tyler cupping Holly's face in his hands and she massaging the back of his neck. As their kissing intensified, Tyler lightly bit Holly's bottom lip, then pulled back.

"I'm sorry," he said. "Did that hurt?"

"No," Holly managed to reply, dizzy with desire. But, before they resumed their kiss, she wanted to ask him something.

"Tyler," she whispered, running her fingers through his hair. "Does this feel strange to you?"

"You mean us kissing?" Tyler asked, his warm breath tickling her ear.

She nodded. "I mean, I feel like it all happened so suddenly."

"I know," Tyler said with a grin. "But sometimes that's how the best stuff in life happens." He put his arm around Holly and drew her into his chest. "It doesn't feel strange at all," he whispered. "It feels *awesome.*"

"Awesome," Holly echoed, and they started kissing again.

This is *awesome,* Holly thought. Their being together felt so natural that she didn't hesitate for a second as Tyler laid her back on the towel. They snuggled warmly, holding each other tight.

For the briefest instant, Holly wondered if Alexa would be upset if she knew what they were doing. But, no; Alexa had ended things with Tyler. Holly couldn't help but wonder why. He was amazing. Holly felt a little sorry for Alexa — maybe she just didn't know how to fully enjoy herself. Holly hoped that her friend would one day experience the exquisite happiness she was now feeling here, on this beach, under the full moon.

Funny. The moon had also been full that night when Diego had kissed her all those years ago. But

Holly felt older and wiser now. Kissing Tyler felt meaningful, but Holly wasn't going to turn this sweet moment into anything more than it actually was. And no matter what happened between her and Tyler down the road, Holly would never let it change the memory of this magical night.

CHAPTER SIXTEEN
Forever

The sun was rising over the ocean, streaking the horizon pink and gold, as Alexa stepped out of Diego's car onto a silent, serene Ocean Drive. She shut the car door, blew Diego one last kiss, then waved him on. She watched, clutching a bunch of orchids to her chest, as the dark-blue Honda slowly pulled away from the curb and drove into the misty dawn.

As Alexa walked under the Flamingo's arch and pulled open the door, she gave a sigh that was equal parts sadness and satisfaction. She was missing Diego already. She crept up the stairs, almost tripping over a stray can of Bud. Her hallway was utterly still. Alexa figured that her neighbors were either conked out, or still drunkenly weaving their way home. *And Holly,* Alexa thought as she turned the knob to Number 7, *is probably sleeping peacefully after her chill dinner with Ida.* Alexa quietly opened the door and tip-toed into the room.

Holly lay on her bed, sleeping in her tank and skirt from the night before. And, nestled at her side, his arms holding her gently, was a boy with dark-blond hair. He, too, was fast asleep, and his bare, muscular chest rose and fell at the same time as Holly's. Alexa froze in the doorway. The sunshine peeking through the shade cast dappled shadows on the couple's blissful faces. If Alexa hadn't known the two people on the bed, she would have thought they made the sweetest, most adorable couple she'd ever seen.

Instead, all she saw was her ex-boyfriend cuddled up with her oldest friend. And all she felt was pure, hot astonishment — and rage.

"What the hell is going on here?" Alexa demanded, effectively killing the idyllic moment.

Tyler and Holly were jolted awake at the same instant. Tyler sat bolt upright, his hair mussed and his cheek bearing the pillow's imprint. He looked from Holly to Alexa in bewilderment. Meanwhile, Holly rubbed her eyes and struggled to sit up, also clearly surprised to find herself in the current situation. They both seemed totally vulnerable and caught off guard, but Alexa didn't care. She wanted some answers.

"I — did we — we must have fallen asleep," Holly

mumbled to Tyler, then glanced at Alexa, who was still standing by the open door.

Alexa crossed her arms over her chest. "You move fast, don't you?" she asked Tyler snidely.

"It's not like that," Tyler protested, his face reddening as he sprung off the bed.

Alexa couldn't believe what she was seeing. Tyler and Holly, together? They hardly knew each other. Alexa wondered, with mounting anger, if Tyler had hooked up with her old friend out of pure spite. Not that Holly had exactly turned him down.

"Yeah? Then what *is* it like?" Alexa spat. "Oh, wait. I'll tell you. It's *gross.*"

"Alexa, don't get mad," Holly added quietly, standing up. "We didn't mean for you to see us like this and —"

The way Holly said *we,* as if she and Tyler were an actual couple, only added fuel to Alexa's fire.

"I can't *believe* you would do this to me, Holly," Alexa snapped. "After everything we've been through on this trip. Some friend you are."

Holly jerked back, surprised by the venom in Alexa's voice. Then she felt her own anger flare up. Alexa was, once again, tainting one of Holly's perfect memories. Did she always have to act like such a diva?

In one fluid motion, Tyler reached for his T-shirt and hoodie on the floor, pulled them on over his track pants, laced up his sneakers, and made straight for the door.

"I'll call you later," Tyler said, giving Holly a soft smile as he turned to go. Then he glanced awkwardly at Alexa. "And I'm, uh, really sorry about this, Alexa. I'll, um, see you, I guess."

And he was gone.

Alexa slammed the door behind Tyler and faced Holly again. Alone in the sun-drenched room, the girls glared at each other, their eyes narrowed and their mouths set in stubborn scowls.

"Why did you *freak* like that?" Holly asked. "You didn't even let me explain —"

"Did you have sex with him?" Alexa cut in.

"That's private," Holly replied, turning cherry-red. "But, if you must know, we didn't, okay?" She rolled her eyes, irritated by the accusation. "God, Alexa. Do you always assume *everyone* is like you?"

Alexa gritted her teeth. Did Holly have to go flinging that issue in her face again?

"No," Alexa hissed. "I'm just realistic. I walk in here, see you on the bed with my ex-boyfriend — how am I supposed to react?"

"But, look, I'm still fully clothed," Holly said. "We met down on the beach, and started talking, and then we came up here to talk more. That's all . . ." Holly's face warmed at the memory of how she and Tyler had cuddled on her bed for hours. Drifting off in his strong arms had felt so comfortable. "Stop jumping to conclusions," Holly added, narrowing her eyes at Alexa.

Alexa paused. *So this is how Holly must have felt that night at the Delano,* Alexa realized with a twinge of guilt. She must have had the same involuntary jealous-girl reaction: He's *mine*!

But Tyler isn't *mine,* Alexa reflected. *I dumped him.* And, despite her moment of weakness the other night, Alexa knew she didn't have feelings for Tyler anymore. She remembered how Holly had selflessly urged her to call Diego yesterday, putting aside her own raw emotions. *Who's being the baby* now? Alexa thought, suddenly feeling a little silly.

Holly watched as Alexa's face softened, and her own anger subsided. She sympathized with how surprised Alexa must have felt, seeing her with Tyler; after all, Holly had been in that same position herself only a few days ago.

"Listen, we're being stupid," Holly said quietly. "We can't get into *another* fight." It was their last full day in South Beach, after all; Holly didn't want their trip to end in more hostility.

Alexa relaxed her shoulders. "Especially not over a boy," she agreed. She felt a smile tug at her lips. "I'm sorry I overreacted," she added.

"Truce?" Holly offered, smiling back.

"Truce," Alexa affirmed. She leaned against the dresser, setting down her orchids, as Holly sat on the edge of her bed.

"So . . ." Alexa said after a moment. "How *did* you and Tyler start talking last night?" Now that she was less pissed, Alexa was extremely curious.

Holly blushed, folding her hands in her lap, as she told Alexa about running into Tyler on the shore, and their instant chemistry.

"But I don't know if it's anything serious," Holly concluded. "I mean, it might have just been a one-time thing." Though she couldn't help but remember the way Tyler had looked at her while he was making his swift getaway. They'd exchanged cell numbers last night, and he was still staying at the Flamingo — they could easily see each other again. And, of course, there was school. Holly shook her head. She had to be careful not to get too invested.

"Well, you never know," Alexa said. She tapped a finger to her lower lip, thoughtful. *Of course.* Holly and Tyler — it suddenly made perfect sense. They had the whole sports obsession in common. And they were both — sometimes annoyingly, sometimes adorably — innocent. Alexa remembered that when she and Tyler had broken up in Oakridge, she'd assured him he would find the right girl for himself. Maybe, in a totally unexpected way, Tyler had done just that.

"The whole thing's so surreal," Alexa said. "I mean, it's *Tyler*. And it's *you*." She shook her head, then gave Holly a half-smile. "And at the same time, it works. Though it'll take some getting used to."

"That's how I feel about you and Diego," Holly said. "I'm still trying to wrap my mind around it."

Alexa laughed at the absurdity of it all. "I guess we kind of . . . swapped boys, huh?"

"The great spring break switch." Holly giggled. She looked at Alexa affectionately, thinking about how far they'd come together. Naturally they were both weirded out by their respective boy situations — who wouldn't be? But they weren't going to let the weirdness ruin their bond.

A knock sounded on the door. When Alexa opened it, there stood a wilted-looking Daisy. Barefoot, she wore a tube top and hot pants and held in her hands the red flip-flops Alexa had loaned her on their first day in South Beach.

"Hey," Daisy whispered. "I wasn't sure if you guys were up but I thought I heard you laughing in here. I just got back from Mac's Club Deuce, and I remembered you guys were leaving this morning, so I wanted to return the flip-flops."

"Thanks," Alexa said, accepting the flip-flops. "We're actually leaving *tomorrow* morning."

"Great!" Daisy said. "So can you guys come to the bonfire and concert on the beach tonight?"

"Of course," Alexa replied. She'd seen posters advertising the concert tacked up around the beach, and had been intrigued. Daisy said she'd see them there, and headed to her room. Alexa shut the door and looked at the flip-flops in her hand, remembering how Daisy had come to their room their first day at the Flamingo. Alexa couldn't believe how much had happened between then and now.

"Hey, Alexa," Holly said gently. "Is it okay with you if I invite Tyler to the bonfire, too?"

"It's up to you, Hol." Alexa shrugged. "You don't need to ask my permission."

"I just wanted to make sure . . ." Holly trailed off.

Alexa walked over to the bed and sat beside Holly, poking her in the ribs. "I know. I appreciate your asking."

"What about you?" Holly asked, leaning back on her elbows. "Are you gonna bring Diego?"

"No. He has to do family stuff tonight. So we already said our good-byes." Alexa stared off, her expression dreamy.

Holly sat up, her eyes round. "Wait," she said, as if something had just occurred to her. "You spent the night at Diego's!" In all the chaos that morning, that fact had barely registered.

Alexa nodded, not offering anything else.

"So . . . what happened?" Holly asked, holding her breath for Alexa's response.

But Alexa only smiled mysteriously, stood, and glided over her to the dresser drawers to take out a towel for the shower. Holly gave an impatient sigh, and Alexa turned to face her again.

"As you said, Hol, it's private, right?" Alexa replied breezily, her eyes sparkling. Then she grinned and drifted out of the room with her towel.

Holly fell back on her bed, secretly relieved. Maybe there were some things best left unknown.

Alexa and Holly spent the rest of the morning packing. Their flight was early the next day, and they wanted to leave their last night free for fun. Alexa felt a twinge of melancholy as she spread her outfit for the plane on top of her luggage: Seven Jeans, a faux-fur chubby, and moccasin boots. *Back to winter*, she thought. *Back to reality*. Holly, who was laying out a hoodie and cords on top of her zipped-up bags, looked equally forlorn.

But, with the packing out of the way, there still remained a full day of sunshine to savor. As he'd promised, Tyler called Holly, and they agreed to go for an afternoon run on the boardwalk. Meanwhile, Alexa mellowed out on the beach and talked to Diego on her cell. Diego told Alexa that he hoped to get a summer internship at Princeton, meaning he might be up in New Jersey as early as June. They also discussed the tantalizing possibility of taking a whirlwind trip to Paris. Alexa was so satisfied with what lay ahead that she was able to tell Diego, sincerely, that she didn't mind his not being able to attend the bonfire that night.

"You'll just have to make it up to me the next time I see you," she teased, before they said good-bye again.

Over on the boardwalk, Holly and Tyler were also talking about that night's bonfire as they ran side by side, keeping pace with each other. Holly had invited him along, and a psyched Tyler said he'd call Holly before he was ready to head out.

Tyler makes things so simple, Holly thought. When they'd met up in the Flamingo lobby before their run, Tyler had kissed Holly hello, and asked if things were patched up with Alexa. When Holly assured him that they were, he'd grinned and they'd headed out. She glanced at him now. In the daylight, with his burnished-gold hair and lightly tanned skin, he seemed to glow. Holly couldn't get over his ridiculous hotness.

"So are we gonna keep this up when we're back in Oakridge?" Tyler asked Holly as their sneakers pounded the wooden slats of the boardwalk.

"What?" Holly gasped, momentarily thinking that he meant their relationship. "Oh, you mean, running?

You bet. I try to go every morning. And I expect you to keep up with me," she added teasingly.

"I hope I can," Tyler said. He slowed down to a walk and gave Holly a long, steady look. "And I hope we see each other, you know, when we're not running, too."

Holly slowed her steps, but now it was her pulse that raced. Tyler stopped walking and took hold of Holly's hand.

"I have an idea," he said, smiling. "I know you're leaving tomorrow, but I think you should change your plane ticket. That way we can go back together on Saturday."

Holly searched Tyler's face, her heart tip-tapping against her ribs. Yes, she'd told Alexa that kissing Tyler might not lead to anything more. But now Holly felt, with utter certainty, that this was already something more. Neither she nor Tyler could deny it.

"I'd love to," she told Tyler honestly. Still, Holly knew she had to return to Oakridge tomorrow. Her parents were expecting her. And, most of all, Holly wanted to fly home with Alexa. They'd made the voyage out together. It seemed only fitting that the trip back be the same.

"But I can't," Holly went on reluctantly. "My parents would kill me."

Tyler nodded. "My mom and dad are pretty strict,

too. They barely even let me come down here. It's like I have to map out a plan of attack whenever I need their permission to do something."

One more thing we have in common, Holly thought, tightening her grip on Tyler's hand.

"So that's cool." Tyler sighed, looking disappointed. "But can call I you tomorrow? What time does your flight get in?"

Holly gave Tyler the details, then kissed his cheek, and they resumed their run. Now that Holly knew they would still see each other in Oakridge, an array of possibilities opened up in her mind: Tyler driving her to school in the mornings. Tyler coming over to her house. She and Tyler making plans for the weekend. And she was sure even her parents would like him. Holly grinned.

Suddenly, going back to New Jersey didn't seem so dreary after all.

By the time Holly and Alexa had returned to the motel and showered, the sun was setting, and the other Flamingo kids had left for the bonfire. When a towel-clad Holly received the call from Tyler, she insisted that he go ahead to the beach without her, and that she'd meet him there. She'd feel bad making him wait around the Flamingo while she got dressed. And, besides, Holly thought, feeling very girl-power, even if Tyler *was* sort of becoming her boyfriend, that didn't mean she needed him to escort her everywhere.

She and Alexa threw on their clothes — Holly in capris and a racer-back green tank, Alexa in a lavender strapless cotton dress. They picked up their bags and towels — in case they wanted to stargaze while at the bonfire — and Alexa locked the door behind them. The girls flip-flopped noisily down the stairs, and crossed Ocean Drive.

The bonfire was being held a few beaches over, and Alexa and Holly decided to walk on the sand for a while, not the promenade, to get there. Holly noticed that the beach nearest to the Flamingo was already empty at this hour; most people were probably on their way to the concert. Alexa and Holly strolled along the sand, and then they both stopped, captivated by the sight of the sun sinking into the ocean. The sky leveled off into different colors: peach, cranberry, indigo. The sun's rays shone very brightly for an instant, and then began to fade softly.

Holly had the most acute sense of time passing. Soon, twilight would shift into night, and night into morning, and then — they'd be gone. "Wow," she murmured, her eyes on the horizon. "That's a nice send-off for us."

Alexa grabbed Holly's arm. "It's not over *yet*!" she

cried. Alexa never liked to admit when her travels were coming to a close; she had to soak up every last moment.

"Almost," Holly said. "Though I wish we had more time here."

"We have plenty of time," Alexa said, still holding Holly's arm. "Time to make spring break official."

"What are you talking about?" Holly asked, a slow smile spreading across her face.

"Remember when I told you to tell your parents that you're supposed to go crazy on spring break?" Alexa said. "Well, we've done a lot on our trip, but I don't know if any of it qualifies as truly crazy."

Holly's stomach jumped as inspiration struck. She looked around to make sure the darkening beach was truly empty, and then gave Alexa an impish grin.

"Have you ever gone skinny-dipping?" Holly asked.

"Tons of times," Alexa replied, laughing. "And you?"

Holly shook her head. She'd missed out on the experience when her friends had gone without her to the Jersey Shore. And, at summer camp, she'd almost done it, but the thought of anyone seeing her naked had been too mortifying. Holly thought back to Aaron walking in on her in the shower; she'd been ashamed, yes, but it hadn't killed her. Standing on the beach this evening, Holly felt much more secure in her own body.

She was, after all, the Pulse TV bikini contest champion.

"Do you want to go *now?*" Alexa asked, accurately reading the mischievous twinkle in Holly's eyes. She, too, scoped out the beach for any witnesses. "Before the bonfire?" she added.

"Well, haven't you gone skinny-dipping *tons* of times, Alexa?" Holly challenged, nudging her friend. "Are you chickening out?"

Alexa grinned at Holly. "Is that a dare?"

"Double dare," Holly said, heading toward the water and motioning for Alexa to join her. "Now or never."

"Okay, but just for two seconds," Alexa said, following her.

Since when am I the cautious one? she wondered as she and Holly raced to the shore.

Stifling their giggles, the girls shimmied out of their clothes, and tore toward the ocean. They shrieked as they dove into the Atlantic, swimming out, and under. The water was surprisingly mild, and the gentle waves lapped against their bare skin. Alexa immediately relaxed, enjoying the sensation of floating totally nude as night fell around her. She and Holly smiled at each other, only their heads visible above the dark-blue waves.

Holly was loving the feel of the water against her skin, and not feeling embarrassed at all. Now she understood skinny-dipping's appeal; it was completely liberating. Intoxicating. Holly spread her arms wide and leaned back into the ocean's embrace, looking up at the endless sky.

When they started getting goose bumps the girls decided to swim back to shore, grateful for the blanket of near darkness — and their waiting towels. Wrapped only in terry cloth, they collapsed onto the sand and broke into gales of laughter.

"Did we really just do that?" Alexa gasped, and Holly could only nod, giggling helplessly.

Once their laughter had subsided, the girls sat still on the sand, listening to the gentle rhythm of the tide. Both of them felt tingly and refreshed, their skin still damp and cool. They let the wind dry their hair as they watched the sky come alive with stars.

"It won't be like this when we're back in Oakridge," Holly spoke quietly.

"Like what?" Alexa asked.

"Like . . . how close we are right now," Holly said, choosing her words carefully. "South Beach is a break from reality. When we're back at school on Monday, all of this will disappear." She gestured to where they were sitting on the beach.

Ever since her run with Tyler that morning, Holly had been thinking about high school. She and Tyler were in different social spheres at Oakridge, but Holly didn't doubt that they could work around that. And there *was* some overlap between their groups because of the sports connection. Holly could easily see Tyler slipping into her world, getting along with her friends.

But Holly couldn't see Alexa in her world at home. She tried to picture the glamorous Ms. St. Laurent sipping smoothies with Meghan and Jess in the high school cafeteria, or accompanying them on Sunday afternoon bike rides. Holly shook her head. Impossible. Away from South Beach, she and Alexa wouldn't work.

"I don't think that's completely true," Alexa said softly, looking at her friend. "It's not like we can just go back to being acquaintances, as if this trip never happened." Alexa, too, was finding it difficult to imagine sporty Holly fitting in with her stylish circle of friends. But that didn't mean that she and Holly still couldn't hang out on their own from time to time.

"That would be dumb," Holly agreed, drawing a line in the sand with her finger. She looked up at Alexa with a small smile.

Alexa gazed at Holly thoughtfully, combing her fingers through her damp hair. "I don't think we'll ever be as close as we *once* were," she said. "You know, like back in grade school, when we were . . ." She remembered her pink bracelet and smiled. "Best Friends Forever."

Holly nodded, hugging her arms to her chest. "That whole *forever* idea is silly, anyway," she said, thinking about how she and Alexa had stopped being best friends after a time. "Nothing lasts forever."

Alexa bit her lip. "Holly, I am so sorry," she said softly. "I'm sorry about how our friendship ended. I wish I could go back in time and do things differently." She reached out and took Holly's hand, feeling choked up. "I know I was the one who . . . changed a lot."

Holly shook her head. "We *both* changed," she said. "But, then . . . I think that we also stayed essentially the same. And that's why we still make a good team."

"You and your sports analogies," Alexa teased, flicking some sand onto Holly's leg. The girls smiled at each other, then got to their feet, wringing out their hair. Wordlessly, they slipped back into their clothes and started up the beach once more. It was time for the bonfire.

"You know what?" Alexa said as they walked along, their arms linked. "I still believe in *forever.* We might not be best friends anymore, Hol, but we'll always be in each other's lives in some way. No matter what." Alexa now knew that her friendship with Holly reached far beyond the petty divisions of high school. South Beach had proven that.

"I used to think of you as the sister I never had," Holly mused aloud. "And maybe that's still true in a way. I mean, we'll bicker and fight and be apart from each other . . . but none of that really makes a difference, in the end." She shrugged. "Just like sisters, right?"

"Like sisters," Alexa echoed happily.

A tall bonfire was blazing in the sand when they arrived at Lummus Park Beach, and a local reggae band was playing on an elevated stage — the exact spot where Holly had won the bikini contest. A mix of locals and tourists were crowded around the fire drinking Coronas, dancing, laughing, loving the warm March evening.

Holly and Alexa set down their bags and towels and were slipping into the thick of the crowd when Holly caught a glimpse of Tyler. He saw her at the same instant, and he grinned. They headed toward each other, and Tyler wrapped her in a big hug, burying his face in her damp hair.

"Did you just go swimming?" he asked, smoothing his hand along her freckle-dusted arm.

"Kind of." Holly smiled, but wouldn't say more.

Tyler encircled Holly's waist with his arms, and they turned to watch the bonfire. Holly spotted the other Flamingo kids nearby. Although the band was playing an up-tempo song, Daisy and Jonathan were slow-dancing. Thomas and Kaitlin were unabashedly flirting over bottles of beer, and Holly wondered if Kaitlin had liked Thomas all along. She noticed Aaron trying to mack on a punky girl with bleached, spiky hair. When Aaron happened to look over and see Holly with Tyler's arms around her, his eyes widened in comprehension. Holly smiled coolly at him. This was the sweetest revenge.

Then Holly saw Alexa dancing alone as only Alexa could, lost in the music. Holly called to her, and Alexa glanced over, smiling first at Holly and then at Tyler. Alexa's expression, when she looked directly at Tyler, clearly said: *It's all good.*

And it was. Alexa had just gone skinny-dipping, the sweet salty air was caressing her skin, and she was dancing near a bonfire as a live band played. *This can't get more perfect,* she thought blissfully, gazing into the crackling flames. The air around the fire was wavy with heat and glowing bits of ember. Suddenly, Alexa saw a familiar, olive-skinned figure emerge out of the halo of smoke. As the firelight illuminated his beautiful face, Alexa's heart soared.

"Diego," she murmured in disbelief as he swept her up in his arms, lifting her off the sand. "But I thought you had important family plans and — "

Diego kissed her. "Nothing is more important than this," he told her.

They wrapped their arms around each other and danced, oblivious to the crowd around them. When the song ended, Diego smiled down at Alexa and squeezed her hand.

"Let me go get a drink," he said, pointing to one of the coolers on the periphery of the crowd. "Do you need anything?"

Alexa shook her head. She had absolutely everything she needed. She watched Diego walk off, then glanced back to where Holly and Tyler stood. She caught Holly's eye, and motioned for Holly to join her. Alexa realized that she didn't need to spend every second with the boy in her life. She could hang with her friends, even *while* her significant other was there.

Holly had seen Diego and Alexa together, and felt surprisingly okay with it. Now that she was falling in love, she wanted the rest of the world to feel that way as well. She waved back at Alexa, then turned to Tyler.

"I'm going to dance," she told him, planting a quick kiss on his lips. "Why don't you grab something to drink and meet me?"

Tyler agreed, and headed off for the coolers. As

Holly was making her way toward the crowd of dancers, she nearly collided with Diego.

"Hey," they said at the same time, smiling awkwardly. Diego seemed about to add something — perhaps an apology — but Holly shook her head.

"It's okay," she told him. "Don't even worry about it."

Diego nodded, his dimples showing. "All right." He started off for the coolers. "I'll see you around, Holly."

"I'll see you," Holly echoed, turning away. She remembered that Diego was starting Princeton next year. So she would see him around, especially if he and Alexa started dating seriously. And Holly could live with that.

"Look at you, hottie!" Alexa exclaimed, kissing Holly on the cheek when she arrived at her side. "You're glowing."

"So are *you.*" Holly grinned at Alexa. It was true. Alexa's white-blonde hair spilled, mermaidlike, down her back and her face was radiant.

"Hang on," Alexa said. She reached for her tote and pulled out her digital camera, holding it at arm's length as she and Holly leaned their heads together and smiled. Alexa pressed the silver button and the flash went off. Then, she flipped the camera over to admire the image she'd captured — she and Holly, smiling on the beach, frozen forever in time. She returned the camera to her bag, satisfied.

Alexa and Holly started dancing together on the sand. A few guys tossed appreciative glances their way, and Alexa acknowledged the boy-attention, but she didn't crave it like she had before. She stood on her toes, spotting Diego near one of the coolers. He was sipping a Corona and talking to, of all people, Tyler. Alexa nudged Holly to point out the surprise pairing, then the girls looked back at each other and grinned. Who *knew* what those boys were talking about?

Night had fallen, engulfing the ocean in darkness, but the stars were very bright overhead. Holly looked down at her watch. The hours were slipping by. Soon, it would be morning, and the girls would be on a plane again, soaring back home. Back to school and parents and ordinary life.

"Can you believe at this time tomorrow —" Holly began.

"Shhh!" Alexa put her hand over Holly's mouth. "Don't say 'tomorrow.' Don't even *think* about it."

Holly smiled. "You're right."

So the girls cast aside all thoughts of home, and boys, and the future. They simply surrendered themselves to the South Beach night: the music, the waves, the fire, and the starry sky. Tomorrow seemed like ages away.

Here's a sneak preview of the sizzling new book

6X
the uncensored confessions

BY NINA MALKIN

Sex. Fame. Rock 'n Roll.

Four bandmates on the fast track to pop-rock superstardom reveal the unfiltered truth about the glamorous, backstabbing world of sudden celebrity.

Introducing . . .

The Voice Sweet, trusting Kendall sings like an angel — and is about to discover her devilish side.

The Body Rich, spoiled Wynn can't keep a beat to save her life. But with curves like that . . . who cares?

The Bitch No-nonsense Stella is all confidence, attitude, style, and smarts. But her relationship with the band's manager might reveal her to be more vulnerable than she thinks.

The Boy A/B has got real talent. Now if only he can keep his mind on the music instead of crushing on his bandmates.

6X Can you handle it?

In stores this June!

chapter one

THE BODY

They call me The Body, though not to my face. Not that I would care. Maybe I would, I don't know. Technically, I know I have a good body. I'm five ten, wear a size four jeans, and my boobs are a double-D. My mother says I should be proud of my body; she certainly is. I'm sorry, does that sound terrible? It's just that I read in a magazine about a girl my age who had a boob reduction — I mentioned that to my mom and she looked at me like I'd asked to be decapitated. Plus she's forever ordering me to stand up straight and put my shoulders back — a drill sergeant in socialite's clothing. When I started to develop, she would brag to her friends. Not that she actually takes credit for my body; in fact, she's always saying things like "It must be something in the water!" But that's how she thinks of me — as her creation.

Or her project. Because before 6X was anything, when it was just a crazy, this-will-never-happen-in-a-million-years idea, my mom was all for it. Not me. Even now, with our video on MTV ninety-seven times a day, it hasn't fully sunk in, since the way it started out was so unreal, so stupid. A big fat joke — with me as the punch line. But like it or not, here I am in front of a camera, spilling all. Uch, I'm sorry, it's just really hard and completely embarrassing — I made *such* a fool of myself.

It was the holidays, and my stepdad's law firm was having a party at the Drake House, very fancy, all the lawyers and all the big clients. There was no reason for me to go — there wouldn't be any people my age, no kids to talk to — but my mother was like, "You're going." Any excuse to get me out of jeans and into a dress by whatever designer currently has her in thrall.

So I went (you do not argue with my mother), and I swear, there is nothing more mind-numbing than watching a ballroom full of old people party. Waiters trudged around with trays of champagne and I thought: *Why not?* Nobody blinked when I took a glass. So I took another. I wasn't drinking to get drunk, though. It's more that I was bored and uncomfortable — holding a glass gave me something to do.

Sipping and walking, sipping and walking — that was my evening. Until all that sipping made walking kind of a challenge. I went to stand by the edge of the stage and watch the band, even though they were Top 40 — definitely not my thing. Soon as they took a break, the drummer came up to hit on me, which was *so* not appropriate. I mean, I'm a guest, and I'm fifteen. Anyway, I didn't know what to say — I'm pretty shy in general, and I get extra shy around guys who consider my boobs tantamount to aurora borealis. But there I am — hello, little drunk girl — telling him how cool *I* thought it was that he played drums, because I always wanted to play drums — which wasn't true, I'd never even thought about it.

Next thing I know, he's leading me onto the stage and sitting me behind the kit and telling me what to do. I just start banging away, but within seconds my mom's unacceptable behavior radar picks up on my unacceptable behavior and she dispatches my stepdad. Only he's not alone; he's with one of his partners, Brian Wandweilder — this entertainment lawyer, a real hotshot, the youngest partner at the firm.

"Well, well, well, Sherman," Mr. Wandweilder said to my stepdad. "I didn't know Wynnie played drums."

My stepdad smirked at him. "She doesn't," he said, then gave the drummer a dirty look and took my arm to help me down. I didn't complain; I was too busy babbling, "That was so much fun! Oh, my God, that was SO FUN!" Such a ditz, I know — but the weird thing was Mr. Wandweilder kept going on about how incredible I was. Under normal circumstances — in other words, not drunk ones — I would have been mortified, but we talked about me playing the drums for a long time. There was something just so earnest about him, pale brown eyes peering sincerely behind little wire-rimmed glasses, sandy hair, not *long* long but not lawyer short — sort of flopping as he nodded with an enthusiasm, an excitement, that was more kid-like than adult. Mr. Wandweilder talking about me and music and the drums made my stupid-drunk-girl act seem not just acceptable but, I don't know, credible . . . cool.

And later that night, in the limo coming home, my mom and stepdad were discussing it.

My stepdad was like: "And if you can believe it, Cynthia, Wandweilder actually said he could put a band together around Wynnie and sell it."

"Why wouldn't I believe it?" my mom said. She had that out-of-breath sound in her voice that she gets when she's irritated. "Wynn is a poised, beautiful, talented girl. And Brian knows the industry. You always say that. Do you think he was joking?"

"No, I actually think he was serious," my stepdad said, loosening his tie. "But he doesn't know Wynn. Really, Cynthia — can you envision our Wynnie bopping around on stage, playing drums in a rock band?"

They're having this conversation with me sitting between them in the limo. They're talking about me, and I'm sitting right there. And it's not like I'm passed out and drooling; I'm just a little drowsy.

"You're not denying that my daughter is poised and beautiful and talented, are you?" my mother said, raising an eyebrow in warning.

"Of course not," he replied quickly. "But Wynnie? In a band? Playing drums? Don't you think that's slightly ridiculous?"

My mom patted my stepdad's hand and called him darling. "What isn't ridiculous?" she said. "Martha Stewart went to jail. One of the Hilton girls milked cows on television. Arnold Schwarzenegger was elected governor of California. We live in the age of ridiculous." She looked at me and smoothed my hair and smiled. "I'm not even thinking about Wynn actually being *good* at it, of her having any kind of success. I simply think it might bring her out of her shell."

"Maybe," said my stepdad. He was quiet for a minute, mulling it over — he's like that, always looks at all the angles. "Maybe," he said again. Then it was his turn to look at me and smooth my hair and smile. "I just hope she doesn't come out of her *shirt.*"

THE VOICE

They call me The Voice. Oh, gosh, no — not officially! That would be so rude. Because it's not like the other kids aren't talented. Because they are. Really. Just sometimes at Universe, our record label, they will say that. It's kind of a slang thing in the industry to say, "She's the voice" instead of "She's the lead singer." Anyway, singing is what I do. Always has been.

Ask anyone in my family and they'll tell you about "the nudge." We were all there in church — my mom and daddy, my grandparents, basically the whole town of Frog Level, South Carolina. And when the singing started, I opened my mouth like everyone else . . . and out it came. My voice. My mom says it was the sweetest, truest sound she ever heard — like an angel — but she had no idea it was little old me.

Well, once she realized it was *my* voice, she stopped singing herself and nudged my daddy with her elbow. He couldn't believe it, either, so he nudged my granddad, next to him in the pew. And then it was like the wave — you know, the wave they do at football games? Like that. The nudge started moving through the congregation until every last person except for the preacher got a nudge and stopped singing and it was just me, three and a half years old, belting out "What a Friend We Have in Jesus" like nobody's business. It was my first solo.

Gosh, that's a back-home story for you. All my family is still down there in Frog Level. That old church isn't there anymore but I can remember it: white clapboard, wooden floor, and so tiny — standing room only on any given Sunday. Isn't memory strange? I think it is. Because even though I can remember that church, what I cannot remember, what I wish I *could* remember more than anything, is my daddy. I cannot see his smile, his eyes, his hands, his hair; I cannot see any part of him anywhere in my mind.

What happened was, he got killed defending our country in the Gulf War. And my mom doesn't have any pictures of him — they went missing because my mom and I moved around so much. It took us a while to get all the way up to New York — well, New Jersey; right now we live in Elizabeth, New Jersey. What happened was, after we lost my daddy, my mom had to work real hard at the Wal-Mart and go to college, but once she earned her degree she kept on looking for better and better jobs. We'd stay in a place for a bit, but if she didn't get promoted, well, then it was "Who can do better?" And for some reason the better the job, the farther up north it was. She's got a wonderful position now; they love her. My mom is serious about her career; she is an *executive* at the top of middle management. As supportive as she is about me being a star and all, she would never up and quit her job. It's *hers*. It's one of the things that make me so proud of her.

Gosh, I could go on and on about my mom — but we're supposed to be talking about me. Well, 'round about the time we moved here, I dropped my first name, LuAnn, and started going by Kendall, which is my middle name. I was entering all these pageants and talent shows, and it just sounded so much more sophisticated and professional: Kendall Taylor. Only when I go back home to visit, I go by LuAnn — my mom says so. LuAnn is my great-grandmomma's name, so it's out of respect. Me going by Kendall, nobody down there even knows about that; my mom says it's our secret. Although, gosh, with all that's going on now — I mean, we're on MTV! — pretty soon the folks in Frog Level will catch wind, and I can't imagine what my mom will tell them all.

Anyway, all those pictures of my daddy. Lost. It's sad, I think, but I don't dwell on it, because I am a very positive person. Plus I know my daddy's up on a cloud, watching all the awesome things that are happening for me. Sometimes I like to think that when I sing, my daddy is starting a nudge right there in heaven!

THE BITCH

Call me The Bitch and you better watch your back. Just kidding! Look, no offense but it's dumb to talk about which "one" I am in the band. Back in the boy-band era maybe that's what they did — he's the poet, he's the bad boy, he's the sex god — but please, that is over. It's just stereo-typing, which I am personally very much against, and which our band is so not about. Because check it out, here's the black girl and she's not in an R&B group and she's not even the singer. Our band is about breaking barriers.

But whatever, if these video diaries get turned into a reality show or some kind of special-bonus-extra content for our CD, and that helps sell records — cool. See, that's how my mind works. I am a businesswoman. First and fore-most. And an artist. An artist and a businesswoman. Besides, it's not like I have a problem big upping myself, and venting is good because I get to have my say. I mean, let's be real: when 6X does press — for a magazine, or a talk show, any of that shit — I'm always gonna get left out. For two very, um, *obvious* reasons, everyone wants to talk to Barbie — oops, I mean Wynn, but it's okay, keep that in; she knows I call her Barbie. And then they wanna talk to Kendall, since she's the singer — fine. And then they wanna talk to A/B, because he's the only boy and they wanna know what that's like; plus he's a cutie in that "Hot? Who? *Moi?!*" kind of way, and all our chick fans wanna hear from him. So by the time the interview is over, oops, they run out of tape and time and nobody gets a chance to ask me a single thing. Which is retarded, because I'm the only one in the band that's got anything to say. I have a *vocabulary*, all right. Do I have to show you my standardized test scores?

Look, I don't mean to be harsh. It's not like I'm in a band with a bunch of morons. A/B is really smart, and he's funny as shit, but he's an eat-sleep-breathe-fill-in-what-ever-bodily-function-you-want kind of music junkie. And Kendall's smart in that bouncy, chirpy, Goody Two-shoes way. On the low, every now and then Kendall will come out with something whack, but mostly she works the little angel thing, which means she is pure vanilla without the bean. Then Wynn, well, between you and me and the whole entire world, I'm not sure what it is with her because I think, I *know,* my girl's got some pretty deep thoughts going on behind those wispy honey-colored bangs, but her favorite two sentences are "I'm sorry" and "I don't know."

Not me. I've got opinions. I've got ideas. I make shit happen. Like that day in school, when Wynn first brought up the band thing in homeroom. We both go to Little Red Schoolhouse. Yes, that is really the name of our school — so cute I could vomit. Personally, I think my parents could spend their hard-earned money on things other than private school for me — and I could definitely live without taking two trains into Manhattan from Brooklyn every day. But my dad teaches math at a junior high that's so ghetto, the kids call it Jay-Z J.H.S. The shit he's witnessed on the job, you know he'd rather sleep on tacks then send me to public school. As to my mom, she believes overpaying for my education will keep me from turning out like my half brother, John Joseph, aka J.J., aka Loserboy. He's the fruit of her first marriage to one of the goombah guys from her old neighborhood, before she went all jungle fever and got with my dad.

Only forget my family — you wanna hear about 6X. Back in the day, Wynn wasn't exactly a friend, but we had a few classes together, we talked. Well, one time she's telling me about some chichi champagne-fueled night out, and this drummer dude who's clearly trying to find a way into her thong. I'm half listening to this shit, but the second she gets to the part about her stepdad's law partner claiming he could build a band around her, I snap to. I mean, I'm riveted. Right away, I'm like: "Really? I play bass."

And that weekend, I learned how.

That's where Loserboy came in. Twenty-five years old, can't even hold a job at the freakin' post office . . . pathetic. My dad does his best to ignore J.J. — which is tough, seeing as how he's been living in our basement since his own father kicked him out — but I love him like crazy, he's my big brother, all right. So he's got this bass (he was in a punk band for five minutes once), and that Friday night we put on *Leave Home* and *Rocket to Russia,* and I strap on his big-ass Fender P and it's coming down below my knees and he teaches me a couple of bass lines. All weekend I practice, and the next Monday at school I'm all over Wynn about the band, the band, the band.

And if that makes me pushy or aggressive or a bitch then, fine, whatever. . . .

THE BOY

Ah yes: The Boy. The dude, the guy, the Y chromosome. That would be me. Most of all, though, I'm the musician. Every band's gotta have at least one. Not to be a complete asshole but, hey, we've all got our jobs.

Wynn's job is to be the babe. Oh, she keeps the beat okay — believe me, when I first heard her, man, I was like "No way," but it's amazing how much she's improved. Only come on, calling her "attractive" is like saying the Grand Canyon is a hole in the ground, and I don't just mean her body, it's the details — her heart-shaped face and those eyes, not quite green, not quite blue. Even her earlobes are hot, her clavicle. She could be up there hitting a bucket with a pair of knitting needles. As to the other half of our rhythm section, Stella, she's also a graduate of the leaps-and-bounds improvement program. Still, playing bass is not her main thing. Hmm, how can I put this? Stella's job is to be the boss. We've got a manager and an A&R guy and a lawyer and a label, but Stella's the boss because she scares the crap out of us. The girl was a Mafia kingpin or a Third World dictator in a former life, I shit you not.

Kendall, obviously, her job is to sing. She's one of those people, you hand them the phone book and when they start singing it, your jaw drops, you get goose bumps, the whole nine. So you could say that Kendall's a musician, too, but I beg to differ. She's something else: a natural. Never took a lesson. Pure gift. Me, I got some gift action going — at the risk of coming off completely obnoxious, I *can* play any-thing — but while Kendall just does it, I have to work at it. You can't hand me the didgeridoo or the tuba and bang-zoom I know how to make zee beautiful music. You got to give me a couple of days alone with it. Not like I've got much else to do since I don't have a girlfriend running my life at the moment. Hey, I'm not Bo-Bo the Dog-Faced Boy, either, but at my school if you haven't stepped right out of an

Abdominals and Fitch ad — if your hair's a little shaggy or your muscles don't have muscles — you're deemed wholly undrool-worthy by the girl-powers-that-be.

Anyhoo, like I said, I have to work at music, only it's not work because I love it.

And the point is, it doesn't matter to me if 6X is chicks or Chihuahuas, I'm just happy to be part of a band that's going somewhere. I'm seventeen years old and I've been in eight different bands, so the fact that we're signed with a hit single out and ready to make our record is, to me, *finally*. Not just "all right!" but also "all right, *already*." Even my mom and dad are resolving their considerable conflicts about my career choice now. Typical Jewish parents: you slide out of the womb and they practically slap you onto the piano seat, but God forbid you actually want to *do* music instead of be a doctor or a lawyer or a nuclear physicist and it's as if you handed them massive two-for-one heart attacks. I don't care — I'll always do music. Say I become the CEO of some enormous bloodsucking conglomerate one day, I'll still do music on the side, and if I got a record deal I'd call a board meeting and be like "Later, dudes . . ."

I was eleven in my first band, a cover band, classic rock. Everyone else was in their late twenties and thirties; I was the gimmick, the little piano prodigy. We'd play bars all over Long Island; my mother was not into it, but my dad convinced her it was okay because his kid brother was in the band. Uncle Dick. And his first name is not Richard, he's just an asshole. We'd do all the alphabet bands — BTO, ELO, ELP, and of course, AC/DC. Miraculously, the

experience didn't turn me off to music. In fact, I loved it —
I still get the warm-and-fuzzies when I hear AC/DC or the
Floyd.

Still, by age thirteen I'd switched to guitar as my main
instrument and started a band with some kids on my block.
Here's the rest of my musical résumé to date: I had a ska-
punk band; an emo band; a very strange duo with this guy
from camp — me on guitar and keyboards and him on
oboe and flute; your basic generic rock band; a very short-
lived nu-metal thing; and two things I can only categorize
with the meaningless tag of "indie rock." Where did they all
go? Nowhere. Guys would move away, or get into sports or
girls or drugs too much; or we would just disintegrate for
some other reason.

So about a year or so ago, while trying to disentangle
myself from the last indie-rock thing without making anybody hate me, I started doing the coffeehouse open-mike
circuit. Just me and my six-string soul mate, Dan Electro,
taking the Long Island Railroad into Manhattan, plugging
in between all these whiny-sensitive acoustic-guitar guys,
doing a set of obscure covers and crappy originals (a master songsmith I am not). Yet somehow that's how I hooked
up with a manager, who turned out to be a major dickwad,
but through him I met this guy who knew a lawyer who
hooked me up with the girls, and now we're 6X, pop-rock
sensation, superstars in training.

Does that sound simple as A-B-C? One-two-three?
Vini, vidi, vici? Yeah, right . . .